Carnival
A Delaney and Murphy mystery
Jack Adams

Atlas Productions

Chapter 1

Then...

Twelve-year-old Adam Murphy liked visiting the cemetery. Unlike most kids his age, he didn't find it spooky or boring – he admitted it might be spooky at night, but in the daytime, he found himself fascinated that so many people lay beneath the earth, beneath his feet. Adam wondered what they looked like now and if they liked having visitors stomping on the earth above them. Walking toward the Murphy family vault with his grandmother, Audrey, he read the headstones. He had come to memorise some from their monthly visit to his grandfather's resting place, and occasionally, he found a new one with the earth fresh and no headstone to mark it. Even Audrey had her favourite graves. She liked the ones with the large angel statues, the older ones, not like the new angel on Sarah Anne Tilley's grave, which they had visited a few times.

'Look, Audrey! Someone's placed flowers on Jeremiah Clay's grave,' Adam said, surprised; she stopped to study the old grave.

'Well, look at that,' she said with raised eyebrows. 'How lovely that he is not forgotten. Perhaps someone has done their family tree, and Jeremiah has been rediscovered.' She gave a small sigh. 'He was so young when he died, and a very selfless death.'

Jeremiah Clay 1871 – 1891
Drowned saving others.

Adam did the maths. 'He was twenty. I'll be twenty in eight years.'

'And let's hope you live a very long life, my boy,' she said, and they walked on.

Adam mumbled the names and dates as they walked towards the family vault on the back row of the cemetery with the garden wall behind it. Audrey liked to walk even though she could drive right up to the grave, but she found it respectful to wander through the grounds and acknowledge the dearly departed. It was pleasant and easy exercise, and a good history lesson for Adam.

He kept up the commentary. 'Matilda Clarkson, beloved wife... Charles Porter, he was old; he died at 92! Claude Billing gone too soon. Why does he have a broken pole on his grave.'

'It's a broken column. It means he was cut down in the prime of his life,' Audrey said.

'It looks damaged,' Adam said, not impressed. 'He was nearly my age, Audrey. I wonder what he was like. I bet he liked cricket.'

'Yes, I imagined he donned his whites and played the game, but he lived long ago,' she said, glancing at the dates. She never spoke to Adam as if he were a child. 'There were lots of diseases in the past century that don't exist today; vaccinations prevent them. Families were big then in the hope that more children would survive.'

'So, did you have lots of brothers and sisters?' Adam asked.

'Yes. There were ten of us – six brothers and three sisters.'

'No!' Adam turned to look at her. 'Where are they?'

She waved her hand. 'Here and there, mostly in England. Some long-dead.'

'But I've never met any of them,' Adam said, amazed that his grandmother could have that many siblings, and he had never met one.

'You have, you just don't remember. Uncle Joseph came over a few years ago.'

'Oh, right,' Adam said, remembering the crusty old man with the accent and lectures.

Audrey chuckled. 'And you met Minnie, Aunty Minnie, before she died.'

'Was she your sister?'

'Yes, one of my favourites.'

'One of my favourite aunts too,' Adam said kindly, remembering the sweet old lady who kept giving him treats and money and patting his face. 'Is she buried in the vault?'

'No, that's just a Murphy vault with your grandfather's ancestors in it. Your father may choose to rest in there when he dies, as will I. You can visit me then, resting next to your grandfather.'

'I'll miss you,' Adam said, then smiled. 'Rest. It sounds so funny, like everyone in there is just snoozing.'

Audrey laughed. 'It's easier thinking of them that way than completely gone from this earth, isn't it?'

He nodded. 'I guess so.' Adam had no knowledge or experience with death. He saw a girl once who went missing, but he didn't know any dead people. Except for Aunt Minnie, he only met her twice, so she didn't count.

'Do you want to visit your favourite grave?' he asked and nodded towards a large angel statue not too far from where they walked. The statue guarded the grave of a young soldier who had died in a war in the past century. The soldier didn't have a military grave, which Audrey said was unusual.

'We might visit after we pay our respects to your grandfather.' They arrived at the large Murphy family vault, and before entering, Adam exclaimed, 'That man waved to me!'

Audrey snapped to look in the direction he was pointing.

'At Mr Armstrong's grave, you know, the new one without the headstone.'

'He'll have one soon; the earth has to settle,' Audrey said, squinting as she looked towards the gravesite in question.

'Look, there he is, he's waving.' Adam raised his arm to wave, and Audrey grabbed his hand. Her eyes widened with recognition. A small gasp escaped her lips before she hurriedly masked her reaction.

'I know, don't talk to strangers,' Adam said, rolling his eyes and lowering his hand.

Audrey's hand hesitated on the vault door as she glanced around.

'Did you forget the key?' Adam asked. 'I can run back to the car for it.'

'No, I have it, my dear. Thank you.' She stared off into the distance. 'I don't think we should go in today.'

'But why? Don't you want to say hello to Grandpa?'

'I do, but I don't think we should stay here alone, not today.'

'But we're not alone though; there's lots of dead people here and that man over there. I can protect you, Audrey,' he said, narrowing his eyes against the glare as he looked to where she was looking – toward the man near Alex Armstrong's grave.

Audrey smiled, her voice sounding calm as if all was well, while her hand hurriedly fiddled with the clasp on her handbag.

'I know you can, darling, you thoughtful boy. And I will always protect you as best I can, even if I am not as young as I used to be.' She opened the tan leather handbag draped over her arm and reached inside, not taking her eyes off the surroundings.

'He's still watching us,' Adam said, and his grandmother pulled a whistle out of her bag.

Adam laughed. 'What are you going to do with that? Can I blow it?'

She handed it to him. 'Yes, Adam. Let's walk quickly back to the car and blow it loud and often.'

He laughed again, thinking it an odd game, and blew it a few times, feeling silly. He hoped no one from school saw him. In the distance, the cemetery groundsman heard the noise and looked up. Seeing Audrey waving at him, he acknowledged and, getting into his work vehicle, drove towards them.

Audrey took off at a fast pace, holding Adam's arm as if she might protect him or die trying.

Chapter 2

E ighteen years later

   Now...

Adam crooked his arm, and Audrey placed her hand through it. She alighted from his black Mercedes and into the chilly autumn day. He wore a dark suit, and Audrey always wore bright colours when she paid her monthly visit to her husband, Edward, and son, James – Adam's father. She usually went alone, but today, Adam was in attendance. It was the anniversary of his father's death fourteen years ago.

'It is very low, isn't it?' Audrey said, glancing back at Adam's black Mercedes SL convertible. 'If your mother had given it some thought, she should have bought you a family car.'

Adam laughed. 'On this occasion, I think Mum got it right.'

Audrey smiled at him. 'Well, I am sorry to hear you may not have a family, but you have found a great love, which is wonderful. And you can always borrow my Jaguar if you need a four-door vehicle.'

As they did when he was a boy, they walked through the cemetery, staying in the sun where possible and enjoying the glorious day.

Adam's eyes were drawn to the graves he used to study each visit. He was thirty now, and when he was a boy, he remembered greeting Jeremiah Clay, the hero, whose headstone engraving had faded considerably. Near him was Matilda Clarkson, the beloved wife whose husband had now joined her. There was Charles Porter, who luckily lived until he was 92, and the boy who was once his age, Claude Billing, who was gone too soon.

'We're a long time dead, aren't we?' he said, and Audrey looked up at him. He noted this as she had always been so tall and slim, but now, his septuagenarian grandmother was becoming smaller, or so it seemed, and he felt that frailty in the hand that gripped his arm.

'A good Scottish proverb,' she agreed with a nod and a smile. 'Be sure to live your life because you are a long time dead. Oh, look, one of my favourite angels has been cleaned. Doesn't she look delightful?'

Adam smiled. 'There's a lot to be said for this interest in ancestry. Personally, my history interests me but anyone else's bores me stiff.'

Audrey chuckled. 'Oh, I'm with you, darling. Shirley from my bridge club keeps telling us about the people she has discovered in her family tree... kings, queens, explorers. I would be more impressed if they were all convicts who made something of themselves.'

'I hear you, but if the ancestry fad means someone is cleaning our vault after we're dead, I'm all for the next generation getting involved.'

Audrey chuckled and agreed. 'I might get a flower or two on my grave yet,' she teased with a glance at her grandson.

'I didn't say I was going to get into it; it might have to skip a generation,' he joked. 'Do you remember when we were followed, and you made me blow that whistle?' He laughed at the memory.

'Oh yes. I was so frightened that day, and I was only in my fifties, so we probably could have put up a good fight, but it all ended well. Today, we would just use our phones to call for help.'

'You mean you're not carrying your whistle?' Adam said, disappointed, and she playfully hit his arm.

'I might be.' Audrey stopped suddenly, pulling Adam to a halt. 'Adam, do you see that?'

At first, he thought she was joking, trying to re-enact that day when she left, shaken, so he played along, looking in the distance, a smile upon his face until it faded. It was unusual to see someone waving to you in a cemetery; most people bowed their heads in silent prayer or contemplation at the gravesite they were visiting.

'Who is that?' he mumbled. 'Do you know him?'

Audrey didn't answer. She freed her hand from his arm and reached into her handbag. For a moment, Adam thought she would get that whistle, but then she reached for her glasses, dropped the case back in her bag and put them on.

'Extraordinary,' she said, looking in the distance. 'I am sure that is him; it's been years, nearly two decades.'

Adam could see what appeared to be a male in a long coat at the gravesite of the man killed near the carnival all those years ago. Adam couldn't remember the victim's name now.

'He's at Alex Armstrong's grave,' Audrey said, and Adam made a sound of recognition.

'Audrey, I'm going to walk you back to the car, lock the doors, and I will investigate,' Adam said, taking her arm again.

'Absolutely not, Adam. We shall see to this right now.'

Adam looked surprised. 'We didn't "go see to this" last time, if you remember.'

'That was different. You were a boy, and I was responsible for your safety. Now, you can handle yourself. Shall we?' she asked and started walking.

'Against my better judgement,' he muttered. 'We could drive there.'

'We're halfway there,' Audrey said over her shoulder. He took the lead, noticing the man was not leaving. In fact, he stood straighter as if ready for a confrontation.

'You will leave this to me, right?' Adam said.

'We'll see.'

Adam exhaled, knowing that arguing was futile. He focused on the man standing in the same place watching Audrey, just like he was when Adam was 12, eighteen years ago. Just like it.

Nathanial Delaney, Private Investigator, had learnt he was only as good as his next case. Good clients came whenever he succeeded and received some publicity or acclaim. Then they fell off as his name was forgotten, and his private investigation agency returned to representing the usual distressed wives with cheating husband cases and workplace investigations of employees faking injuries. None of which he enjoyed or found satisfying. Fortunately, his researcher, Danielle, enjoyed the covert work—any work that got her out of the office—and he gladly handed them over to her. But the case that walked through his door this morning made it all worthwhile.

Laura Armstrong sat opposite him in the Delaney and Murphy meeting room in Stones Corner. The Delaney part looked after investigations, and the Murphy part was Adam Murphy, a psychologist – his closest friend and a brother in every way but DNA.

She was a woman with an interesting face, a square jaw and pointy chin, full lips, straight sandy-coloured hair cut to shoulder length, and parted in the middle. Her sharpness and bright, large brown eyes gave character to her face.

'I'm not asking to boost my self-esteem,' Nate said, 'but given the high-profile nature of your case, I'm interested as to why you selected me. Plenty of more experienced private investigators would jump at the chance to work with you on this.'

'Probably, but you had a career in the police service, so I'm guessing you will have networks.'

'I do.'

'Plus, your last case was a cold case. You might call my case the same, except no one but me thinks it is.'

'Because they believe justice was served with the coroner's finding?' he suggested, and she nodded. 'And yes, Holly Castle was my last case. It was very cold.'

'And Audrey recommended you.'

'Really?' Nate said and then laughed. He guessed the woman before him was in her mid-20s, yet she had crossed paths with Adam's grandmother and had been familiar enough with her to receive a recommendation. 'I didn't see that coming,' he said.

'I contacted her during my initial research; you know she was involved in the case eighteen years ago.'

'I didn't know.'

'I hear you also work with Audrey's grandson, a psychologist; that appeals to me. I think that could be very handy,' Laura Armstrong continued.

'Yes. Adam. He doesn't charge me to consult.'

'I would like him on the case if he is willing. I will be paying him for any hours he puts in. I'm a solicitor, Mr Delaney, and everyone working on this case is a professional and will be paid accordingly.'

He raised his hands in a manner of acceptance. 'Then you should brief us both, and please call me Nate.'

'Nate,' she said as if trying out his name. 'Can we make a time to do that?'

'Yes.' He liked Laura's clipped, direct manner of speaking and found himself parroting her. He often became a chameleon and took on the likeness of his clients in his dealings with them. Nate rose, went to the door and asked Jessica to assist them. Introductions had already been done earlier.

Jessica entered, clicked on her iPad and scrolled through the diary while Laura looked at her phone.

'Nate and Dr Murphy are free tomorrow at 11.30 or 3.30. Too soon?'

'No, 11.30 is perfect, thank you,' Laura said, tapping in the appointment and looking to Jessica with a smile and nod of thanks as the office manager—also Nate's girlfriend—departed back to her desk.

Putting her phone down, Laura said, 'I'll be off then. But before I go, please consider there are risks for both of us if you take this case on.'

'Yes,' Nate agreed. 'I saw the story in the press. But if I only took on cases that guaranteed my safety or that I came out of looking good, I'd be comatose with boredom.'

She smiled, satisfied with his response.

Nate continued, 'I accept there may be some danger, plenty of deception and cover-up, and hopefully, the right outcome.'

Laura Armstrong nodded and drew a shaky breath, letting down her defences. 'Thank you. I'm counting on it.'

Audrey pulled up to her full height and, with her air of superiority, looked quite confronting.

'And here you are, again, after all these years.'

The coat-wearing man opposite smiled. His face was thin and lined. Adam estimated he was probably only in his mid-forties, but the likely addition of sun, drink, and smoking put extra years on his face.

'It's back,' he said.

'So, I read.'

'Read? I think you know more than that,' the man said.

Adam cleared his throat. 'We haven't met,' he said, studying the wiry man who looked bigger from afar due to his coat. Audrey reluctantly introduced the men.

'Gerardo Dobrev, my grandson, Adam.'

Adam gave him a nod. Neither extended their hand to shake.

'Gerry's my name. I remember you. You may have heard of me?' he said and pulled his coat closer around his shoulders as a small breeze chilled the area.

'I'm afraid I haven't,' Adam said. 'Have we met before?'

'Yeah. It must be fifteen or sixteen years ago.'

'Eighteen years ago,' Audrey said with a look to the grave Gerry stood in front of, the grave of Alex Armstrong.

Gerry did the same and sighed. 'So, he'd be 42 now.'

Adam saw the dates on the headstone. Alex Armstrong was 24 when he died, and he read the poignant message:

ALEXANDER ARMSTRONG
Father, husband, son, brother
His memory will live within us.

'You were a boy when I saw you here with Audrey,' Gerry said and laughed. 'Blowing that whistle like I was going to harm you.' He shook his head at Audrey.

Adam remembered the day this man had his grandmother hurrying him away from the cemetery before they visited the vault.

'Shall we go, Audrey?' he said, wanting the back story from his grandmother.

'Why are you here?' Audrey asked.

'I'm visiting Alex,' Gerry said as if it were obvious.

'Is that so? I wonder what his family would think about that.'

Gerry shrugged. 'They obviously visit, but I've never seen them here,' he said, noting the grave's cleanliness. 'His daughter might keep it clean, or his wife.'

'You know a lot about him. Do you visit often or only today when you know the case is to be re-opened and I would be here for the anniversary of my son's death?'

He laughed. 'You've caught me out. I can't say I've visited poor Alex too often.'

'How many hours have you waited?' Audrey drew a breath.

Gerry smiled. Adam could understand why his grandmother disliked the man. It was a sinister smile, and on this occasion, it said Audrey was right in her character assessment; this man was not to be trusted.

'Not long. I knew you would come early.'

Audrey gave a false laugh that rang hollow. 'And what were you hoping to achieve?'

Gerry's chin went up; he wasn't one for being laughed at. 'I wanted to remind you to leave it alone; there's nothing in it for your community group.'

'I pulled out back then and won't take up the mantle again now. I've washed my hands of it. However, I support the young lady and her quest to find the truth,' Audrey said haughtily.

'Do you want to know what happened, Adam?' Gerry Dobrev turned his attention from Audrey.

'Adam, let us go,' Audrey snapped and turned, putting her hand on his arm and bringing him along with her. They walked away at a good pace. 'Do not look back.'

'Why? Will I turn into a toad? I need to be sure he's not following us,' Adam said, keeping pace with her.

Audrey looked up at him and laughed. 'You are right, darling, it was all a bit dramatic, wasn't it?'

'But he frightens you.'

Audrey hesitated. 'Yes, he does. He did then, and nothing has changed.'

Chapter 3

At three pm, with no clients in-house and everyone in attendance, Nate's new case was discussed. Danielle arrived bearing the group coffee order that Jessica had placed with their favourite café downstairs. Rob, Adam's mentor, who worked with the company several days a week on class actions, joined them. The small party draped themselves around the reception area.

'I can't believe you scored this case,' Danielle said.

'Thanks,' Nate said drily, and she laughed.

'No, I don't mean you don't deserve it; I know you are good enough. But it will get a lot of publicity if she does the podcast.'

'I know, and you're right. It surprised the hell out of me, too. Mind you, she hasn't signed the contract yet.'

'She will,' Jessica said loyally. 'It's exciting to have another high-profile case.'

'Audrey recommended me to her,' Nate said to Adam. 'It was good of her, but what's her connection?'

'Have we time to start at the beginning and tell me what you're talking about?' Rob asked.

'And me,' Danielle agreed. 'I've only read the newspaper article about the daughter seeking justice.'

'Sorry, righto,' Nate said, sipping his coffee before starting. 'There's not much to tell yet. The client, Laura, will brief us tomorrow. But what I know is that eighteen years ago, a new neighbourhood was built called Riverside Park – it's an estate not far from where we grew up,' he said with a nod to Adam. 'Nearby was a large and permanent attraction called *Dobrev's Carnival World*, which had been there for some time and took up a considerable package of prime land.'

'We loved *Dobrev's Carnival World*,' Adam added, and Nate grinned.

'Yeah, I beat Adam at Dodgems many times there.'

'And yet I can't remember that,' Adam said, and the group smiled at their antics.

Nate continued. 'The new residents of Riverside Park decided the carnival was bringing down the value of their properties, and a vocal group of them wanted it gone. There was a lot of pressure put on the council and the owner, Rayco Dobrev, who was in his sixties then, to shut it down. Then a scare campaign began.'

'Who was scaring who?' Danielle asked.

'The Dobrevs were doing the scaring, allegedly. It was not Rayco, but his son, who was in his twenties then. Gerry Dobrev pushed back against the neighbourhood group and tried to scare new buyers out of the area with riots and driving down the value of the properties. One night, during a protest, a man was killed. No one was ever charged with his death; it was a night of confusion, and with no witnesses, it just went away.'

'I remember it,' Rob said. 'It was over as quickly as it started.'

'Yeah,' Nate agreed. 'From what I've read in preparation for my potential client, the cops closed the carnival for a week while investigating. No one was ever really in the spotlight, and the death was declared accidental.' Nate looked at Rob. 'What more do you remember?'

'Not much, except it was a witchhunt for a brief time,' Rob said. 'There were multiple suspects amongst the carnival workers and picketers outside the carnival. Next, it was blamed on the neighbourhood mob, and then, as you said, it was deemed an accident, and it all went away.'

Jessica spoke up, reading from her laptop screen. 'The coroner ruled that no definitive finding could be made.'

'That's how I remember it,' Rob agreed, 'And I'm fairly sure the area dropped in value after that, and the carnival stayed. Now it's a ghost site.'

'Is it?' Adam looked curious. 'I haven't gone past there in years. Is the Dobrev family alive? Do they still own it?' he asked Nate.

'Yes, to both questions. *Dobrev's Carnival World* is closed for business, but it is sitting there like a white elephant on expensive land,' Nate said. 'I cruised by this morning to check it out.'

Jessica shuddered. 'Creepy. I bet the ghost house has squatters at night.'

'Wasn't the victim a young man with a family?' Rob asked. 'You boys would have been 11 or 12.'

'Right on both counts. Alex Armstrong was his name,' Nate said.

'Yeah, I remember now,' Adam said. 'We went to the grave when it was a mound of dirt.'

'We rode our bikes over it,' Nate said, waiting for the reaction and wasn't disappointed when Danielle and Jessica flared up. He held up his hands. 'Just kidding. We went to the grave but didn't jump over it.'

They all looked to Adam as if Nate was untrustworthy, and Adam confirmed, 'It's true. We'd never do that.' He tried not to smile, diverting the conversation. 'Nate and I went to *Dobrev's Carnival World* quite a few times,' he said.

'Yeah, at least half a dozen, birthdays included. What's Audrey's connection?'

'Ah, that goes back to the time of the death of the victim,' Adam said. 'Audrey said she would come in and explain her involvement if you got the case, but it was connected with her community work.'

'Excellent,' Nate said.

'Tell Rob the best part,' Jessica said, finishing her coffee and leaning forward slightly in anticipation.

Nate shot her a small grin. 'My potential client is the daughter of the victim, Alex Armstrong. Laura was six when her dad died. She's 24 now and has just completed her law degree; I suspect she's done extensive work on the case during her university years and found faults in the investigation or legal proceedings. She could have chosen any number of big investigative firms, but she's our new client, and it's already making headlines.'

'Everyone's fascinated with crime, especially cold cases,' Jessica said.

'It's a shame she couldn't get her degree earlier,' Danielle said, deflating Nate's big moment. 'Because someone's got away with murder for all that time.'

'Well, she was a kid when her father died, so she had to grow up and study for six years,' Nate said as if it were obvious.

'I know, I'm just saying,' she shrugged. 'So, if that was 18 years ago, what's with the riots happening there now?'

'Yeah, I'm keen to hear Laura's take on that,' Nate said. 'I believe it's because the area is being gentrified, and residents want the ghost carnival gone. It's an eyesore.'

'What's gentrified mean?' Danielle asked.

'Basically, it's becoming trendy,' Nate said. 'People with money move in, do it up, make it fashionable, and the existing poorer or older residents can't afford to live there anymore.'

'How sad,' Danielle sighed, 'but inevitable. Given Riverside Park is reasonably close to the city, I can imagine it would be a good buy.'

Nate laughed at the idea. 'When we all moved into that area, it wasn't considered close to the city. It was well and truly the burbs. Now that urban sprawl has caught up, it's desirable,' Nate concluded, looking at Adam. 'Dr Murphy, Laura requests your input and will pay you for services rendered.'

'She thinks I'll be rendering services?' Adam asked, surprised.

'I suspect there are a lot of heads to be read,' Nate said, finishing his coffee. He aimed for the bin, sinking the cup perfectly and raising his arms in victory.

'What is she like?' Adam asked, keen to hear first impressions.

Nate looked to Jessica for her thoughts.

'Polite, direct in her speech and to the point, very smart, you could just tell, and really determined,' Jessica said. 'She looks like a young Jodie Foster.'

'Who's she?' Nate asked, his eyes narrowing as he thought about their client list.

'The actor,' Jessica said with a roll of her eyes.

'Oh, right. Yeah, she does a bit. My impressions were the same and not that it's important, but as Mum would say, "She's as plain as an Arrowroot biscuit", though I quite like Arrowroot biscuits, particularly with butter.'

'Me too,' Adam agreed. 'Remember the ones with icing we always had at your birthday parties?'

Nate grinned. 'Yeah, with jelly bean faces – "Funny Faces" they were called. My aunt couldn't cook, so she'd make those.'

Jessica joined in, 'They're pretty hard to stuff up. All she had to do was stick on some icing and smarties or jelly beans for eyes and the mouth.'

'I'd love a "Funny Face" right now,' Adam said, remembering them.

Rob cleared his throat, an amused look on his face.

'Oh, you're all still here,' Nate said, feigning surprise. 'Okay, so I believe Laura is convinced her father was murdered for his part in trying to drive the carnival out. She's hiring us to help prove it.' Nate addressed Rob. 'Why did you say it was a witch hunt?'

'From memory, the neighbourhood group raised a small reward for information which brought several shady people out of the woodwork.'

'And Carnival World's owners, the Dobrev family, might be the shadiest of them all,' Adam said.

'How do you know that?' Nate asked.

'Because I met one of them this morning in the cemetery.'

'Oh, sorry,' Nate cut in. 'I forgot what day it was.' He had thought Adam had been a little flat and distracted and now put it down to the anniversary.

'It's all good,' Adam said, continuing. 'Gerry Dobrev was there, and he confronted Audrey. I'd say he knows quite a lot about this case and is not keen on it reopening.'

Chapter 4

The library manager, Kelsey Bickley, looked so surprised to see her boyfriend's grandmother walk through the library doors just after 11am that Audrey gave a small laugh.

'I promise you, darling, I have been in a library before,' Audrey said, kissing her on the cheek.

'Of course,' Kelsey laughed, 'just not my library. It's lovely to see you, is everything all right? I am sorry, today is a sad day of remembrance for you.'

'Everything is fine. Thank you, my dear. Adam and I had a lovely visit to his father's grave this morning. I caught up with my dear husband while there,' she said with a wink and a smile. 'Well, this is a rather impressive library; you have done well being appointed manager at such a young age.'

Kelsey blushed slightly, unaccustomed to praise. 'Thank you, Audrey, although I am 33.'

'Only 33! Now you're just showing off,' Audrey teased, making Kelsey laugh.

'It is a lovely place to work, and we're fortunate to have great resources.'

'I hope you don't mind,' Audrey said, 'but while driving this morning, Adam told me about your promotion.'

'Oh, it is just a contract for the year to set up and launch a new multi-visual library in Sydney. Many librarians were capable of the job, but because I had just launched this one,' she said, waving her hand around, 'I was offered the job.'

'You have earned it without a doubt. I apologise for my directness, but we love you, and I hope it won't mean the end of you and Adam. Long distance relationships can be tricky; I personally have never been one for absence makes the heart grow fonder. I often feel it is a case of out of sight, out of mind, but perhaps that is just my attention span.' Audrey did not wait for a reply from Kelsey. 'Now, I am hoping you can help me.'

'I'd love to. What can I do?' Kelsey asked, grateful that the senior Murphy member wasn't pushing her for answers she didn't have.

'Thank you, dear. Something from my past has resurfaced, and I hoped some old newspapers from that time might prompt my memory.'

Kelsey breathed a sigh of relief. Next to Audrey, who was tall and thin, Kelsey looked equally as willowy, her wavy red hair tied back loosely with a hairband and her pale grey-blue eyes studying Audrey with concern. It was nearly two years since she had started dating Adam, and Kelsey considered the Murphy family rather eccentric. For a young lady who liked privacy, she got the wrong man and family.

Audrey continued. 'I will need to go back a considerable number of years.'

'We have newspapers on microfilm and a collection of hard copies, plus there's the National Library online called Trove, which has out-of-copyright newspapers right up to the 1950s. The microfilm and hard copies go back as far as 1846.'

'Goodness, that won't be necessary; my past doesn't go that far back, only 18 years.'

Kelsey laughed. 'That's recent history. So, exactly what year and which newspaper would you like to call up?'

In no time, Kelsey had Audrey comfortably seated at a desk with several newspapers in front of her and a cup of tea, which no other client was offered, but this was personal. Kelsey left her turning pages of the hard copy newspapers for the year in question while she went to assist another client, always keeping an eye on the most eccentric member of the Murphy family as if she might do something odd at any moment.

'I think I am finished, thank you, dear,' Audrey said as Kelsey rejoined her an hour later.

'Would you like a copy of anything?'

'No, I remember it well, especially now that the article has brought it all back. But perhaps if you wish to copy this article and send it to Adam, he may appreciate it. Thank you, dear.' She tapped on the article in question, and rising, Kelsey saw her out into the warm afternoon where Audrey's pristine jaguar car was parked nearby. From the library stairs, she gave a wave as Audrey drove off.

Her stomach whirled with anxiety. She had consciously applied for the position, and it wasn't because she loved Adam any less than the first day they met. But she saw him being Uncle Adam to Nate's daughter Matilda the other evening, and her heart ached for him. He should be a father, but she had no desire to be a mother. With her checkered history, nothing would change her mind. Not even her love for him. Plus, she had not mentioned there was someone else, someone with her interests, and she needed to step away to think. Kelsey knew she was being cowardly but hoped putting distance between them would make separating easier.

Kelsey returned to the newspapers, curious to see what Adam's grandmother had been reading. She checked the date; it wasn't the year Adam's father, James, died or Adam's birth year, but the story was on the front page and continued for several pages into the Sunday edition. Kelsey dropped into a chair at the reading desk. Why would Audrey have an interest in the death of a man 18 years ago? She began to read.

DEATH AT CARNIVAL WORLD

YOUNG FATHER BRUTALLY STRUCK.

Unrest in Riverside Park's growing estate has taken its first casualty as tensions continue to rise between *Dobrev's Carnival World* owners and the burgeoning suburb's new residents.

Alexander Armstrong, 24, a father of one, was declared dead at the scene, a victim of a riot in Fairground Lane and Bougainvillea Street between dissenting residents and supporters of the Dobrev family and their carnival. Mr Armstrong recently bought a house in the new estate, intending to raise his family in the modern suburb. But the noise of the carnival and the traffic it created had proven problematic amongst the new residents who were paying top prices.

Police Sergeant Frank Lyons said Alex Armstrong was the chosen representative of a newly formed neighbourhood action group.

'The riot was over quickly, and when the police arrived, it was quelled,' Sergeant Lyons said.

'No one recalled seeing Mr Armstrong during the outbreak. We are asking anyone with information to come forward.'

Long-term resident Beryl Cooper was shocked by the riot and death.

'My family has lived on Bougainvillea Street long before the land was subdivided and Riverside Park Estate was established. We were here decades ago when the carnival was constructed, and the road was renamed Fairground Lane. We've always co-existed,' she said.

'There was a time when all the families on the bigger rural blocks knew each other and looked out for each other,' Mrs Cooper said.

'That's not happening now. It's all about getting the biggest house onto your land and complaining about hard-working people who have built and run their business here for years.'

Sergeant Lyons said the territorial conflicts had been building for some time and now resulted in the tragedy of the loss of a young life.

'Alexander Armstrong was a young cabinet maker with a six-year-old daughter and wife. Mrs Susan Armstrong said her husband was involved in the group to protect his family and investment.'

While members of the Dobrev family were seen at the riot, the family declined to comment.

Kelsey used her phone to scan the story and sent the image to Adam, who replied with his thanks and said that he would tell her the full story of Nate's new client tonight.

She sat back and closed the paper before her. The death may have happened 18 years ago, but the case still raised the hairs on the back of her neck. If Kesley were not in a public library, she would have risen and locked the door.

What was Audrey's connection? More to the point, what was she inviting back into her life?

Chapter 5

Then...

'We're here!' Nate exclaimed excitedly, bouncing on the backseat of Audrey's Jaguar. 'Wow, there are lots of people here; we're going to have to queue for a ride.'

'It will move quickly enough,' Charlie, Adam's security officer, assured them, turning around slightly from the front seat where she sat next to Audrey. Nate was in love with her, and Adam thought she was really cool. 'They get about twenty people or more on each ride,' Charlie said.

Audrey had a brief meeting with the Carnival owner, and the boys were excited to come along with Charlie while the meeting was underway.

'There's a car spot, Audrey,' Adam said, pointing further up the street to where a car flashed its right indicator. 'He's pulling out.'

'Well done, Adam, very good spotting,' she said, hurrying up behind the driver and putting the indicator on. Audrey always secured parking on the street, even if it required several circles of the block, as she flatly refused to pay for parking when 'businesses should be welcoming your custom'. *Dobrev's Carnival World* offered a large area for car parking, which was nothing more than an oval, and it charged five dollars for the privilege. Money was no object, but it was the principle of the matter for Audrey.

'There's another!' Nate yelled from the back seat beside Adam.

'Mine is better,' Adam said, 'it's closer to the carnival.'

'But mine is on the right side of the road, so you don't have to cross,' Nate said. 'Mum doesn't like driving in traffic and always tries to get on the right side.'

'You are both correct, fancy being spoilt with two good spots!' Audrey reverse-parked the Jaguar, and the four alighted, waiting for the lights to cross the road. Behind them was a string of shops, including a café with large timber booths and next door to it a bakery.

'Charlie, can we go on the ghost train first?' Adam asked.

'We should do the dodgems first. I bet I could beat you around a lap,' Nate said.

'No way. We've got to do the Ferris Wheel too,' Adam said, looking up at the tall ride that could be seen across the suburb from where it whirled at the back of *Dobrev's Carnival World*.

'Yeah! But we can't do the carousel, that's for babies,' Nate said.

'I like the carousel,' Audrey said, smiling at the vintage ride visible through the gates. It featured beautiful horses and carriages intricately painted.

When the walk sign came on, they walked across, the boys on their best behaviour, largely because they feared and respected Audrey – a good, healthy fear. They waited while Audrey gave the man at the gate the four vouchers to get them in.

'Thank you, Mrs Murphy.'

'My pleasure, Nathanial,' she said with a smile and a nod at his politeness.

'You can call Audrey by her name, Audrey, you know,' Adam reminded him.

'Mum said not to, and she'd know if I did.'

Audrey laughed. 'Yes, we mothers and grandmothers have eyes in the back of our heads.' She could tell the boys were thinking about that momentarily before she laughed.

'That's creepy,' Adam said as they moved in, and Audrey gave Charlie a wad of cash to treat the boys while she went to her meeting.

They walked her toward the administration building, checking out the rides and booths as they weaved through the customers. Adam read the name on a booth near them. 'There's a tarot reader. Is that like a fortune teller? Have you been to her, Audrey?'

'No darling, I don't believe in that. So, if I die, please do not try to contact me. I'm sure I'll have nothing to say that I haven't said to you already.'

Charlie laughed. 'If you wish to contact me, I am sure I would have a word or two to ensure you are both behaving,' she said, and the boys grinned.

'There you go, contact Charlie at your own peril,' Audrey said with a smile to the sassy security officer.

'Look, she's coming over,' Nate said, and they watched a small woman in a black dress with a red cloak leave her tarot table and walk towards them. She wore her hair dark and short, and her dark eyes seemed to size them up.

'How are you today, Mrs Dobrev?' Audrey asked.

'Very well, Mrs Murphy, thank you. And are these your beautiful grandsons?'

'Just the one. This is my grandson, Adam, and his companion, Nathanial, and their carer, Charlotte. This is Mrs Dobrev.'

The boys greeted her as expected, and then the tarot reader said.

'Why don't you come over for a reading, Mrs Murphy? I have a message for you from your husband.'

'Thank you, Mrs Dobrev, but he knows where to find me if he wants to tell me anything.'

Charlie hid a smile, but Adam studied the woman with curiosity.

'Are you here to discuss the charity event with my husband?' Mrs Dobrev asked.

'Yes, you are both most generous in considering hosting it for the community,' Audrey said.

'I assure you, Mrs Murphy, it is not my choice.' She leaned forward slightly to be closer to Audrey and added, 'If I had my way, not a cent would go to the community.' She pulled back.

'It appears you have a customer,' Audrey pointed out as a young couple approached the fortune teller's table.

She hurried away with a wave of her hand and a smile to the boys, which neither boy reciprocated as they studied her with curiosity.

'She's scary. I bet she works in the ghost train,' Nate whispered, and Audrey repressed a smile.

'I will be about thirty minutes, no longer, hopefully,' she told them. 'After your rides, we will get a milkshake across the road at the cafe.'

'They make the best ones ever,' Adam told Nate but stopped his grandmother before she walked away. 'Don't you want to get that message from Grandpa, Audrey?'

Audrey smiled at him. 'Darling boy, I don't believe in speaking to the dead through cards. If Edward had a message for me, why wouldn't he come and give it to me? Why would he tell Mrs Dobrev to tell me? He was always very straightforward when he was alive.'

Adam looked worried, and Audrey added, 'He'll be telling me to ease up on the Jag accelerator and spoil you more often.' She shook her head. 'It's all fakery, in my opinion.'

'Fakery,' Adam said, committing the word to memory. Audrey was pleased to see their attention easily diverted by shouts from the ride called the Zig Zag, which had just started up and was tipping its riders upside down.

Audrey whispered to Charlie, 'I don't trust that woman as far as I can throw her, as the saying goes. Do keep the boys away from her, and I shall see you soon.'

'Strawberry milkshake is better than chocolate,' Nate said as the boys left for their first ride with Charlie.

Now...

Nate was uncharacteristically nervous about his meeting with Laura Armstrong and pleased that the team, especially Adam, would be sitting in. He tried to analyse his reaction and gave it away for fear of becoming Adam.

'This is our second cold case,' Danielle said excitedly, joining Nate and Jessica as they prepared for the meeting. 'Wouldn't it be great if we got a reputation for solving them, and that became our bread and butter?'

And that was it, Nate thought, the source of his anxiety. What if they couldn't close the case?

'I'd feel better if Adam was here,' Nate said, glancing at the clock. It was nearly 11.20am, and the client was coming soon.

The buzzer on Jessica's desk sounded, and she answered it, opening the underground carpark and directing Laura Armstrong to park in the Delaney and Murphy visitor spot.

'Adam's car is in the carpark,' Jessica said, surprised. Moments later, he was at the door, coding in the number and rushing in.

'Cutting it very fine,' Nate said.

'Sorry. I had to swing by the mental health facility. One of my patients…' He waved his hand, his voice trailing off as if that were explanation enough, and he accepted Danielle's coffee with thanks.

'Is he or she all right now?' Danielle asked.

'That kid's never going to be all right,' Adam said with uncharacteristic despondency. 'I'll drop in and see him again late this afternoon.'

'Dane?' Nate asked, and Adam nodded.

'The client is on her way up the stairs,' Jessica told them.

'I drove past *Dobrev's Carnival World* on my way home last night,' Adam said, heading to his office to drop off his gear. 'You can feel the tension in that neighbourhood.'

'Can you hurry up?' Nate called after him and headed into the meeting room with Danielle, leaving Jessica to greet Laura and his best friend staring after him.

Adam threw his belongings on his desk, took a deep breath, and centred himself. He hurriedly returned to the meeting room before Nate self-combusted.

'I'm sorry, Adam. He's a little tense,' Jessica said sympathetically as Adam passed her desk.

'It's all good,' Adam told her. Upon entering the meeting room, he sat where Nate directed him and asked, 'What's wrong?'

'Nothing.'

'Something,' Adam shot back.

Nate exhaled, his cheeks puffing. 'Nope, I'm just fine.'

'You've got this,' Adam said to him in a low voice as Danielle rose to meet Laura at the door.

Nate did the introductions, and Laura took a seat amongst them. Jessica took the seat closest to the door to exit if the phone rang. Adam studied the new client. Jessica was right; she looked like a practical, confident, intelligent woman.

'It must be hard doing what you do with a high-profile mother,' Laura said, declaring that she knew who Adam was and his pedigree.

'It has its moments; it's hard on Jessica, too, with some of the fake appointments and calls we get.'

Jessica smiled. 'I've learnt to sift between those needing help and the nutters,' she joked.

Laura grinned. 'I bet. Before we start, I best declare up front, that I have a podcast.' She held up her hand. 'I'm not recording anything. It's a podcast I started when I was at university and researching my father's death.'

'Has it brought in any results?' Nate asked.

'No, it isn't live yet. I've just been recording it as I go, and when I prove Dad was murdered and get justice, I'll edit it down to a dozen episodes or so and launch it.'

'Can I ask why?' Danielle said.

Laura bit her lip for a moment before answering. 'To be honest, when studying law and the riots in Fairground Lane, I became a bit overwhelmed with it all. Recording my notes helped me to clarify my thinking, and later, I thought it would make for an interesting podcast, you know, to give hope to those who have lived with miscarriages of justice.'

'Does who you appoint hinge on their willingness to be interviewed for the podcast?' Adam asked abruptly and felt Nate bristle near him, not wishing to lose the case to his media-shy best friend.

'Not at all,' she answered. 'I would love to interview all of you as we go along, but if you don't wish to, that's fine too. I won't record without your permission, and you can sign off on your edited interviews before I air them if that makes you feel a little more comfortable with the idea.'

Adam nodded and said nothing. Nate moved the meeting along, reassured that she was speaking as if the case was already his.

'We've read up on it, of course, but you've got the floor,' Nate said. 'What can we do for you?'

'Thank you,' Laura said, confidently looking at all the faces around the table; she invited them to interrupt at any time with questions and began.

Chapter 6

A podcast for the love of God. Everyone is seeking their fifteen minutes of fame, Adam thought to himself. He was sure he didn't say that out loud, but nevertheless, he felt Nate nudge his foot under the table to pay attention now that Laura had set up her laptop and a projection on the wall as part of her brief. Adam would have walked away from the case when she said podcast, but Nate wanted it, so he'd do his bit for Nate's sake.

'My father died eighteen years ago,' Laura was saying. 'I was six then, no other siblings. But Mum remarried three years later, so I have a couple of stepsisters.'

'How does your mum feel about you investigating your father's death?' Nate asked.

'She'd rather let sleeping dogs lie. So would my stepfather. My sisters don't care one way or the other. I'm nine years older than Casey. She's 17 and likes the podcast idea; Angie's 13 and has no thoughts on it one way or the other. You know,' she said and smiled, 'I'm the same age now that Dad was when he died.'

'That's poignant,' Jessica said.

Laura agreed and continued. 'Mum said they were so excited playing adult, as she called it, and buying into the new estate in Riverside Park. It was the great Australian dream – a brick house, a big yard for the kids to play in, and everything new and sparkling. Except for *Dobrev's Carnival World.'*

'We know it,' Nate said. 'It wasn't far from the new estate my parents bought into that offered all the same shiny dreams.'

The office phone rang, and Jessica departed to answer it.

'It's fine, keep going,' Nate assured her, and Laura continued.

'May I?' she nodded at the projector remote, and Nate passed it to her, rising to turn off the overhead light.

Images of *Dobrev's Carnival World* over the years appeared on the wall. Laura stopped it when she reached the year of her father's involvement.

'When we moved into the estate, this was how it looked then.'

'That's how I remember it,' Adam said and Nate agreed. 'We went there a few times,' Adam informed Laura.

'I did too,' she admitted. 'It was fun, but it was a bit of an eye sore, and it created traffic in the street and noise until 10 o'clock when it closed, or so Mum tells me. There was the noise of the music from each of the rides, the spruikers on a microphone, and people noise. The developers of our estate tried to buy them out, but the owner and head of the family, Rayco Dobrev, didn't want to sell.'

'How long had he owned it for then?' Adam asked.

'Thirty-five years,' she answered without hesitation.

Adam assumed she knew this case inside and out, that it had occupied every waking moment when she hadn't been studying for her law degree. He wondered how she would cope if Nate didn't get a result. He made a mental note not to mention that to Nate, who was already worried about the outcome and his reputation.

'Rayco Dobrev was 65 then, so he could have taken a big payout, and he and his wife, Gerta, retire comfortably, travel the world, and do whatever they wanted,' she said with a wave of her hand.

'Perhaps he wanted to keep running the business that was his legacy and not be forced out by the new development,' Adam suggested. He couldn't help but feel sorry for the Dobrev family.

Despite Nate's look that he read as *"Shut the hell up"*, Laura smiled.

'Don't worry, I'm not that black and white that I can't sympathise with Rayco Dobrev. I get it. I love my live music, which is being pushed out by all the unit dwellers moving into Fortitude Valley complaining about the late-night noise; they are ruining the vibe. But Dad, Mum, and the other buyers into the new estate had not factored on the noise and traffic from the carnival, or perhaps they hoped it would go away.'

Adam regarded her anew. Good. She was smart and compassionate and might see both sides of the story. Nate raised an eyebrow in Adam's direction and received a small shrug in reply.

'And Rayco Dobrev is still alive?' Danielle asked.

'Yes.' Laura clicked through to another image, and all eyes turned to the wall where it was projected. 'This is *Dobrev's Carnival World* or Dobrev's abandoned carnival now. I took this shot last week. The old fairground has been closed for years. Rayco Dobrev is still the head of the family and refuses to pass it down the line, sell it, or manage it. So, it has gone into disrepair. It's like history repeats itself because the residents are up in arms again.'

'Odd timing with your case launching,' Jessica agreed, having returned quietly some time ago.

'It is. A recent story in the newspaper featuring it in its glory days may have sparked the unrest. I'm unsure if their protests will hinder or help my investigation,' Laura admitted. But residents want it removed.'

'It's a major eyesore,' Nate agreed. 'But if Rayco Dobrev is still alive, where is he?'

'He is in aged care. He has dementia and scattered memories of the carnival. I don't know if he has a will; I'm not privy to that information,' Laura said. 'I'm led to believe the son might inherit the carnival, and I know for a fact that he wants it sold now.'

'You'd just bulldoze it and sell the land, surely?' Danielle said.

'Therein lies the problem,' Laura nodded. 'The son wants to do that. However, according to the local newspaper, Rayco Dobrev does not want his legacy destroyed. It would cost a bit to get the carnival up and running again, and the neighbourhood does not want a functioning carnival or museum relic on their doorsteps.'

'That land is worth a tidy sum,' Nate said. 'So, if the residents want it gone and Gerry Dobrev wants it sold, the only one standing in the way is Rayco Dobrev, who might not even remember he owns it.'

'That's it in a nutshell,' Laura said.

'If the council could afford it, it would make prime parkland for a built-up community. Perhaps they could name the parkland after Rayco to keep his legacy alive,' Adam said.

'What a lovely, altruistic thought,' Nate said, smiling at Adam. 'But back to reality.'

Laura laughed, and Adam restrained himself from biting back. He knew he wasn't in a good frame of mind – it was the anniversary of his dad's death, a creep from the Dobrev family threatened his grandmother, his patient, Dane, was having an episode, and Kelsey was moving out for a year. Just great.

'Regardless,' Laura said. 'It distracts from my investigation because I don't want anything sold or demolished until I can find out if Dad was murdered. Who knows what evidence might be on-site or who might come out of the woodwork with a memory? If it is sold and cleared away, then...' she shrugged.

'You know it is unlikely that anything of value to your case would still be on the site,' Nate said.

'Yes, but it makes it so final if it is gone, and I've waited all these years to pursue the investigation.'

'Then let's get to it. What's our part? What do you want from us?' Nate cut to the chase as the slides flicked between images of the old-fashioned, broken-down horses on the carousel, the decrepit ghost house and cracked clown faces.

'Freaky,' Danielle shuddered.

'Don't mind her,' Nate said. 'She's not scared of men, snakes or spiders but finds an old carousel scary.'

'It's true,' Danielle grinned, and the group laughed, breaking the tension in the room.

'So, the history in a nutshell,' Laura said sobering, 'Dad and the other new residents decided they would petition to have *Dobrev's Carnival World* moved out of suburbia or have the hours restricted. I don't remember much except being frightened and told to stay inside when protests were on our streets, but I believe Rayco Dobrev's son, Gerry, was very vocal and aggressive. Several residents had windows broken, cars scratched and dinted, and Rayco Dobrev denied it had anything to do with the carnival.'

'I guess he couldn't say it was done by carnival attendees as that would play right into your dad's hand – that it needed to be moved out of suburbia,' Danielle said.

'Exactly,' Laura agreed.

'How many residents were up in arms about it?' Adam asked.

'Of the 650 new homes, there were over a hundred or so protestors. The estate was full of young families then, too, so no one wanted the vehicles or strangers coming in daily, let alone the carnival workers hanging around.

Many of them were transient. The residents formed a committee, and Dad was one of the leaders trying to effect change. He was a big guy, and Mum said he didn't mind a fight. The night of his death, there was a huge group of homeowners, mostly men, up against the carnival staff led by Gerry Dobrev.'

'Was Rayco involved?' Nate asked.

'Not according to any of my sources,' Laura said. 'Dad was in a fight, and the carnival folk said he fell and struck his head on the sidewalk. It was ruled death by misadventure.'

'And you don't believe it was?' Danielle confirmed.

'No, but I've got nothing to substantiate that. I've spoken with people still living in the area who claim to have seen nothing. They may still be too scared to say otherwise.'

'Or they saw nothing,' Adam suggested.

'Over 100 people were in the fight, and no one saw anything... bit odd, don't you think?' Laura asked Adam.

'I do,' he agreed, to Nate's relief.

'I wonder if we would get a different response from them,' Nate mused, leaning forward.

'I suspect you won't while there's still lingering tension in the area,' Adam said.

'According to the local paper, threats are flying between Gerry Dobrev and the current residents,' Jessica agreed, tapping on a manilla file featuring press clippings.

'Why, if he wants the same thing as them?' Danielle asked.

'That I can't tell you. I've only really investigated my own case,' Laura said.

'It's about what happens to the land when it's sold,' Adam said, and they all turned to look at him. 'Audrey knows a bit about it.'

'Your wonderful grandmother,' Laura said and smiled. 'She's terrific.'

'We'll get her story later then, and stick to your brief for now,' Nate said, knowing time was limited.

'There's one more thing,' Laura added, and Nate nodded for her to continue. 'I want to be involved. I know that's probably not how you work, but I want to be part of the investigation. This is my life's work.'

Nate thought on this for a moment before answering. 'Okay, what does that look like?'

'Well, I'm not going to ask for a desk in your office,' she said with a quick grin. 'Bet you are relieved about that.'

'We can't say that until you leave,' Nate joked, and she laughed again.

'Thanks. Since graduating, I deliberately took a part-time legal job so I had time to work on my father's case. Once I solve it or take it as far as possible, I'll return to full-time hours, but for now, this is my focus.'

'Where do you work?' Adam asked.

'I work for *No Fears No Tears*.'

'Ah,' Adam nodded, 'that's where you met Audrey.'

'Yes, she's on their board.' Laura turned to the group. 'It helps teenagers who need legal support on various issues. It's not-for-profit, and I do it three days a week.'

'I'm surprised you haven't met Adam in your work travels,' Jessica said.

Adam gave a shake of his head. 'I've only got one teen client, and he's institutionalised.'

'That's sad,' Laura said and sighed as if she knew only too well what that involved. Addressing Nate, she said, 'I'll do my best not to be a pain in the butt client, and I'll try to help more than hinder. I want to consult every couple of days. Come in, see it all on a whiteboard, and go with you on interviews or surveillance if it doesn't compromise the investigation.'

Nate tried not to grimace.

'I'll do any legals for free, of course.'

'No filming, only recording with permission?' Danielle asked.

'Yes, correct,' Laura said, then turned to Adam. 'And will you help where you can? I know you're working on your own clients, but I'd appreciate your input.'

Nate held his breath, but Adam answered pleasantly enough, 'Sure, happy to consult, but I don't charge to help Nate out.'

Laura shook her head. 'I need to pay consultancy rates, but I'd welcome a discount.'

'We can live with all that,' Nate said. 'It's going to be hard to separate the past from the present for now.'

'What do you mean?' Laura asked.

'If there's tension building there now, it could be in our best interest to investigate that to find out who the players are and tap into them, their history, and what they know. If we go in just focusing on a death 18 years ago, we're going to be finished and out on our arses pretty quickly, especially if people are nervous.'

Danielle agreed. 'If we can approach it like we're investigating disturbances in the area and then work in your historic questions, we'll get more people willing to talk.'

'I see what you are saying,' Laura said and thought for a moment. 'What do you think?' she asked Adam.

'They're the experts,' Adam said, nodding to Nate and Danielle. 'But the residents will be more concerned about their current dramas. It's not a bad way to tap into them.'

'It makes sense,' Laura agreed.

'So let me kick off by asking about the son, Gerry Dobrev. Do you think he played a part in your dad's death?' Nate asked.

Laura nodded. 'I think he's the number one suspect.'

Chapter 7

Nate looked smug as he wandered into Adam's office. Finding him absent, Nate wandered back out again.

'Where is he?' he asked Jessica.

'He's gone downstairs to get another coffee. I offered to go, but he said he needed some air.'

'I forgot about his dad's anniversary, and then he had the patient drama. He was like a dog with his bristles up. But Laura didn't seem too worried.'

'She's a lawyer; she's used to disagreements. Plus, she's smart, and I suspect she gets where he's coming from – she's doing the best for her family, and so was Rayco Dobrev. Even if the son sounds like a deadbeat,' she added.

'Yeah. Still, I hope Laura and Adam will not be at loggerheads if he works on this.' Nate sighed. 'I feel like a deer in the spotlight. There are so many things to do, I don't know where to start.'

'Well, let me suggest something,' she teased.

'Sure,' he looked pleased, thinking a liaison might be on the cards. They were alone in the office, and he could always close his office door.

'Burnsy has just arrived, so let's see what he can find out about it for you,' she said with a smile and nod to the car park TV monitor.

Nate groaned. 'Yeah, I was hoping for a more exciting suggestion than that.'

Within moments, Sergeant Matt Burns—a former police colleague of Nate and Jessica—appeared at the door, and Jessica buzzed him in. His feelings for Jessica were well known, but Nate won her hand and heart; it didn't make the men's contact uncomfortable.

'Just in the neighbourhood?' Nate asked after greeting him.

'No. News travels fast,' Burnsy said, removing his police hat and running a hand through his thinning brown hair. 'I heard you just got the Armstrong case. I'm working the same... not the cold case,' he hurriedly added. 'The current drama in Riverside Park.'

'Perfect,' Nate smiled. 'Step into my office.'

'I'll bring you both in a coffee since I want another too,' Jessica said.

'You are too good to us,' Nate said, and she agreed. 'If you see Adam, tell him I want to catch him when he's free.'

The men sat by the window at the small table in Nate's office.

'Interesting case,' Burnsy said. 'How did you get it?'

'Beats me,' Nate joked but added, 'she heard about our cold case success with Holly Castle and knew Audrey—Adam's grandmother—who recommended me.'

Burnsy looked impressed. 'Good on you. I'm on the case for a different reason. Maybe we can share what we know.'

'You know I'm always up for that, mainly because you've got better resources.'

Burnsy chuckled. 'At least you're honest. Tell me what you are doing for Laura Armstrong?'

Nate gave him an overview of their almost impossible brief to prove her father was murdered during the riot and it wasn't death by misadventure. 'She wants his killer to pay.'

'Yeah, good luck with that; my job's easier,' Burnsy snorted before sobering. '*Dobrev's Carnival World* is a ghost park now, but it still sits intact and derelict. You know that, right?'

'Yep, seen the pictures, driven past, and I'll check it out again.'

'Apparently, the park has been coming to life several nights a week, scaring the locals witless and when a few have taken it upon themselves to investigate, they've been assaulted. There are rumours of drug deals happening there and gangs meeting – not ideal if you have a young family living in the area. Several locals have sold up and left,' Burnsy said, handing Nate a copy of the file. 'You can have that if you keep it quiet. I've included the historic case.'

'Brilliant, thanks,' Nate said gratefully and grabbed for it in case Burnsy changed his mind.

'I heard the son's an angry thug who may or may not inherit it. Do you think the spooking is his work to buy some local properties cheaply?' Nate asked.

'Good theory.'

'Better call Ghostbusters,' Jessica said, overhearing and entering with their coffee.

Nate was momentarily distracted by her smile and pale pink dress. She also leaned over him to put his coffee down before departing. When he looked back at Burnsy, he saw the look of amusement on his face.

'Don't say it.'

'Ah, young love.'

'Yeah, you had to say it,' Nate grimaced.

'Forget it. I'd be unable to function in the same office,' Burnsy said.

Nate exhaled, took a sip of coffee and got back on track. 'I think I should start with some good old-fashioned surveillance and see who-is-who in the zoo, or rather in the remains of the carnival.'

When Burnsy left, Nate wandered over to Adam's office again and found his best friend tapping away on the keyboard of his laptop. Adam looked up, which Nate took as an invitation to enter.

'All right?' Nate asked.

'Yep. You?'

'Yep.'

The men would not win awards for communication, but they knew each other long enough to recognise when something was wrong.

'I'm sorry about this morning, I forgot it was the anniversary—'

'It's no drama. It was a long time ago,' Adam cut him off, his eyes not leaving his screen.

'So, is everything okay with your patient then?' Nate tried a different angle.

Adam shook his head. 'Nope. Won't be in a hurry.' Adam's answers were short and clipped.

Nate took a seat uninvited in front of Adam's desk. 'I get the impression you didn't like Laura,' he persisted.

'She's all right. I'd do the same in her position.'

Nate sighed. 'Right. Could you ask Audrey to come in and brief us, or we can visit her?'

'I've already organised that, and Jessica has put it in the diary. Audrey has her bridge game at eleven, so it's first thing in the morning.'

'Great.' They sat in silence for a moment. 'Do you think you can work with her?'

'Who? Laura?' Adam asked.

'Yeah.'

He stopped working and said, 'I don't see why not. You know you don't have to use my services just because we share an office.' Adam rose, took his coffee cup, and headed to the window. 'I can recommend a dozen good people.'

'You know that's not what I mean.'

'Sorry, I've got a lot on my mind. What do you mean then?'

'Nothing, forget it,' Nate said, rising, annoyed by their tension. He strode out of Adam's office, then turned and re-entered, closing the door behind him.

'You're back,' Adam sighed.

'What's happened?' He wandered over, seated himself on the windowsill furthest away from Adam, and studied him. He waited. 'If I've done something, just spill it.'

Adam slumped slightly. 'It's not you – just a shit morning. Plus, Kelsey's accepted a contract in Sydney for a year to set up and launch a library there. Some new multi-visual hub that's being rolled out.'

'Oh wow, right. And you're only telling me now?'

'I only found out myself on the weekend.'

'So, you're going with her?'

'No.'

Nate exhaled with relief before adding, 'Why not?'

Adam turned to look at him. 'I have patients who will go backward if I just leave. I've got Audrey here, and she's not getting any younger. You and I are sharing offices...'

'Don't get me wrong, I don't want you to leave, but I'd get it if you did,' Nate said. 'Don't stay because of this,' he said, waving a hand around the office area. 'I can look after Audrey; we're living next door to each other, so to speak.'

'I don't want to move to Sydney.'

'Right. Me either,' Nate said. 'Kelsey will be home on weekends and holidays, though.'

'Supposedly, she won't have a lot of those. It's a tight schedule for the launch with a lot to get done.'

'You can go down to see her.'

'Yep. Just the life I wanted, just like my parents. Me living in a different state,' he said, the irony not lost on him. Adam said in a low voice, 'Read between the lines.'

After a moment, Nate said, 'No. Not you two. I don't believe it.'

'It's about kids, and futures, and weird families.'

'Bullshit. She's had plenty of time to leave if that were the case,' Nate said.

Adam gave a small huff of laughter without humour, turned, and binned his coffee cup. Grabbing his keys, phone, and laptop, he said, 'I've got to go see Dane.'

With that, he departed, leaving Nate standing in his office, not as sure now that everything solid in his life a minute ago would last.

Chapter 8

Then...

While waiting outside Adam's school to collect him, Charlie scanned the arriving parents and cars, always alert for anything untoward. She learnt many years ago, during training, that the worst mistakes are made when you become familiar with your job. Her teachers showed the trainees—of which she was one—photos to prove their point: that hurried last job of the day, the Friday rush to get out of the office, or the routine patterns where danger is forgotten because it never happens. Then bam! It happens. Adam's former security officer, Tom, was a classic example. Too busy thinking it was a boring gig and seducing Adam's mum, and bam! The kid was abducted by the man known as Uncle Allan. She didn't want to think of what might have been. She had grown to love Adam and his best friend, Nate.

Then Adam came into sight, walking with some of his school friends, their bags over their shoulders as they made their way to the gate in their blazers, long pants and hats. Adam didn't seem so different when he was amongst his friends at school. Some were boarders who only saw their parents on school holidays; others, like Adam's friend Stuart, with whom he played cricket, lived with his mother most of the time. His parents were divorced, and his father—a politician—spent a lot of time travelling and attending meetings in Canberra. There were lots of kids like that. But it didn't mean they liked it; they just didn't know anything different until they met a traditional family. Like Nate's household.

She saw the moment he spotted her leaning on the bonnet of her car, which she used of an afternoon to pick him up. It was fast and had good security. He waved, and she noticed his friends checking her out.

'Hey,' she greeted him and waved at his friends as they passed.

'They think you're hot,' Adam told her as they entered the car.

'I am hot today; you must be in that blazer too,' and she winked at him before he could explain the meaning. Charlie locked the doors as soon as they were in.

They drove past Nate's school, and sure enough, he was waiting for them. He loved it when Charlie did the pick-up, and he could get in the car with her and Adam in front of his friends, even better if she was driving the Jag.

'Nathanial, hello,' Charlie said, 'belt up.'

He laughed at the use of his full name, like Audrey did, and leaned forward to punch Adam's shoulder to say hello.

Charlie asked after his day and, after glancing at Adam a few times, asked, 'You seem down. What's up?'

He smiled at her small joke and then said what was on his mind. 'If Audrey died, what would happen to me?'

'Oh, Adam,' she said, glancing at him sympathetically. 'You're not an orphan, kiddo. You'd go and live with your Mum and Dad wherever they are, or if you really didn't want to leave your school or Nate, I imagine you could even board and keep going to school here.'

He nodded, taking that in.

'What would happen to you, Nate?' Adam asked.

'Mum said I'd live with my godparents if anything happened to her and Dad because Nan lives overseas. My godparents live near the city, so I'd probably change schools. I don't want to because they have three girls.' He grimaced. 'Who's your godparents?' Nate asked Adam.

'My godmother is Audrey, and my godfather is Jack. He's a singer, so I don't think he'd let me go on tour with him.'

'What's brought this on?' Charlie asked.

He shrugged. 'Today, one of the seniors got called to the office; his parents were in an accident. So, it got me thinking.'

'That's a coincidence because I've been thinking too. Audrey's got a board meeting this afternoon, and I've got three leftover passes for *Dobrev's Carnival World.'*

'Yeah?' Adam's eyes lit up.

'Can we go? I'd have to call Mum,' Nate said, leaning forward in the back seat.

'Luckily, I've already asked Audrey and your mum, Nate, and they both said yes.'

The boys whooped pleased, and Charlie was glad to see Adam light up again.

'You're a genius,' Nate said.

As she drove towards *Dobrev's Carnival World*, Charlie agreed, making them laugh. 'It's just that when you were racing each other on the dodgem cars the other day, I was pretty sure I could beat you both.'

Adam laughed. 'No way, but you're on.'

'Challenge accepted,' she said slowly in a gaming voice, 'and I'm game to go on the ghost train ride if you are both brave enough?'

'Sure, that's nothing,' Nate said with false bravado.

Charlie drove towards the new estate under construction—Riverside Park—behind the expensive houses on the river where Adam lived and the estate that was new not that long ago where Nate lived.

'Lots of new homes are going up,' she said.

'Yeah, there was trouble here the other night. Audrey and I heard the police sirens, and Nate's dad said there was a fire in one of the streets.'

'He didn't go down to check it out though. Mum wouldn't let him,' Nate said.

'It's about the carnival, I think,' Charlie said. 'Some of these new homeowners want it gone.'

'But it was here first,' Adam protested.

'It was. It's a bit sad.'

Charlie drove onto the secured oval near the carnival and paid to park; unlike Audrey, she didn't want her car on the street or to be bothered circling for a carpark. The three went in. It was quieter on weekdays, and the after-school crowd that often dwindled in with their annual passes was just arriving. As Adam was "starving," they got an ice cream and walked around checking out the stalls, laughing at some of the rides and people's expressions when they got on and off.

'There's the fortune teller again,' Adam whispered to Charlie as they approached her booth. Charlie began to steer Adam and Nate away, but it was too late; the tarot reader, Mrs Dobrev, recognised them and came toward them.

'Hello there, it's Charlotte and Adam, isn't it?' she asked.

'And Nate,' Adam added.

'Hello, Mrs Dobrev,' Charlie said. 'You must excuse us; we have to keep moving.'

The older lady, in her sixties with a lined face, smiled and looked at Adam.

'Your grandmother probably doesn't want you talking to me, young man, because she doesn't believe in an afterlife.'

'That's right, Mrs Dobrev,' Adam said politely and honestly. 'She doesn't think Grandpa would be sending her messages.'

'Bye then, Mrs Dobrev, take care,' Charlie said, moving Adam and Nate along, but the woman followed.

She called after them, 'You tell your grandmother for me, Adam, that her group isn't getting anything.'

Adam turned to hear what she was saying, but Charlie hurried him along. 'There's the dodgems. Let's get a ticket.' She turned to give Gerta Dobrev a warning glance.

The fortune teller kept following. 'Tell your grandmother and her group to back off, or else.'

Charlie spun around, moved toward the small woman and hissed, 'You back off right now.'

Gerta Dobrev held up her hands in surrender, smiled at Charlie, saying she had said all she wanted to say, turned, and left.

Charlie schooled her features and, smiling, rejoined Adam and Nate. 'Goodness, she's a pushy one, isn't she?'

'What did she mean about backing off?' Adam asked.

'Her husband has some plans for the carnival, and he wants to help the charity that Audrey works with, but it appears Mrs Dobrev doesn't want to help. I'm sure she has her reasons,' Charlie said, staying neutral.

'I'd better tell Audrey.'

'We'll tell her when we get home. But now, prepare to be beaten,' Charlie said, giving the boys a determined look and making them laugh. She looked back and saw the tarot reader still watching them.

Sinister was the word that came to Charlie's mind.

Now...

Nate parked away from street lights, found a dark corner, and pulled up in front of a parked car. He killed the car's lights, and with Danielle, they waited to see if an overzealous community watch group member was watching them instead of the other way around. After a short while, they relaxed.

'Ah, surveillance,' Danielle said, 'you either love or hate it.'

'Which one are you?' Nate asked, pleased for the company as they started work on Laura Armstrong's case by observing what was happening around *Dobrev's Carnival World.*

'I like the downtime, getting paid to sit, think, watch. But I know a lot of people can't stand the endless hours of stillness.'

'I did surveillance a few times with Burnsy when we were both cops,' Nate said with a smile, thinking back to his younger self. 'I like doing it on my own, but we weren't allowed to; we had to share shifts to keep each other awake and offer backup. At least you and I don't have to talk. Burnsy talked the whole time... the whole time. Sigh.'

Danielle laughed. 'Really? That surprises me.'

'Keeps him awake, apparently. But he did bring food and drink on surveillance. Just a thought if you want to write that down and take action on it.'

'Danielle laughed. 'You should take a leaf out of his book then.'

He made a scoffing sound. 'If I told Audrey I was doing this, we'd be sorted for the night. She would have catered.'

'She's a great old girl,' Danielle smiled, thinking about Adam's eccentric grandmother. But then she tensed. Nate, reading her body language, followed her gaze.

'Was that a light? In near the carousel?' she asked.

The pair was parked far enough away from the abandoned carnival park not to be seen but close enough to spot movement or lights. Nate squinted as he focused on the site for the next ten minutes, but nothing.

'It must have been a reflection,' Danielle said with a shrug as a car passed, momentarily blinding them.

'Creepy, that place at night,' Nate said.

'Yeah, you can say that again.'

In the half-light, they could see the old buildings with askew signs, the broken horses on the carousel as if tormented and trying to escape, graffitied posts, and distorted laughing clown faces. The pair sat in silence again until Nate offered Danielle some gum.

'Better than nothing, thanks,' she said, accepting a few pieces.

'Do you think Adam can work with Laura?' Nate asked out of the blue.

'Hmm,' she mused. 'He seemed testy today, but I thought he was stressed out by his patient and thinking about his dad being gone all those years.'

'Yeah, he was,' Nate said.

'Does it matter if they don't get on? You've got a signed contract now,' Danielle said with a shrug.'

'That's true,' Nate said. 'But I prefer one big happy family.'

Danielle chuckled.

'Kelsey's going away. She took a year-long contract down south,' Nate revealed.

'What?' she whirled to look at him. 'No way!'

'Way,' Nate nodded.

'Do you think it's... you know over?'

'I don't know, but I think he does.'

'Why didn't you say so? That explains his mood, poor Adam. They seemed so in love.'

'I thought it's his news to tell, but then, knowing Adam, you'd probably die waiting to hear it from him.'

They sat silently for a short time, listening and watching before Danielle said, 'He probably won't want to live in his house alone. Do you think he'll want to move back into the mansion? I can move out of your place if you're coming home.'

'I never thought of that,' Nate said with a weary sigh. 'See, it's all changing again. It's like whenever things are good, someone shakes the snow globe.'

Danielle chuckled at the image. 'That's good. I'm going to use that.'

'Thanks,' Nate smiled. 'I'll ask Adam if he wants to move home, but you don't have to move out. Even if I return, we could flat together like we planned.'

She gave him a wry look.

'What?'

'And do I buy earplugs for the nights that Jessica stays over? No thanks. I'll get a place if need be.'

He chuckled. 'I forgot about that aspect.'

'How many nights do you want to spend on surveillance?' Danielle asked.

'Worst-case scenario, three – two consecutive days, then maybe Friday night. After that, I want to go in.'

'Yeah?' she brightened. 'Count me in.'

While they sat in silence, Nate thought about Adam. He reached for his phone and called him, but it went to the message bank.

'What was that?' Danielle said, and Nate dropped his phone and reached for the binoculars.

'Where?'

'That light, inside the carnival,' she said, filming the area with her phone.

Nate searched the area, squinting and scanning it with the binoculars. 'I can see shadows moving, but that's it. Probably kids.'

They both jumped as something thumped against the roof of their car, and Nate instinctively moved to exit; Danielle caught his arm.

'Wait, watch,' she hissed.

There was no movement around the car or any sign of what struck his vehicle. Nate made a low growling sound. 'If someone's damaged the Audi, a broken-down old carnival will be the last of their worries.'

'I know,' she rolled her eyes. 'Be afraid, be very afraid.'

Nate smiled, and they sat and waited, watching and being watched.

Chapter 9

J essica was excited that the day's first meeting at the Delaney and Murphy office was with Audrey. She had spent quality time with her at the wedding of Adam's mother, the *IT* girl Winsome Keeley and his godfather, rock star Jack Bernham, but had rarely seen her since, even though Jessica spent half of her weeknights at the riverside mansion sharing Nate's bed. Audrey lived in her own wing, and came and went at random times to her bridge club, charity work, and theatre group. Some nights, they heard the gate opening long after they had gone to bed, and Nate would rise to check if the Jaguar was driving in and to ensure she was okay. He would give her a wave from the window as the garage door closed her in. It seemed very uncool to admit they were in bed before 79-year-old Audrey.

Because of Nate's surveillance shift last night, Jessica had not slept over, and Nate and Audrey arrived together just after 9am.

'How odd to be driven here by you, Nathanial,' she was saying on entering. 'I can remember you sitting in the back of my Jag on the way to school like it were yesterday.'

'I'm relieved you didn't make me answer questions from the news today like you used to, Audrey,' Nate said, faking relief, and she laughed.

'I only wish I had remembered too,' she teased him before greeting Jessica, and the three made their way to the meeting room. Danielle arrived next with their morning coffee order, for which Audrey had already requested tea, and Jessica put a pot and China cup before her.

'You are putting us to shame, Audrey,' Jessica said. 'Your social life is better than ours.'

'Not at all, dear. When I was working, I didn't have time to be out at all hours of the night playing cards, going to the theatre and drinking good port. I was home in bed at a good hour. You will have plenty of time to make up for it.' She patted Jessica's arm. 'Where's my grandson?'

They heard the outside door open and voices as Rob and Adam arrived. Rob stopped to greet Audrey, and Adam rushed in after depositing his keys and jacket in his office.

'And what hour do you call this?' Nate asked, making them laugh.

'Sorry, Mum,' he said to Nate and greeted the ladies, kissing his grandmother on the cheek.

'Sorry I'm late,' he said but did not give a reason. 'I know Nate's normally the late one, so you are probably all a bit shocked.'

'It's one of the things I do well, and I don't like having you try and take it from me,' Nate said, giving him a serious look.

Jessica was pleased to see Adam's sense of humour had returned; Nate had told her about Kelsey.

'Before we start, I want to tell you all something,' Adam said, and his seriousness gained their attention. Before starting, he accepted the cup of coffee from Danielle, who thought he might need it.

'If you don't already know,' he said, glancing at Nate, whom he suspected had spread the news, 'Kelsey's accepted a contract in Sydney and left this morning.'

The group gasped at the suddenness of it, except for Audrey, who spoke with Adam last night.

'Despite my profession, no, I don't want to talk about it or analyse it to death,' he said with a small smile that fooled no one, given his pain.

'That's fine, but—' Nate started and was interrupted by Adam holding up his hand.

'There's more. We've broken up.'

'But if it's only for a year, why—,' Danielle said and again stopped on seeing his expression.

'It's not for a year. Kelsey has been doing her masters in research for the last eighteen months. She's been working with a mentor…' he stopped; no one said a word, and composing himself, continued. 'He's ten years older, has a passion for national archives and her, apparently. It's mutual; quiet, bookish souls – her words,' he mumbled as if hearing them again was too much. Adam inhaled sharply. 'Kelsey wants me to meet someone younger, have a family, all the things she can't be for me.' He looked around. 'That's it.'

'I know what Kelsey means,' Danielle said, thinking aloud. 'You're three years younger than her; you could be dating girls much younger.'

Jessica nudged her under the table, and Danielle added, 'Not that you wanted to, of course.'

Adam sighed. 'No, and before anyone says it, let's not go there. No saying, "I *need to get back on the horse*", or I should "*put myself back out there*", "*her loss*", "*You'll be snapped up in a minute*", or any other similar, stupid saying.'

'Well, that's me out,' Danielle said, throwing her pen on the table. 'They're the only sayings I know.'

Adam chuckled, and Audrey said, 'It's the thought that counts, good try, Danielle, dear.'

Nate cleared his throat and filled the silence. 'We'll have a drink and—'

Again, Adam cut him off, holding up his hand to silence Nate.

'No, Nate. We're not going to do that either. No drunk therapy, matchmaking, changing your weekend plans to incorporate me,' he looked around the table. 'I don't want everyone looking at me like I'm some poor, sad bastard who is going to go off the rails. If that's what I have to face coming in here every day, then I may have to resort to murder. Sorry Audrey,' he apologised for the swearing.

'Quite all right, my boy, I've heard worse,' she assured him, making the group smile, including Adam.

'Sorry,' Nate put up his hand this time, 'but you are some poor, sad bastard, for a while anyway, so just own it. And murder is not ideal,' Nate said. 'Bodies are getting harder to hide these days in a built-up city. Or so I've heard,' he added quickly when Jessica gave him a weird look.

'That might be, but I'm not ruling it out,' Adam said. 'Right, the case…'

'You're coming on surveillance with me tonight,' Nate said.

Adam threw his hands up in the air. 'It begins.'

Nate shook his head. 'Dan did it last night with me, but she can't do it tonight. Since you're free, you're in. It's safer with two.'

'It's Eric's birthday,' she said of her new photographer boyfriend, brother of the late Holly Castle, whose case they recently solved. 'I'm taking him to dinner.'

'Yeah? Happy birthday from us,' Adam said including the group. He turned to Nate, 'Okay, count me in.'

'Oh, wait,' Jessica startled them all. 'Before you begin, Audrey, one moment, please.'

She raced out of the room while the group drank their coffee or tea and talked of things that weren't about Adam despite the elephant in the room. When she returned, Jessica saw everyone sneaking looks at Adam, trying to read his emotional state. She opened a Tupperware container and announced, 'Ta-da! Last night, I made funny faces!'

The group laughed, and Jessica filled Audrey in on the background – 'Nate said that Laura Armstrong was as plain as an Arrowroot biscuit, and his aunt made funny faces with Milk Arrowroot biscuits.'

'These are as good as Nate's aunt,' Adam said, not taking one despite Jessica's prompting.

'Do you want me to turn that jelly bean smile upside down to a frown for you?' Nate asked Adam, making him grin, and Jessica hit his arm.

'That's hardly supportive,' she scolded him.

'It's what Adam expects from me,' Nate assured her. 'He can't take sympathy.'

'No. Funny that given a psychologist spends his day being sympathetic,' Danielle added.

'I'm right here,' Adam said drily.

'They're delightful, Jessica,' Audrey said, accepting a white one while Danielle took one with pink icing and blue Smartie chocolates for eyes and a jelly bean mouth.

'I made ones with black eyes and smile for you,' Jessica said, knowing Nate liked black jelly beans.

'I wouldn't say she's plain,' Audrey said of Laura. 'In my day, she would have been called a handsome young woman. Strong face, intelligent eyes, and being quick to laugh can add a lot to one's beauty.'

Again, all eyes turned to Adam as if Audrey were matchmaking, and Nate hurried the conversation along. 'Audrey, thanks for coming in. What can you tell us about the Dobrev family and their Carnival World?'

Audrey set her teacup down and began. 'The head of the Dobrev family, Rayco, is a lovely, gentle soul. He had a dream when he started that fun park. The family is Bulgarian, and his parents came here without any English language, worked hard and did their best. Rayco, or Ray as he preferred to be known, learned his work ethic from them. He wanted to create a park that would bring families together, provide a fun, affordable day out, and that people would return to for years and bring their children.'

'He achieved that,' Adam said.

'He did,' Audrey agreed. 'His son and wife worked in the park, and you boys went there, as did many families.'

'And then the area was developed?' Jessica asked.

'Exactly so,' Audrey nodded. 'It seemed a long way out of the city when they first built there, and it was, but the city crept up on them, and soon the train and bus networks were put in place, and the land became very desirable. We were all part of the new estate dream.'

'Our place was in the release before Riverside Park was developed,' Nate said.

'Yes. Riverside Park was the final package of land and house sales, and it was right on the doorstep of *Dobrev's Carnival World*,' Audrey said. 'Ray was offered a generous package to sell up and leave, but it was his life's work.'

'Was Gerta, his wife, as passionate about the business?' Adam asked.

'No, Darling, she wasn't, but nevertheless, she worked in it every day. Gerta wanted to take the offer, sell and go, but Ray had his dream. So, he decided the best way forward was to appease the new homeowners and developers by making themselves an even bigger part of the community,' Audrey said. 'That's how we met. He contacted many community groups and wanted to hold functions for the schools, the needy, and the sick kiddies. He also had a vision to give some of the land to the community for parkland and affordable housing; he was very generous.'

'Did you think at the time it could work?' Danielle asked.

'Yes, I did. I thought the community might adopt it. He was also prepared to adapt the business hours to reduce the noise and accommodate residents.'

'So, are you saying that Laura's father and the neighbourhood group he led were unreasonable?' Nate asked.

'Not in context. The negotiations initially travelled along nicely, and I was happily involved. But then Rayco and Gerta's son, Gerry, and some of the invested carnival workers started to fight back.'

Adam nodded knowingly. 'Gerry threatened us that day in the cemetery when I was about twelve.'

'You're kidding?' Jessica said, shocked. 'That's scary.'

'It was, dear,' Audrey agreed. 'Gerry Dobrev was waiting at Laura's father's fresh grave as if warning me what he was capable of doing. I am not one to back away from a good fight, but I did with this. I had a young grandson to protect, and James—Adam's father—was away a lot; it wasn't worth the risk. I told Ray I was sorry, but it was too controversial for me and pulled back.'

'Gerry would have been pleased,' Nate said.

'Yes, no doubt, and he threatened other community members too, telling them to back off or there would be trouble.

'So,' Nate mused, 'Gerry, the son, wanted the carnival to continue as well? It was only Gerta who wanted to take the money?'

'No,' Audrey said. 'Gerry wanted to sell. Unlike his father, Gerry didn't want the community to get any land or even discounts. It was a sordid affair.'

'Yesterday, he was there again at the cemetery, eighteen years after his last visit,' Adam said. The surprise looks on everyone around the table made Nate realise this would be more complex and dangerous than he first realised.

Audrey nodded. 'And, it is all starting again; I suspect the fight is still the same. The residents want *Dobrev's Carnival World* gone.'

'I don't understand,' Danielle said. 'It's closed down now. There's no noise or traffic, and if Rayco Dobrev is alive and in aged care, it can only be a matter of time until he passes and it can be sold.'

'Yes, one would think so,' Audrey agreed, 'but Gerry threatened us to keep quiet and not get involved again. So perhaps there's more at stake than we know. Perhaps he thinks we will try to claim some of the assets for charity based on his father's verbal promise. But last time, a young father lost his life, and no one wants to see that repeated.'

'I think this case is going to get a lot bigger than Laura's father's death,' Nate said.

'And now we're part of it,' Danielle agreed.

As the meeting ended, the front door buzzer sounded, and Jessica rose, returning with Laura Armstrong.

'Audrey!' she proclaimed, and the ladies hugged.

'I was just sharing my background information for your case. I am sure Nathanial will update you,' Audrey said, retrieving her handbag to leave.

'Nathanial?' Laura said, 'Oh, Nate. Oh my, are they funny faces?'

'Have one,' Jessica said.

'Thank you, I love these. My aunty always said I was as plain as an Arrowroot biscuit, so I have an affinity for them,' she said and chuckled.

There was no exchange of looks as everyone averted their eyes.

'Well, I've got to see a patient,' Adam said, rising.

'Adam's doing surveillance with me tonight,' Nate said.

'I'd like to do a night as well. Can I come along with both of you?' Laura asked.

'Why don't you come along on the Friday night shift with me,' Nate said, wanting to talk with Adam tonight. 'Danielle will be along too.'

'Done,' she agreed. 'I'll bring snacks.'

'And that's how it's done,' Nate said to Danielle, who rolled her eyes. 'I'll drive you home, Audrey. Danielle can update you, Laura.'

'I can take Audrey,' Adam said. 'Give me a minute to grab my stuff. I'm heading that way to the health facility anyway.'

'Lovely,' Audrey said. While she waited for her grandson, she studied the young lawyer. 'Be very careful, Laura dear, won't you? A guilty man will go to extremes to protect his freedom.'

'Do you think we might need security?' Laura asked.

'We know someone,' Nate said, glancing at the door.

'Not him, not Tom,' Danielle said with a shake of her head.

'We'll see. He's available, knows us all and the lay of the land, and is affordable,' Nate said. 'I'll suggest it to Adam tonight when we're in the car for hours so he can work through his explosion.'

Audrey smiled sympathetically. 'My poor grandson. A rough time indeed.'

Chapter 10

A dam dropped Audrey off at the riverside mansion—his childhood home—and ensured she was safely inside before he drove out of the huge gates and headed to the mental health facility in the neighbouring suburbs. He had to admit, the mansion was looking good. Their gardener and pool guy were doing a great job, and having Nate living on the premises let him not worry about Audrey around the clock.

Thinking about his own timber character home, he felt the same emptiness he did when he thought of Kelsey. He would be home alone in the house he thought would be his and Kelsey's marital home. It might have been the house for a couple of kids, but he accepted long ago that she didn't want to have any, and as an only child, he refused to have just one child; it was two or more, or none at all. His first marriage to Stephanie was fuelled by sex and attraction, but he loved Kelsey and had been fiercely protective of her.

Adam was disappointed in himself; he didn't see it coming – not a hint. He thought he was good at reading people, but clearly not. Although she promised nothing had happened with the archivist, she wanted to pursue it. Apparently, the pair had a deep connection and were cut from the same cloth. He was cut from a different roll, he thought, trying to amuse himself.

In the space of a few nights, his whole life and the future he had mapped out had changed, and he wasn't sure where to go from here. Nothing familiar was the same; all of it seemed undesirable, leftover, like he'd been left behind. Had she been thinking of her mentor while sleeping beside him? At the wedding, was it duty that made her attend? Was she sizing him up against this other guy for months on end? And when he was away for a few days with Nate on the last case, was she alone at night?

His mind went over the same questions as if an answer might present itself. With the thoughts intruding, it took all his concentration to talk with Audrey on the way home. He had known Kelsey since he was a teenager. She was part of his past and present, and he didn't know how to cut her out. But Audrey knew him and had stopped talking before he realised it.

'I'm sorry,' he mumbled, and she gave a small shake of her head and a smile.

'My darling, do not be. Grief takes a while to settle.' She had not spoken for the rest of the trip home and touched his face tenderly on departing.

Adam arrived at the Mental Health Facility without remembering the drive. Checking in, he made his way to the meeting room for his appointed time with Dane. The sixteen-year-old was brought in; his neck tattoo and short hair made him look rougher than his true nature. Dane's perpetual suspicious look added to his air of aggression.

'Hi,' Adam said. 'You look better than when I saw you yesterday.'

'You look awful. I'm supposed to look wasted, not you,' Dane joked, plonking himself onto the couch opposite Adam and crossing his leg onto his knee.

'Get out of here; I look fine,' Adam retorted, trying to be light-hearted.

'Are you taking?' Dane asked.

'Of course I'm not taking anything,' Adam shot back with a look of disbelief.

'Sniffing?'

'No.'

'Drinking?'

'No. I'm not snorting, inhaling or sculling anything. Let's talk about you,' Adam said, rolling his eyes and making Dane laugh. 'I'm the psychologist; you're the patient. Remember?'

Dane grinned. 'I just thought you might like a change from bleating patients.' He folded his arms across his chest, becoming increasingly comfortable in Adam's presence.

'I'd be happy if you did some bleating,' Adam said. 'It might make you less inclined to do some damage.' Adam referred to the day prior when he was called in as Dane ran amok.

'Ah, that,' Dane said.

'That,' Adam agreed.

As often happens when things go bad, the universe prods your pain, and Dane asked the one question that would cut like a knife.

'Got a girlfriend?'

For a moment, Adam bristled and caught himself about to answer yes.

'Nope. Do you?'

'Nuh. But jeez, if you can't get a chick with your looks and money, there's not much hope for the rest of us.'

'Not while you're in here,' Adam said, bringing it back to Dane. 'But you've got a lot to offer.'

'Ha! Like what? Trey gets lots of chicks,' Dane said.

The boy from an abusive background with a Dissociative Identity Order was speaking of one of his personalities, Trey, the model.

'He's always boasting about it. But the guys like him more. He's really popular with the men. He's been paid a lot to give them what they want,' Dane said, his voice harsher, spit building as he hissed the words. 'I told him he's not doing it anymore. He's been freaking out about it; he's freaking out now.' His voice rose as anger welled.

Adam wanted to stay with Dane; he would deal with Trey another time.

'Dane, do you remember how we spoke about doing an exercise with eye movement?'

'Yeah, changing how my memories are stored in my brain.'

'That's right,' Adam said, pleased but not surprised. Dane was bright, but that was the tragedy of his childhood, that it was derailed. 'I think it will help Trey, too. It's helped others I've worked with.'

'He needs it,' Dane scoffed. 'Are you going to zap him?'

'No. Remember we talked about how it is done with hand and eye movements?'

'Yeah. Trey says, "Whatever". He doesn't care.' Dane had his petulant look on but was protective of Trey. 'He doesn't trust men much.'

Adam nodded. 'If you had to tell me how Trey was feeling now, how you are feeling, in a couple of words, what would those words be.'

Dane's eyes narrowed as if it were a trick. 'He's angry. Like he wants to kill them.'

'Okay, so you feel angry at them, but can you find a word that describes how you feel about yourself? Or how Trey feels about himself. For example, if he had to describe himself to me in one word now.'

Dane thought for a moment. 'Useless.' He spat the word out.

'In that situation with the modelling agent and the other men, you or Trey had little control. But didn't you do the best you could? That's not being useless.'

Dane scoffed. 'I just put up with whatever they dealt me. Didn't even fight back.'

Adam noticed he hadn't referred to Trey this time; Dane was the victim, the true victim.

'You did what you thought was best, given you were outnumbered. You made that decision because it was the right one for survival that day. Can you believe that about yourself?'

Dane's lips thinned as he thought about it. What Adam was saying was right, but... 'No, I'm a mute whore, that's all I am.'

Adam controlled his breathing; the despair came off the boy in waves, and he tried not to reflect it along with his own misery.

'Answer me honestly, Dane, without flogging yourself for what happened. Think back on that day you were modelling with the men present. Can you accept that you did what you had to do to get through the day?'

Adam could see the boy's resistance, but Dane nodded briefly.

'Say it,' Adam encouraged him. 'Acknowledge you did the best you could when you had no choice.'

'I did the best I could when I had no choice,' he parroted, and Adam waited. Dane sighed and said it again with more sincerity.

'Yes, you did, as many others like you have done before. Now that we know that to be true, what emotion are you feeling? Fear, pain, hate, anger, or something else?'

Dane rubbed his chest. 'Pain. No hurt.'

Adam nodded, intending to desensitise that feeling. 'Hurt. I want you to think about that incident again, Dane. It'll be okay. I want you to think of being used and where it hurts now.'

Dane drew a deep breath. 'Say it again.'

'Think about the men, how they made you feel used and where physically you feel that hurt.'

Dane did not speak but rubbed his heart with his palm as if massaging an ache.

Adam continued. 'Now, follow my hand with your eyes.'

Adam engaged in left-and-right hand movements for thirty seconds, not speaking and ensuring Dane followed with his eyes. He put his hands down at the end of the set of eye movements. 'Dane, take a deep breath, and I want you to let all those feelings go.'

Dane took a long, deep breath and exhaled, releasing the breath and, Adam hoped, some of the anxiety.

'How do you feel?'

Dane bit his tongue while he thought. 'Mixed up,' he eventually said.

'That's fine.'

'It sucks that I let them get away with it.'

'But you didn't. They didn't get your heart or soul. You went into self-preservation mode and survived. You did your best.'

'I did my best,' Dane said with a nod and a shudder in his voice.

'You're better than you thought, braver,' Adam said.

'Different,' Dane conceded. He raised his chin. 'Stronger.'

'Yes, you are strong. We will do this exercise again and think about how strong you were then, the choices you made that day and how capable you are now.'

Small steps, Adam thought. He could still control this part of his life even if the rest was off the rails.

Chapter 11

Adam tried not to react when he found out Laura was coming along on surveillance, but it was fair to say he was not happy. They planned to start a little earlier to study the neighbours and street before it was dark. Then, they would settle in for the night shift.

'The more the merrier,' Danielle said, having dropped in briefly to see Nate before calling it a day.

'There's safety in numbers,' Nate agreed.

Adam looked to Jessica, who said, 'I've got nothing,' making him laugh.

'You don't really need me along then,' Adam said.

'I do,' Nate disagreed. 'Laura is just observing. Dan, Jess, get out of here; it's nearly 5.30.' They didn't need much encouragement.

'I'm meeting Eric at the gym,' Danielle said, rising and stretching. 'The couple that works out together stays together.'

'We're doomed,' Jessica joked with a glance at Nate.

Rob wandered out of his office, hearing the discussions and preparing to leave for the day. He usually clocked off earlier to beat the traffic home but was catching up post-holiday.

'Still here?' he asked Nate and Adam.

'We're just waiting on the legal minion,' Adam said unenthusiastically. Then, he winced when he saw Jessica's eyes widen as someone entered behind them.

'Legal minion reporting for duty, sir,' she said and laughed. 'The door was open.'

'Hi Laura, that courier guy didn't close it behind him,' Jessica said.

Adam turned to see Laura equipped with a video camera and iPad and dressed head to toe in black. She looked good – black boots, jeans, and a sweatshirt. Her hair was tied back in a small ponytail, and her brown eyes appraised him.

'Well, that's awkward,' Nate grinned, enjoying the scene.

'Let me rephrase that,' Adam said, trying to cover for the comment as the office team grinned like it was the greatest joke. 'Thanks for the warning, you lot,' he said under his breath.

Laura laughed again. 'Don't sweat it. I've been called worse; I work in law.'

'Ignore grumpy,' Nate said, giving his client a warm, welcome smile. He clapped Adam on the shoulder. 'He likes to do surveillance alone so he can analyse himself.'

Adam rolled his eyes.

'Thanks, Nate, for *tolerating* me on this mission,' she said, with an amused glance at Adam. 'I'll do my best to be seen and not heard.'

'Are we off then?' Adam asked, cranky that his relaxing night with his oldest friend was now a night with a client, and he would have to be on guard. Hopefully, Nate didn't watch them all night to see if they had a spark, given Audrey was already dropping less-than-subtle thoughts. Just what he needed.

On the way down to the parking garage via the stairs, Nate politely read Laura the riot act. 'If anything starts to go down, follow our lead and instructions to the letter. Plus, there are no flashes, no lights from phones, cameras, or anything of that nature. Turn your phone on silent, too.'

'Got it,' she said. 'I'll be making notes, so if anything is completely off the record, just flag it.'

'You're not recording anything for the podcast, are you?' Adam asked and saw Nate flash him a look not to annoy his client.

'Of course not,' Laura assured him. 'If I wanted to use anything with you guys in it, I'd get you to sign off on it. You have my word.'

They arrived at Nate's car, and he opened the back door for Laura.

'Which side do you want me on?' she asked Nate.

Preferably where I can't see you, Adam thought miserably.

'Why don't you sit behind Adam? If anything eventuates, I can catch your eye and signal you, plus there's more legroom. He's shorter than me.'

Adam scoffed. 'You may be two months older, but I am one centimetre taller.'

Laura's laugh drifted from the back seat. She laughed a lot, and Adam liked that about her.

'Sorry to just invite myself along,' she said, 'but I can't come Friday after all, and I didn't want to miss seeing what surveillance was like.'

'Sure,' Adam said, 'no problem,' his answer devoid of sincerity. As Nate drove them toward *Dobrev's Carnival World*, Adam caught Nate glancing at him, trying to read his best friend.

Laura's phone rang and she apologised. 'I'll put it on silent, but I just need to take this.'

Nate glanced at Adam again and asked, 'Are you all right?'

'Sure.'

'Sorry about—'

'It's all good.'

'Okay.' Nate persisted in endeavouring to have a conversation. 'How did you go with your patient?'

'Yeah, interesting, we're getting there... somewhere, but moving forward, I think.'

'That's something.' Nate cleared his throat. 'I'm going to say something, and I don't want you freaking out or leaping from a moving vehicle.'

Adam could hear Laura speaking on the phone, so he nodded for his friend to continue.

Nate began quickly and in a low voice, 'I've seen you deal with break-ups a few times; we've both been through it. I know this is the closest you've got to commitment since Stephanie, but the way you've shut down is unnerving. So, I was thinking,' Nate said, continuing while he had the floor, 'do you want to move back home?'

Adam snapped to look at him. 'Why would I want to do that?'

Nate shrugged. 'A change of scenery. You could rent your house out and move back in. I could move home, and Danielle would be happy for the flatmate. Or I could move into the other wing; we wouldn't see much of each other if you were worried I'd get sick of you.'

Adam gave a huff of laughter. 'I don't want you to move out. I hadn't thought about staying or going, to be honest.'

'Come home,' Nate said, pleased Laura was still on the phone so they could talk. 'Even with Jess staying over, it's a big place for four people.'

Adam said nothing for a moment. He was thinking of his ex-wife Stephanie and their break-up. He had called it off, and now he felt her pain and humiliation, not to mention her fear of losing her job as Winsome's publicist. At the time, he'd been clinical about it, burnt out with the effort of maintaining her. His mind drifted back to Kelsey, and he checked the rearview mirror to ensure Laura wasn't listening. Her dulcet tones floated over the front seat as she maintained a quiet conversation.

'I can't believe I didn't see it coming,' Adam said with a slight shake of his head. He rubbed a thumb across his lip in thought. 'I'm clearly good at analysing people.'

'Why would you see it coming?' Nate said quietly. 'You were both in love, and you trusted her. She didn't break that trust. You believe that, don't you?'

'Yeah, I do. Kelsey wouldn't do that. But now she's free to...' The words trailed off, tinged with bitterness.

'Mate, I know it's hard—'

Adam leant back and stared at the car's ceiling. 'Nate, do not start.' His emotions rose to his throat, and Adam couldn't speak; he turned his head away to look out the window. Nate sighed knowingly next to him and said nothing more.

Laura half listened to her mother issuing the same warnings to her and studied the boys at the same time. She thought that was one bonus of being on surveillance; she could observe them with full license. Laura mused that if Adam were a private investigator like Nate, he would be Agent Aloof. At least he looked sufficiently embarrassed by the minion comment. Adam was beautiful physically; she could imagine his mother's disappointment that he didn't follow in her modelling footsteps. And he was different with Nate – a lot less intense, maybe more himself, but other times seemed so hot and cold. She heard him laugh at one of Nate's jokes. Arrogant didn't describe him, nor did aloof, in fairness. He was annoyingly undefinable.

Nate, on the other hand, was very laid-back, quick to smile, and full of bravado. He was in charge of the case but didn't pull rank on her or Adam. But tonight, Laura thought, she intended to do her job to the letter – sit in the back and be quiet, take notes, take a few pics, yep, pretend she's not even there.

After a few more minutes, she hung up. 'Sorry about that. Mum's nervous about me being involved in all this.'

'Understandable,' Nate said. 'I'm nervous about it too,' he joked.

'To be honest,' Adam began, 'I thought you would be sombre and find this all very draining, but you seem to have a good grip on it.'

'Is that a professional analysis?' she teased.

'A professional observation,' he said, turning a little to shoot her a smile.

Laura shrugged. 'I guess it has been 18 years since Dad's death, and I was only a kid; I barely knew him. I'm seeking justice, not revenge.'

'And your mum never wanted to leave the neighbourhood, not even after your dad's death?' Nate asked.

'I thought that was odd too. But Mum had friends in the neighbourhood who looked after her. Plus, it was her dream home.'

Nate pulled the car to the side of the road a little further away from *Dobrev's Carnival World* and killed the lights and engine. The traffic had delayed them, and night had fallen; only tinges of red dusk remained.

'Okay, give me the surveillance run down,' she said enthusiastically from the back seat.

'It gets exciting from here,' Nate joked. 'Now, we scan the area and set up markers in our minds of what is there so we hopefully notice if anything changes.'

They sat in silence, Nate pointing out things to observe, jokingly referring to Laura as the civilian in the back seat.

'Where exactly did your dad die, do you know?' Adam asked.

'Yes. On the corner to your right is where he allegedly hit his head. Weird, isn't it, to think someone's life is snuffed out right there, and life goes on?'

Adam returned to his state of quietness, and Laura wondered if she shouldn't have come along. Maybe they wanted to talk about guy things, whatever that included. Another thirty minutes passed, and Nate exhaled. 'Having fun yet?'

Laura laughed. 'It's like a boring law lecture. I love this car. Is this your first Audi?'

'Yep, I love it too. Winsome gave it to me for my 30th birthday, Adam's mum,' he added in case she didn't make the connection.

'Wow, you're kidding? What did you get then?' she asked Adam.

'A Mercedes,' he said.

'Wow. I can tell you what I'll get for my thirtieth: fifty dollars in a birthday card from the cheap shop and a promise to have me over for dinner as soon as my stepfather is away on one of his golf trips.'

'You don't get on?' Adam asked.

'We get on well enough; I quite like him. But Mum is all about keeping him happy.' She said nothing more about that, but after studying the car in some detail, Laura added, 'Very extravagant.' She ran her hand over the cream leather interior and snuggled into the seat. 'Have you slept in here yet?'

Nate turned and gave her a strange look. 'No. Why would I?'

She shrugged. 'But you could if you found yourself out of work and homeless. Several of my clients have had to resort to that. Mainly women,' she added. 'One lady and her three kids under ten were sleeping in her station wagon.'

'What do you drive?' Adam asked, lightening the conversation.

'A Peugeot, an old one,' she clarified. 'But I love it. It's white with a sunroof and in good nick. I've got a huge student debt to repay, so I won't be driving anything flash for a while. But I'd look really good driving this,' she joked.

'Yeah, I look really good driving it, too,' Nate said and grinned.

'Might help you get a girlfriend,' she teased. 'I bet it's a chick magnet.'

'Can't hurt,' Nate added. 'I'm seeing Jessica.'

'Oh, your office manager. Nice.' Laura nodded. He was the boy next door; she could understand Jessica's attraction to him with his positive outlook. She noticed Nate quickly changed the conversation from relationships, for Adam's sake, no doubt. Jessica had subtly told her of the break-up, so Laura didn't put her foot in it.

'It's much more sinister here at night,' he said, switching gear.

'I'd love to go in,' Adam said, looking towards the derelict grounds, the faded sign bearing the Dobrev name and the rides visible through the fence.

'Yeah, I was thinking maybe tomorrow if nothing happens,' Nate said. 'I will speak with some of the residents in the morning. See who has been here since the estate opened, find out what they remember, and what this new scare campaign is about.'

The three sat silently for a while, and then Laura reached for the bag at her feet. 'If it's allowed,' she said for Adam's benefit, 'I have coffee, milk, sugar and three varieties of biscuits.'

Nate kept his eyes glued to the fairground. 'I'm impressed; you can come on surveillance anytime.'

She laughed. 'What will it be?' Adam took a coffee and declined a biscuit; she wondered if he had eaten at all today.

'It's so creepy at night,' she whispered after a while.

'It is that,' Adam agreed. 'But Nate will protect you, he's an ex-cop.'

Nate chuckled. 'Yep. Lock the doors, and if anything happens, I'll accelerate.'

They finished their coffee and biscuits. Hours passed. The men spoke of their trips to the carnival when boys, Adam and Laura swapped tales of

Audrey's endeavours, and Nate updated them on his parents' caravanning adventures. It was nearing eleven o'clock, and nothing had happened.

Laura broke her rule to be quiet and unseen... that novelty had worn off not long after they parked. 'Not even a flicker of light out there. Is the neighbourhood only terrorised on nights with a full moon or what?' she asked, amusing them again.

Nate and Laura discussed the case for a while, and Adam checked his phone several times, searching for something that never came.

'Another half hour will do us, but you two can leave whenever you like. I can get a Uber to pick you both up on the corner,' Nate said. 'As you said, nothing much is happening and we're only doing surveillance so I can manage it.'

'What? And miss out on all the fun, no way!' she said.

And then there was a movement.

'Heads up,' Adam said, and Nate grabbed the binoculars from the consul between them. Laura spun around, grabbed her phone, and began to film.

'There's a shadow, something moving near the carousel,' Nate said quietly.

Then, a few moments later, his breath hitched. Laura gasped, and Adam froze, watching with fascination.

The carousel with the tormented and broken horses started. Slowly, in the moon's shadow, it did one full circle and stopped.

'Creepy,' Laura said in a hushed voice and pressed down on the lock on her door to ensure it was locked.

'It's okay,' Adam said, glancing her way. 'You're safe here.'

She nodded and, like him, hurriedly turned back to watch.

'It's stopped after one full rotation,' Nate said.

'Should we go in?' she asked.

'No—'

'Not tonight,' both men answered in unison.

'We don't know what we're dealing with,' Nate said. 'We wait, watch, record, and tomorrow I'll ask questions.'

Nothing more happened, and no one was visible. At midnight, Nate started the car, and they dropped Laura off at her mother's place nearby, as she had arranged earlier. Nate departed after seeing her enter the house and headed to the Murphy riverside mansion in the neighbouring suburb.

Adam exhaled. 'Well, that was interesting.'

'Stay the night,' Nate said to Adam, who nodded his agreement.

Once they were in the gates and out of the car, Nate turned to Adam. 'Beer?'

'Yeah, why not.'

'And we'll talk.'

'Do we have to?' Adam asked.

'Said no psychologist ever,' Nate quipped. 'And yes, we have to.'

Adam followed Nate inside, just as he always did.

Chapter 12

'**M**iss us, Boss?' Larry Ridgeway, 38, a tattooed roof tiler, gym junkie and in prison for throwing a colleague off the roof after an argument, asked. He was the unofficial leader of the men in Adam's therapy group.

'Like you wouldn't believe, Larry. Coming here is the highlight of my week,' Adam shot back as he joined the waiting group. He sat amongst them in his suit with no tie and slip-on boots with no laces, running on adrenalin after a night of surveillance and several nights of no sleep.

Larry laughed. 'Yeah, we're happy to see you too, but you'll never top arriving with that wedding cake,' Larry said with a shake of his head, remembering Adam bringing in a small layer of Winsome's seven-tiered wedding cake after some coercion and sympathy. 'That's what I'll remember you for.'

'He bangs on about it all the time,' Baz, a friend of Larry's, said.

'Best fruit cake I've ever had,' Larry said and sighed. 'Anyone else you know who is getting married so we can score some more cake? What about you?'

It never ceased to amaze Adam how the universe conspired against him when he was in pain. If Larry had asked that question at last week's session, he would have laughed and said any day now. Now it cut like a knife.

'You'd starve waiting for that day, Larry. Righto, the week that was,' Adam directed them.

'Can I go first?' asked the least likely group member to speak up. David Yates was an accountant gone rogue. Amongst the young, rough, and well-built men in the therapy group, David, 45, looked like he should be the therapist; he was thin, conservative, and wearing steel-rim glasses.

'Sure, Dave, please do,' Adam said, as he usually had to elect and persuade someone to start.

'I had an epiphany this week.'

Adam sat forward with interest.

'What's that mean?' Gary, the fidgeter who always sat next to Dave, asked.

'I had an illuminating discovery, an intuitive perception, you might say,' Dave explained.

Seeing Gary's blank expression, Adam added, 'He realised something big.'

Gary shook his head. 'Why didn't he just say so?'

Adam withheld a sigh. It was going to be a long session, but at least he was distracted. 'Go ahead, Dave, thanks.'

'When I was charged with fraud, my wife left me, my business went bust, and I ended up in here. For the first year, I thought my whole life was over. If I could have topped myself, I would have.'

'Yeah, I felt that way when I came here too,' Larry said. 'Not the topping part; I was going to kill someone else.'

'You got decades with no parole; that's why you felt like that,' Gary said unhelpfully.

'I didn't feel too bad about coming here,' Tim said with a shrug. 'Probably because two of my brothers are in here. The other one's on the outside now.'

'Yeah, it helps if you know someone,' Larry agreed, crossing his tattooed arms. 'But we've been your family, Dave.'

'You have, Larry, and I am truly grateful for that,' Dave said sincerely.

'Your epiphany then?' Adam moved him along.

Dave pushed the steel rim glasses further up his nose. 'For months and months, I mourned the loss of my old life, worrying that I would never be able to recapture it. But the other night, out of the blue, I realised I didn't want my old life back. I don't want to be with my ex-wife, live in that house, or run that business. So, I got to thinking about how much of what I was doing was self-sabotage.'

'I get that,' Tim empathised. He was the youngest member and was inside for theft and violence. 'My father said I did my crime just to get noticed.'

'Yeah, something like that,' Dave agreed. 'But maybe I wanted out of that life and wanted to be caught. I was acting recklessly towards the end, not covering my bases. I honestly believe I felt so trapped that I was desperate for change, even this.' He looked at Adam.

'So, before your crime, you weren't impulsive or took risks?'

'That's the thing. I don't know because I can't remember who I was before years of marriage and striving to make the business work. I was under the thumb, meek, even subservient.'

'So, this breaking out of character and your actions were truer to your personality than you might have realised, without the crime element, of course,' Adam suggested.

'I think it might be. I know to look at me, I'm mild-mannered, but I'm my own man now.'

'Yeah. You've got to wear the pants,' Larry said, encouraging him, 'or sheilas—and blokes, too, for that matter—will walk all over you.'

Adam continued talking with David. 'But you knew the consequences of your actions when you started stealing funds; you were fully cognitive of the outcome?'

'Sure. Like everyone knows the consequences of speeding. But did I think I wouldn't be caught for embezzlement, or did I want to be caught?' Dave asked, and Adam enjoyed having one prisoner amongst the group undertaking some intellectual discourse.

'Can you recall if you were unhappy with your life when you first decided to steal or only after you got down the track and realised there was no going back?'

Dave nodded. 'I thought about that too. I think I started stealing because I was miserable and wanted out of my life. It was as if I were challenging myself to break out and push the limits.'

'Well, you're a success, Davey. You got sent here, so that's big time out,' Larry said, and Dave chuckled.

'Always glass half full, thanks, Larry.'

'So that's your discovery, what now, Dave?' Adam asked.

'I've decided to start over when I get out of here in less than a year. I'm going to be completely different,' Dave said. 'I'm going to live a whole new life and won't allow myself to be trapped again. I'm going to change career, my relationships will be kinder and better matched, and I'm going to be true to my nature,' he said with a small smile.

To Adam, it was as if Dave was asking him questions about his own life. Had he just been cruising with Kelsey because he felt safe with her? Did he believe she needed him so he would never be abandoned? Could he honestly say it was the best match for him? Did he somehow sabotage the relationship by inviting Kelsey to his mother's very public wedding, knowing she would hate it? Was he hoping that might be the outcome? Adam stored Dave's epiphany away for later when he could have a good, hard look at his own life in the same context.

'There's something in that for all of us,' Adam said, clearing his throat and returning to the now. 'Thanks, Dave.'

'Thank you, Adam. Your discussion last week about life directions really stirred me up,' Dave said.

'I want to have an epiphany too,' Baz said. 'How do I go about it.'

Adam smiled. 'It'll just come to you; you can't force it, Baz. But let us know when it happens.'

'Will do, Boss,' Baz agreed.

Adam doubted Baz would recognise an epiphany, let alone be able to spell it, but at least today, one of his group members was lighter of heart and had a future direction. And it wasn't him.

Adam threw up his hands in mock frustration as Nate raced back to the reception desk to answer the phone. After a night of surveillance, they agreed to close the office at 3 p.m. and go for drinks with the team – or rather, Nate suggested and pushed for it.

'That'd be right!' Adam complained to Jessica. 'Nate has been nagging me to finish up early and to head across the road for a drink for as long as I can remember, and here I am—' he stopped talking, tapped his watch and looked around with false dramatics.

She laughed at his antics. Nate made a face at him and held up his hand in a wait signal.

The door opened behind them, and Danielle entered. Eric followed, and the men shook hands.

'It's good to see you again,' Adam said to Eric before Danielle abruptly asked, 'Are we going?' She looked at Adam, who traditionally made excuses to come down later, as if he were holding up happy hour drinks.

'I know. Trust Nate to keep us waiting,' he said, and she laughed and gave him a look that said she had seen right through him. Adam leaned over, looked at the phone panel at reception, and, seeing Rob was off the phone, said, 'Now that you're both here, I'll get Rob.'

'We'll go across the road and get a table; Laura's coming too,' Jessica said, taking charge, and departed with Danielle and Eric.

Adam tapped on Rob's door, opened it and stuck his head in. Rob rarely came for drinks but, having heard of Adam's break-up, decided to come along and make up the numbers. It was fair to say he was worse than Adam when it came to being social – a greying vampire in his sixties who never saw the sun.

'Ready? We're going for drinks.'

'Is it three o'clock already? Logging off then,' Rob said, closing his laptop with a glance at the clock. 'This is a good idea of Nate's; we should both vow to do more team bonding and work-life balance.'

'We say that every week; it's good to have goals,' Adam said with a smile.

Rob laughed. 'True. I know you're not much for socialising.'

Adam shrugged. 'I'm surrounded by people all day at work. I don't need them after hours.'

His mentor rose, grabbed his jacket off the back of the chair and headed toward Adam. 'Before we go out there—'

Adam stopped. From Rob's tone, he could tell that he was going to get a wellness check, and he braced for it.

'I'd suspect you were avoiding me if I didn't know better, but is everything okay?' Rob continued. 'I heard about your break-up with Kelsey and know you're not the type to talk about it, but...'

'Yep, all good. Thanks for asking. She just decided an older academic was more her type.'

'Is she right?' Rob asked.

It was a question he hadn't been asked, and it stopped Adam in his tracks. Before dismissing the idea, Adam recognised the exasperated look on Rob's face; he knew he'd have to give him a few breadcrumbs.

Rob continued. 'You don't have to answer, but I'm available whenever you want to talk. In the interim, stay busy and try to get out.'

'Thanks, but I'm thirty, not eighteen; I've done my share of partying and drinking; I'm handing over the baton to the young ones and staying in.'

'I'm not suggesting you get right back on the horse, but be open to friendships, outings, even just casual sex if it gives you a release,' Rob said candidly.

'Really? That's what you're advocating now?' Adam said with a smile.

'You said it yourself. You're not eighteen.'

'If it were possible to sleep with someone and not have to commit or read about it in the press a week later, then I'd consider it.'

Will that do? Lecture over. But no, no such luck...

Rob scoffed. 'Somehow, I doubt you could ever do that anyway. As nice a lady as Kelsey is, perhaps she isn't the right lady.'

'And yet I thought she was. If she was looking for someone older and bookish, perhaps she picked the wrong guy from the start,' he snapped. 'Let's go.'

Rob looked surprised.

Nate came to the door. 'Are we going?'

'Yep,' Adam strode past him, not seeing but knowing Rob and Nate would be exchanging looks behind his back.

On the walk over, Nate lightened the mood. 'You're his mentor,' Nate said, 'You should put on his performance review that he has to step out with the team at least once a week.'

'I'm stepping,' Adam called from in front.

'I think he should move home too,' Nate was saying.

'That's a good idea,' Rob agreed.

'Thanks, Dad and Dad,' Adam groaned.

Is groaning part of his job description?' Nate asked.

'It's not ideal. I'll make a note,' Rob said in jest.

They arrived at the hotel and saw Danielle waving to them from the far corner of the room.

'It was too busy outside – traffic,' she said by way of explanation, and they sat, their drink order arriving at the same time as Laura.

Adam rose, putting a hand on Nate's shoulder to keep him in his seat.

'Sit here, Laura. What are you drinking?' He headed to the bar with her chardonnay order, watching the group as he waited. He saw them all randomly watching him, especially Nate, so he turned his attention to some sports replay on a large TV screen. The bar was filling up with locals – male and female, some in work gear, some in nightclub gear starting their nights with drinks in the suburbs, and a handful of casual people in jeans; it'd been a while since he had been in a bar as a single man. He returned with Laura's wine.

'Thanks, Adam,' she said. 'Lucky I'm like a camel; I thought it would be ages with that crowd at the bar.'

He chuckled, and the group toasted good health. Then, he drifted in and out of conversations while he thought over David's words in the prison group today. What did he really want if he were honest with himself? He caught Nate studying him again and sighed.

Nate leaned toward him, speaking quietly so no one else could hear in the crowded bar. 'Are you all right?'

Adam rolled his eyes. 'Yes. For the love of God, focus on your girlfriend. I'm not going to self-combust.'

'If you do, could you do it in that direction,' Nate said, brushing down his tie. 'This is new.'

'Very nice,' Adam agreed.

'But seriously, what are you thinking about? Moving home?'

Adam looked confused. 'No. I'm focusing on being my social best.'

Nate flashed him a grin. 'Needs a bit of work.'

'I'm pretty sure I can get to the exit in seven long strides,' Adam said, looking happier at the thought.

Rob attempted to involve him in his group's conversation, but after Adam made a few comments, he turned back to Nate.

'Something is happening here. I don't want to flag a conspiracy theory, but you and Rob need to stop doing your best to make me social.'

Nate took a sip of his beer and said with emotional honesty, 'I feel like you're bleeding, and all I've got on me is a tissue.'

Surprised, Adam's eyebrows shot up at that imagery. 'That's very good.'

'Thanks. I read it online when I googled, "How to help your poor, sad bastard best friend".'

Adam laughed and saw the looks of relief around the table. He decided to lift his game. There was no point in dragging everyone else down just because he was miserable.

'This place has a good atmosphere,' Laura said, looking around the bar.

Adam leaned closer to her and Nate. 'Don't both look at once, but that guy at the bar, the short one with the crew cut, is Gerry Dobrev.'

Nate turned immediately. Laura waited for her turn, subtly glancing over when Nate looked back.

'What's he doing here?' Nate said in a low voice.

'Following us, I suspect,' Adam said. 'Stay here. I've met him once this week; I'll renew the friendship.'

Adam was up before Nate could protest, taking his vodka and lime and walking towards the man sitting at a bar stool. He turned to face Adam as he approached.

'You're a long way from home,' Adam said, and Gerry Dobrev, the smell of cigarettes lingering on him, smiled with his stained teeth from years of smoking.

'I read in the paper that a private investigator was taking the cold case. Didn't know it was a cold case,' he said and sipped his beer before adding, 'I wanted to see the office location for myself.'

'Why?' Adam asked, lowering himself on the bar stool opposite.

'Is that her, the lawyer daughter?' Gerry nodded in the direction of Laura.

'You've seen her photo in the paper and surely seen her visiting her mum in the neighbourhood. You know it is,' Adam said.

Nate joined them, and Adam looked up at him, making the introductions.

'Good to meet you,' Nate said. 'Saves me seeking you out tomorrow. Can we talk now?'

Gerry Dobrev shrugged and looked at his half-empty glass. 'If you shout me a beer.'

Adam caught the barman's eye and ordered the drink. Nate pulled up a stool.

'What are you expecting to find after all this time?' Gerry asked, and Nate gave a small shrug.

'Too early to say. Alex Armstrong's death might have been an accident, it might be more, or it might be too hard to tell after eighteen years, but if it were your dad, wouldn't you want to know?' Nate asked.

'No,' Gerry huffed. 'Good riddance to the old bastard, I'd say.'

'Where's your dad now?' Nate asked.

'In aged care. Senile. Don't expect to get anything that makes sense from him.'

'What do you want at the end of the day, Gerry?' Nate put the question back to him.

'I want all this to go away,' he waved a hand at the two men and the woman at the table waiting. 'I want the old bastard to die so we can sell the property and move on with our lives.' He took several large gulps of his beer.

'So, you'll inherit the carnival?' Adam asked.

'What carnival? That dump. I'll inherit the land and clear it all, and the locals can get their wish. Carnival World will be gone faster than you can say "carousel". They have my word.'

'Did you see Alex Armstrong that night, eighteen years ago, during the street riot?' Nate asked.

'Of course I did; he was one of the leaders. He was a big guy, full of himself, ranting and waving signage as he came down the street.'

'Did you see what happened to him?' Nate asked.

'Nuh. It was crazy that night. He didn't mind throwing around his weight and throwing a punch or two, so it didn't surprise me when he fell and struck his head.'

Gerry had almost drained his beer, and Adam knew the interview would soon be over. He had no wish to fill him up with more grog. Nate didn't offer, so no doubt felt the same.

'Do you know why some residents are being threatened now?' Nate persisted, trying to get in as many questions as he could before Gerry Dobrev walked.

'I have no idea. It's never been the friendliest of neighbourhoods. I've been there for decades and still don't feel welcome. So let me give you a tip: it's a good time to walk away because the place isn't getting any friendlier.' Gerry pushed his glass away and said again, 'Walk away.'

'Or what?' Nate asked as Gerry Dobrev rose to depart.

'Well, you wouldn't want history repeating itself.' Looking at Adam, he added, 'Tell your grandmother that too, if she doesn't want to see me in the cemetery in the future.' He departed, a sneer on his face.

Nate rose and returned to Laura and the group to explain what had happened. With them distracted, Adam finished his vodka and lime in one large gulp and slipped off into the night.

Chapter 13

Laura had never expected to visit Rayco Dobrev at his aged care home, which was only about twenty minutes from his life's work – the carnival. Nate had requested Adam to attend with him, and when Laura asked to come along, he had to be convinced.

'There's no danger in me coming, surely?' Laura had said at drinks yesterday afternoon.

'How do I say this diplomatically?' Nate said, looking at the hotel ceiling.

'Just say it,' she shrugged. 'We'll work better together that way.'

'Okay. I don't know what your agenda is with the Dobrev family. Do you hold Rayco Dobrev responsible as the head of the family, and will you be putting the old bloke on the spot or harassing him? He's got dementia, and I've no intention of distressing him any more than necessary.'

Laura gave a short laugh of surprise. 'Righto, good you didn't hold back.'

Nate grinned sheepishly.

'From my research, I believe Ray Dobrev was a good guy,' Laura explained. 'He was hard-working, well-intentioned, and honestly doing his best to fit in with the suburb changing around him. My goodwill does not extend to his son or Ray's wife, Gerta.'

She could tell Nate was still not keen on the idea, but he agreed that having a female present might be less intimidating for Rayco.

At 10.30am the following morning, they drove out of the Stones Corner office in Adam's Mercedes; Laura insisted on sitting in the back seat despite Nate's chivalry. She sat behind Adam, the driver, to converse more easily with Nate.

'It's my job to be observant, silent, and watch you guys in action. Like I'm not here unless I can be of use,' she said. 'Think of me as making a documentary without the cameras.'

'It would be an all-star cast,' Nate said.

'Bound to be,' Adam agreed with a glance in Nate's direction. 'Academy award-winning material in the category of real-life drama.'

Laura laughed along. She knew Nate and Adam didn't quite know how to take her. They most likely expected a hostile law graduate with an axe to grind.

'If it became a movie,' Nate was saying, 'I couldn't play myself because my cover would be broken – who could play me?' He pondered the question with a straight face. 'Hard to think of someone both strong and smouldering.'

'Will Ferrell might be free,' Adam said, and Nate gave him a smirk that was far from smouldering.

'You two obviously go way back,' Laura said, laughing and shaking her head at their antics.

'Brothers from different mothers,' Nate said, using his favourite explanation.

'And fathers,' Adam added. 'Not brothers at all, actually.'

Nate continued: 'I'm thinking Chris Hemsworth – blonde, muscly, you'd struggle to tell us apart. Australian too.'

Adam laughed. 'I need someone like a younger Tom Cruise. Maybe Ryan Gosling could play me. He's not as good-looking, but he's versatile, like me,' he added with a look at Nate, challenging him to disagree.

'Can't see it,' Nate shook his head.

'If I sell the rights, you guys will be the first to know,' Laura jokingly promised them.

'Let's get down to business,' Nate said. 'Danielle and I had a few wins this morning.'

She saw firsthand how they went into professional mode as if someone had flicked a switch – both men were immediately focused.

'A quick overview,' Nate said. 'Rayco Dobrev has dementia. He's eighty-three, and according to some insider information that Adam got his hands on, Rayco has scattered and unreliable memories of life at the fairground. Danielle spoke with Rayco's solicitor yesterday about organising our entry today, and he thought two wills existed. But Laura, you think no will might exist?'

'That's what I've heard,' Laura agreed.

Nate continued. 'According to the solicitor, in one will, the fairground is left to his wife, Gerta, and son, Gerry, whom we met last night – but apparently, Rayco didn't have much faith in either of them.'

'No surprises there,' Adam said.

'Exactly,' Nate agreed. 'So allegedly, another will was done that left it all to a select number of community groups.'

Adam nodded. 'That's where Audrey comes into the picture.'

'Yes, but the problem is that Rayco's legal team can't ask Rayco because he's not medically capable, and Gerta and Gerry are saying nothing.'

'Where there's a will, there's a relative,' Laura said.

'I promise you we are still working your cold case here, but we need to turn over a few stones to get there,' Nate said.

'I know and understand. Who's to say what we might unearth,' she agreed. 'I bet they're keen to see the poor old guy die.'

'Gerry said as much last night,' Adam agreed, and she noticed he was more inclusive of her today and more into the conversation, not as morose.

'Feel free to ask questions,' Nate said with a glance behind at her.

'Okay. Does anyone have Enduring Power of Attorney?'

'Good question,' Nate said. 'The solicitor has nothing lodged with him, but that doesn't mean it doesn't exist. Like most people, he suspects they never thought to do it until it became too late.'

'Although in fairness,' Adam added, 'I heard from a medical contact of mine that Rayco's decline was quite rapid.'

'During my research, I found out that Gerry has a shady past,' Laura said. 'He's faced court for theft, assault, carjacking, the usual rap sheet but hasn't done time in jail. A few charges got thrown out, and he got community service for the others.'

Nate scoffed. 'He probably thought working at the carnival was community service.'

'No doubt. But that's why he is my number one suspect for Dad's murder, amongst other things.'

'It's understandable why Rayco wouldn't want to leave his life's work to his deadbeat son,' Nate said.

And then Rayco Dobrev's aged care village came into sight – aptly named Hopetown.

'There's nothing much to hope for here but a quick passing,' Nate muttered as Adam turned the car into the grounds.

'So,' Nate continued, turning in the front seat to face Laura, 'today we're trying to find out if Rayco knows anything about the death of your father or if he knows of an agenda or any tension related to the fairground – no easy task and I'm not expecting results. I will talk with management about who has visited him in the last few months. You and Adam will visit with Rayco.'

'Really?' she asked surprised.

'I want to interview him, don't get me wrong,' Nate assured her, 'but the only way I could get his sister to approve our entry was to tell her I was bringing a psychologist to check on Rayco's welfare. Handy to have one on the team.'

She nodded. 'Right. Do you want me to smile and nod, or should I play along if he asks me questions?'

'Play along definitely. Rayco's more likely to be forthcoming with you than me and Ryan Gosling here,' he said with a grin. Adam chuckled.

'Got the letter?' Adam asked as he parked and cut the engine.

Nate reached inside his jacket pocket and gave it to Adam. 'Permission from his sister,' he explained to Laura. 'She's not quite with us mentally either. There's no way Gerry or Gerta would have agreed to us seeing him.'

The group exited the car and made their way to the office. Adam handed over the letter at the reception. Nate was led one way, and a young caregiver—who Laura noticed gave both the boys an appreciative glance—led Adam and Laura to Rayco Dobrev's room. Can't blame her, Laura thought, there's no eye candy in this place. But once upon a time, she bet they were all go-getters.

Adam gave Nate a *good-luck* look and turned his attention to Laura as they followed the caregiver down the hallway. The place was clean and sterile, and all the staff trained to say hello and be super friendly, or so it seemed. It was a good idea to bring Laura, Adam thought, and he was pleased Nate made the right decision in that regard – hopefully, Rayco Dobrev wouldn't be inappropriate or try anything on if he were to have flashbacks to his younger self. Adam glanced at Laura and decided she could capably take care of herself. He never felt that way about Kelsey, even though it was probably true. *Stop thinking about Kelsey.*

The pair followed the caregiver into a room on the right of the hallway, two rooms from the exit stairs; it was good to know these things. The room was small, with a single bed on locked wheels, a private bathroom, and a small private balcony that was sun-drenched where they sat. Rayco Dobrev offered a wrinkled hand to both of them, and they gently shook it. Adam noticed the old fellow still had a sparkle in his watery blue eyes and a tuft or two of silver hair on his scalp. But he was a small man, slightly hunched, who could do with a little body padding. Adam helped him into a chair on the balcony.

'After about eighty, it's all downhill,' he said to Laura with a wink.

'So, when do you turn eighty then?' she asked him, and he laughed.

'Ah, you'll go a long way, young lady,' Rayco said. 'Is he a charmer?' Rayco asked Laura with a nod in Adam's direction.

Adam was about to open his mouth to say they were just work colleagues when she smiled and said: 'I suspect it takes one to know one, Mr Dobrev,' and gave him a smile that would melt the most hardened hearts. He chuckled and touched his nose as if she had that right; it appeared she already had him wrapped around her finger. This could go well for the interview, Adam thought. He didn't recognise her as Susan's and Alex Armstrong's daughter, and Adam was relieved.

A caregiver wheeled a trolley into the room, and the guests accepted the offer of tea and biscuits. Laura rose to help her distribute the cups. The tea wasn't that hot, but Adam assumed, being this far from the kitchen, that it had travelled a bit. Eventually, they were alone again. The visitors made some small talk. Mr Dobrev was lucid enough to converse on any subject but seemed to forget a few minutes later that he had already talked about the weather, the noisy buses going past, and his favourite biscuits after the plate with several choices had been offered. Poor old fellow, Adam thought.

'So, you young people work at my carnival, do you?' he asked.

'No, not right now, but we're here to talk about it,' Adam said.

He sighed. 'It was something in its day.'

'It still looks pretty amazing, just a little... abandoned,' Laura agreed. 'Why didn't your son want to take over the fair?'

She gave Adam an apologetic glance, remembering he intended to lead the interview, but he gave her a little nod of encouragement.

Rayco Dobrev huffed. 'My son doesn't want to work at the carnival, our family legacy. There's no chance to make a quick buck,' he said, with a hint of bitterness about his voice. 'He was always a bit wild, and Gerta encouraged it.' He shook his head. 'Don't know where we went wrong with that boy. I have a daughter, too, but she has no head for business. Flirting, clothes and make-up, that was about it. Not much for budgets and timetables. She upped and married a long time ago.'

He seemed to have forgotten the daughter was deceased, and Adam had no intention of reminding him. Studying the man before him, Adam found him reasonably lucid when talking about the past and asked, 'I imagine using staff and contractors doesn't always work – no one has the same passion for a family business as the family.'

'You got that right, son,' Rayco said. He turned to look at Laura. 'You're a beautiful young lady. I knew a young lady like you once. Her name was Mary. Are you married?'

Laura's eyes widened with surprise.

'Not yet, Mr Dobrev. I've been studying.'

'See, you've got a good work ethic. I bet you have, too, son. That's a nice suit you're wearing,' Rayco said.

'My grandmother is Audrey Murphy, Mr Dobrev.'

'Audrey!' His eyes widened, and he smiled. 'Dear Audrey, what a lady. How is she?'

'Very well, still working with her charities,' Adam said.

'Of course she is. Call me Ray. Is she still happy with Edward?' he asked after Audrey's husband, Adam's grandfather, who passed away decades ago.

'He passed away, I'm afraid,' Adam said, having no reason to hide that detail. He offered the biscuit plate again to Laura and Ray who took one. Adam realised he was hungry too, not remembering when he last ate, so he helped himself to a shortbread biscuit.

'Well, I'm sorry to hear about Edward.'

'Thank you, Ray,' Adam said. 'Laura's father passed away too; do you remember Alex Armstrong?'

Rayco Dobrev's eyes widened. 'Armstrong. Had an accident during the neighbourhood riots.' His body slumped. 'I remember him.'

'Do you think it was an accident, Ray, or someone harmed him?' Laura asked softly.

He shook his head. 'I thought he would hit me a few times; he's a big man.' Ray went in and out of the past and the present, resurrecting the dead and burying others. 'I was surprised when he was the one who ended up dead. Wouldn't have picked that.'

Adam glanced at Laura, warning her not to react, and her chin went up a notch in acknowledgement.

Ray spoke on. 'I tried to talk to him. I offered to change a few things at the carnival and support his kid's school with a fundraiser. He said I was a dinosaur, and no one wanted carnivals anymore.' He blinked, his eyes moist, and Adam felt a wave of pity for the old man who had built his dream. 'Three decades we'd been there before the new development began.'

'I went to *Carnival World* lots of times and loved it,' Adam said, and Rayco Dobrev looked up and grinned.

'Did you, son? What was your favourite?'

'It was a toss-up between the dodgems and the zipper ride.'

Ray laughed. 'That zipper ride. The kids loved to be scared stiff. The ghost house was a favourite, too, but Gerry always took it too far. Scaring people witless, it's not what it's about. It's supposed to be fun and just a little spooky.'

'Audrey took me along,' Adam said, trying to keep the conversation in the era of the riots.

'Audrey's quite a catch. Like my Mary, she was a good sort,' he said, returning to his former conversation and sighing at the memory. 'She used to call me Teddy. Said I looked like one.' He laughed and then coughed a few times, catching his breath again.

'Was that before you met your wife, Gerta?' Laura asked, refreshing his teacup. Adam declined, and she filled her own. He watched her manage the senior man with empathy and warmth. It was not what he expected from someone with a grudge against the Dobrev family; their carnival changed her life.

'Yes. I knew Mary first, but her father wouldn't let us marry. I wasn't Catholic, and he didn't like the carnival business. It broke both our hearts. Gerta's family is Bulgarian like mine, so we often socialised together. It was a marriage of convenience. They don't have many of those these days,'

Then Adam realised they had lost Rayco as he talked about his past, love, and life. Adam tried to steer the conversation again, not wishing to push the old man too far. He bid his time until the carnival was mentioned again.

'It was a great dream and gave many youngsters like me lots of happy hours, Ray, thank you.'

The old man nodded and smiled. 'Music to my ears when I hear it over the bus noise,' he said. 'Thank you, young man.'

So, what are your plans for your fairground in the future when you're not around?' Adam asked gently.

Ray blinked, looked confused, and muttered something about hiring more staff for the coming holiday season. Laura gently stepped in.

'Teddy,' she said softly, using Mary's nickname, 'what will become of the carnival?'

At that moment, Adam could not see anything plain about her. She had warmth in her eyes and a face full of empathy as she looked at Mr Dobrev with compassion. Ray appeared entranced by her.

'Oh, darlin' Mary,' he said, 'that son of mine wants to take it, sell it, and put up all these concrete apartments on the land. Floor on top of floor, no garden, no lake, no playground. It will break my heart. Remember when we had our first kiss on the enchanted carousel.'

Laura smiled. 'The beautiful carousel.'

'You were the beautiful one,' he said.

'But I'm not Mary, of course. You know that,' Laura said, touching his hand.

Adam braced. Rayco Dobrev was confused and might strike out. He was aged, but an unexpected hit would still hurt her. He readied himself to step in if he had to do so.

'You want to keep the carnival as it was for all to enjoy?' she asked.

'On no,' he said, talking to Laura. 'I'm giving the land to the city. Public housing, lots of green space for the kids to play, you know, put a roof over everyone's head – Dobrev Community Village, I've even got the plans drawn. That useless son, he's trying to sell it to developers. He's trying to buy up land all around. He's got a few already,' he said, spit flying from his mouth as he got angrier. 'Him and Norman, well over my dead body.'

'Norman?' she asked. Adam hadn't come across that name this early in the case, and he gathered neither had Laura, according to her reaction.

Mr Dobrev continued: 'Gerardo never worked a day in his life for an honest dollar, and it could have been all his if he had shared my passion. He just expected it to fall in his lap after all my years of hard work. His mother supports him.' He shook his head in disappointment. 'Mary, he's been trying to wheedle it from me for years. Trying to make me give it to him. But no. My folk were honest, hardworking people, and I built the carnival into something with their backing. It's going back to people like them. People like you and me, Mary and the Dobrev name will live on.'

'Like us,' Laura agreed and allowed him to hold her hand. 'You've got a good heart, Teddy.'

Ray Dobrev chuckled, and then he began talking about his art classes and the food they served him. Adam knew they had lost him now and didn't wish to push on any further, but thanks to Laura, they had something. Then, after a few minutes, she had another go at getting him around.

'Where's Norman these days?' Laura asked.

Adam gave her a small smile. *Well done.*

'He's there now; it didn't take him long to get his claws in.'

Before they could ask anything further, a caregiver looked in to check all was well.

'Mary's visiting,' Mr Dobrev said to her. 'We had some happy times, didn't we, Mary?' he asked and looked at Laura like she was the most beautiful woman he'd ever seen – Adam was seeing her in a new light, too. She was an interesting woman with many dimensions.

'We had some very happy times indeed, Teddy. We were lucky.' She blinked back tears from her eyes.

He nodded and smiled, and then the conversation loop began again as a bus passed and he complained about how noisy they were. Adam and Laura extricated themselves, thanked him, and promised to return soon.

Adam could tell Laura was shaken. It was hard not to be, to see this old guy in a loop waiting to die; his family unreliable, and Mary, the love of his life, gone before him. It made Adam think of his parents and wonder if his mother's loss was as great when his dad died. It made him think he was missing out.

Chapter 14

Affected by Rayco Dobrev's reminisces, Laura blinked away tears as they exited, Adam holding the door open for her. There was no sign of Nate yet, so the pair waited under a white flowering tree in the corner of the front garden. A little bench sat underneath.

'Are you okay?' Adam asked once seated.

Laura blinked again, clearing her eyes and gave a small laugh. 'I'd make a terrible investigator – teary on the job. But those kind old eyes looking at me full of love and remembrance, so very sad and the son who is so disappointing.'

'There's nothing good about aging when the mind and body are gone, and life just lingers on,' Adam agreed, and Laura looked at him, surprised by his perceptiveness.

She cleared her throat, not trusting her voice, 'You've had some experience in this?'

'I've done some palliative care work with senior patients and their families,' he explained. 'I'd offer you a handkerchief, but I don't have one. I'm more Ryan Gosling than Cary Grant.' Adam shrugged.

Laura laughed. 'Both are just fine.'

Nate called out: 'Hey, good to go?'

The pair rose and caught up with Nate, heading to Adam's car. He was carrying a small box and a few sheets of paper he didn't go in with; Laura hoped he scored something useful. They took the same seats for the trip back.

After they had driven out of the gates, Nate asked: 'Why so glum? What happened?'

Laura left Adam to answer, and when he was finished, he added, 'I thought you held it together really well, Laura, especially when Ray spoke of your dad being threatening.'

Laura groaned softly. 'It's not easy to hear your dad was a bully.'

'You don't doubt Rayco?' Nate asked.

'No. But it's not my memory of Dad. He was always fun and playful with me, but Mum, my uncle, and some of Dad's friends told me he could be... hard work.'

'Do you think that's why your mum doesn't want you pursuing it, because it might besmirch your memories?' Adam asked, turning the car back into the traffic.

'Maybe. Or perhaps she doesn't have such fond memories of him,' Laura said. 'But I have to have justice. I have to know one way or the other, even if Dad wasn't Mum's greatest love like Mary was to Ray.'

'Mary?' Nate asked, turning in the front seat to face Laura.

'Yes, it was really sad. Rayco thought I was his lost love, Mary.'

'Yeah, those places can be like that,' Nate agreed. 'Well, I'll cheer you up, Mary. I just happened to be passing the kitchen on my way out, and the old girls were helping the chef in the kitchen. It's International Hug Your Hound Day—'

'—there's such a thing?' Adam cut in.

'Apparently,' Nate confirmed, 'and I said I was here with two friends...' he opened the box, and there were three very cute cupcakes, each with pink icing and a doggy face created in icing on the top. Nate offered Laura the box, then stopped. 'Are we allowed to eat in the Merc?' he asked Adam.

'Sure, it's International Hug Your Hound Day!' Adam joked. 'Life's too short not to eat in the car.'

'Nothing like a trip to senility to make you want to live in the now,' Nate agreed and handed out the cupcakes.

'Just don't drop them icing side up,' Adam added, and Nate rolled his eyes. Laura laughed as Nate pretended to drop his cupcake but saved it in time.

Adam shook his head. 'I'm getting an ejector seat for your side of the car, and you'll be the first to trial it,' he threatened. Nate just laughed and pretended to drop it again.

'You guys,' Laura said, cheerier now.

Then...

Adam's security officer, Charlie, had suggested to both Audrey and Nate's mum that dinner might not be required for the boys tonight as the three enjoyed a stick of fairy floss and the view from the Ferris Wheel.

'Why is it called a Ferris Wheel?' Adam asked.

'Mum calls it the Giant Wheel,' Nate said as he sat beside Charlie; Adam sat opposite as the Ferris Wheel lifted them high above the suburbs where they lived. The question was soon forgotten, and Charlie had no answer.

'There's your place,' Nate said, pointing out Adam's roof on a riverside house.

'There's Stuart's further up, the one with the red roof,' Adam said. 'There's yours!'

'Is Dad home?' Nate joked.

Adam leant over the edge as they went the full circle and neared the bottom to alight. Charlie nudged him back.

'That's the guy, Charlie, over there,' Adam pointed, and Charlie followed his gaze. 'He was in the cemetery with Audrey and me, and Audrey didn't like him.'

Charlie watched as the man seemed to watch them in return before turning and departing. From a distance, she put him in his late 20s or early 30s, wiry, with tattoos visible on a leg and arm.

'Who is he?' Nate asked, twisting around to see what they were looking at behind him.

'I believe he works here. He's Mrs Dobrev's son,' Charlie said. 'Let me know if you see him again, but don't speak with him.'

'Why?' Adam asked, his expression anxious.

'Because Audrey wouldn't like it,' Charlie said, thanking the operator as they stepped down from the ride. 'We should get going, it's nearing five o'clock.'

'Can we do the ghost train before we go?' Adam asked.

'Please, Charlie? Last ride, we promise,' Nate begged.

'I thought it might be too scary,' Charlie said, making a ghostly noise. The boys laughed.

'Nuh, we're not chickens,' Nate said.

'All right, then. You two will be in the carriage in front of me, and I'll sit behind.'

'You'll be trying to freak us out,' Adam grinned.

'Cross my heart, I won't,' Charlie said with a smile. 'I'll keep the ghosts from your back.'

She glanced around again, not seeing Gerta or Gerry Dobrev, and relaxed a little. They stood in a short queue for the ride and boarded, taking seats in the small carriages.

'Are you sure you won't have nightmares?' Charlie teased.

'Nuh,' Adam said with false bravado.

It wasn't long before the train started to move inside the ghost house, and Charlie had to admit she was nervous, even if the boys weren't. She placed a hand on both boys' shoulders.

'I'm leaving my hand there, so don't try to shrug me off,' she warned. 'It might get dark inside, and I've got to be sure you don't get flung off.'

Neither boy admitted they were happy for her to grip their shoulder, but there was comfort in knowing she was there. They heard ghostly sounds and the rattle of chains. The girls in front of them sitting with their mother screamed, and Nate rolled his eyes.

'It hasn't even started,' he said in a low voice, and both boys laughed and then were quick to grimace as what felt like a spider web brushed their faces.

The train continued along the track, and it became darker; they were looping now as a skeleton and a witch with a horrific laugh flashed by them. Charlie's grip tightened on the boys as she heard them laughing, but she knew Adam well enough to know he didn't like the ghost train.

Something flew at them, and the girls in front ducked and screamed.

'Bats!' Nate yelled, teasing them, and they screamed some more.

A bony hand trailed over their heads from a skeleton hung above them, but all Charlie could focus on was the man in the corner, the torch lighting his face, and the sinister smile he was giving her. Gerry Dobrev. And no one else saw him.

Chapter 15

Now...

The Riverpark Estate had lost its sparkle. Once shiny and new, eighteen years later, it looked tired. Many families that had moved in when the estate was new were grown and gone. A few remained; some residents were now grandparents, and others had sold up to downsize or try a different lifestyle.

'Want to drop in and surprise your folks? They're only a few blocks away from here, right?' Danielle asked Nate as they alighted from the car in the street where Burnsy had been speaking with residents about the strange happenings at night.

'They're on the road. Mum posted a photo from Forrest Beach on Facebook last night. She loves Facebook, all her cronies sharing their adventures,' Nate chuckled.

'Where's Forrest Beach?' Danielle asked.

'Near Ingham.'

She gave him a blank look.

'About ninety minutes to Townsville.'

'Ah, nice.'

He shook his head. 'And you're supposed to have ancestral roots to the land.'

Danielle scoffed. 'That doesn't mean I'm a walking map. It's a big place, Australia.' She stopped when he did and asked, 'Where do you want to start?'

They studied the quiet street. Most residents were at work, the children were at school, and Nate hoped to get a few seniors at home who may have been here when the estate opened eighteen years ago.

'Wait for it,' he said, 'someone will check us out shortly if we start walking.'

Sure enough, they had gone less than a few metres when a curtain moved and shortly after, a door opened. A woman in her sixties glanced around the door. Her hair was cut short, and she wore gym clothing, showing a slender and fit build.

'It's good that you are here,' Nate said under his breath to Danielle. 'She might have run if two men had arrived.' He raised a hand. 'Morning.'

They walked toward the resident, who stepped outside on her small veranda. Embellishing the truth a little, given he was sharing information with Sergeant Matt Burns, Nate did the introductions.

'Nate Delaney and Danielle Walters, we're working with the police and Laura Amstrong about—'

'Oh, I read about that in the paper. I'm Karen McRae.'

'Would you have ten minutes to talk with us, Ms McRae?' Danielle asked.

'Of course, and call me Karen. I was just about to make a coffee.' She invited them in, closing and locking the front door behind them and leading them to a sunny kitchen and back deck.

'This is nice,' Danielle said.

'Best place to be in the morning,' Karen agreed.

'I grew up in one of the new estates not far from here,' Nate said. 'This is pretty similar to my home.'

Karen smiled. 'They are all carbon copies. Just change the colouring or the type of garage door and call it a village. It was lovely in its day.'

'It still seems lovely to me. Neat and well established,' Danielle said, taking the milk jug and plate of biscuits as Karen grabbed the coffee pot and three cups. Nate was directed to bring the sugar pot and teaspoons.

They settled themselves, and with coffee poured and biscuits selected, Nate asked about her history in the area.

'I've been here since the estate opened,' Karen stated. 'I was in my early forties when my husband, Paul, and I moved here. The kids were teenagers just starting high school. We were a bit older than many families that bought homes here with young ones or intended to start a family. Now, my kids are long gone and doing their own thing, and Paul's about to retire.' She glanced around. 'We'll sell up then. It's become... rougher,' she said after considering a word to describe the neighbourhood.

'Do you remember Alex Armstrong, his wife, and his daughter, Laura, from when you first moved in? Laura would have been six then,' Nate said.

'I knew them by sight only. My kids were older than Laura, so they didn't play together. But I read she thinks her father was attacked that night, that it wasn't an accident, and you're trying to uncover the truth?'

'Precisely,' Danielle said.

'I should tell you,' Karen declared, 'I'm a retired journalist. I was very interested in the riots at the time.'

'Excellent,' Nate said, lighting up, and Karen laughed.

'It was a long time ago,' she added.

'Can you tell us what you remember about the night of his death?' he asked.

'I'll do my best. It was nearly two decades ago, and honestly, the drama was a flash in the pan. We all moved in within a few months of each other, and several residents started complaining about the carnival. I never minded it,' she gave a small shrug. 'We took my teens there a few times, and given we were at work during the week and the kids at school, the carnival's activities never greatly affected our life. It was closed by 6pm on a weeknight and 10pm on the weekend. It just wasn't a big deal.' She shrugged.

'What about the traffic, hooning, the workers, the noise? We heard they were real issues,' Danielle said.

Karen shook her head. 'The traffic was mainly around the carnival area. A lot of these residential streets are cul-de-sacs, so there was no major thoroughfare. There were annoying sounds like the repetitive sounds of bells when someone won a prize and a band on Saturday night, but the Dobrev family offered to tone all that down.'

'Are you saying the protests were over the top?' Nate asked.

'That's how we felt, Paul and I. I did the stories for the local paper; you'll find my byline.'

Nate opened his folder and huffed. He had already printed out several of her articles. 'Karen McRae! There you are.'

Karen laughed. 'My reports will tell you more than I remember. But on the night Alex Armstrong died, we were securely locked in the house. I didn't want Paul to go outside, so he agreed to stay in to protect the kids and me. He's an art teacher, not a fighter. You could hear glass breaking, cars screeching around, yelling, we saw fires being lit. Alex Armstrong was at the forefront of it all. He was also wary of me.'

'Why do you say that?' Danielle asked.

'Because some of my news stories flattered him, some were brutally honest and said thuggery was in action. He steered clear of me and had one of the other protestors answer my questions. That was fine by me.'

'Do you think he could have been murdered?' Nate asked.

'Yes,' Karen said without hesitation. 'He wasn't popular. The Dobrev owner's son, Gerry, was also a nasty piece of work. His father was kind and diplomatic, but Gerry and Alex Armstrong were alphas and clashed. I also thought Laura's father was rude to the senior Dobrev, Rayco, and told him so.'

'How did he take that?' Nate asked.

'Not well. Alex didn't like women telling him anything; I felt sorry for his wife,' Karen said honestly. 'We're not talking the sixties here; he should have known how to handle professional women.'

'Some never do,' Danielle said.

Karen agreed and continued, 'Alex rubbed people the wrong way. The men in the neighbourhood would get the cold shoulder if they didn't support him. He gave Paul plenty of that.' Karen sipped her coffee and asked, 'Is Laura prepared for what she might learn about her father?'

'I think she knows, but not to the extent you have just detailed,' Nate said.

'I was quite shocked by his death, but it would be an exaggeration to think anyone in the neighbourhood mourned him. It was the same when the carnival closed for good about ten years ago. It was a relief. The sooner it is cleared away, the better.'

'You don't think they might re-open it?' Danielle asked.

'Council would be bombarded with complaints. The area is too built up for that now,' Karen said. 'Not to mention, the land would be worth a fortune to a developer. You'd never make that money with an operational carnival.'

'True,' Nate agreed. 'Moving forward to now, we've heard there's been some disturbances at night. Street gangs, maybe?'

Karen shook her head. 'I doubt it. It's him again, Gerry.'

'Gerry Dobrev? Why?' Danielle asked.

'I understood he wanted out,' Nate said. 'He's waiting for his father to die so he can sell the land the carnival sits on, and he and his mother can take the money and walk away.'

'Rumour has it he's not going to inherit it,' Karen said.

'You're well informed,' Nate said with a small smile, and she tapped her nose to indicate she was "in the know".

'Old journalist contacts die hard,' Karen told him. 'I believe he's trying to run down the area and buy up cheap, which tells me he thinks he'll inherit and eventually have an enormous estate.'

'Has he got enough money to buy distressed property?' Danielle asked.

'I couldn't say, but he's got business interests and allies with money – he always did have. That's why the carousel turns at night, and people's cars are damaged. The kids and the older residents are scared. Prices are already not what they were. That Dobrev family...' she shook her head.

'Is there a resident you know by the name of Norman?' Nate asked.

Karen thought for a moment. 'I can't say I know anyone named Norman on the street. Perhaps he's a new resident. Why?'

'Rayco Dobrev mentioned his name to a colleague of mine, but Rayco is not completely with us these days,' Nate said. 'Well, it's been great speaking with you, Karen. Thank you. Is there anyone else on the street who has been here since day one that we could talk to?'

Karen nodded. 'Try Derek. He lives in the house nearest the carnival on the corner. He's been here since the estate opened. If anyone should complain about the noise, it's him.'

Nate and Danielle thanked her again and made their way down the street to a neat house with a well-tended garden. Departing thirty minutes later, they learned very little from Derek—a mousy, nervous man—other than that he tried to keep out of trouble. They called on six more properties and were admitted to three, but the story was much the same.

'So where are the people complaining about the Carnival?' Danielle asked on their way back to the office. Nate tapped the steering wheel as he thought, a habit that drove Adam nuts but didn't seem to bother Danielle, who spent a lot of time in the car with him.

'Maybe no one is complaining anymore. Maybe Gerry Dobrev is trying to resurrect the sentiment the neighbours felt when they tried to drive his family out eighteen years ago to see if he can get any bites. Maybe he is trying to distract attention from Laura's investigation. We need to know who his friends are... I'll see what surveillance on Friday night turns up.'

'I'm free to help.'

'Thanks, Dan, but go and have a date night with Eric,' Nate said. 'I'll take Adam. He'll have nothing to do, and Laura can't come, so I can have some downtime with him.'

'Do you think he's okay?'

'Hard to tell with Adam.'

'Is he thinking of moving back home?' she asked.

'He hasn't said.'

'Do you like Laura?'

'Yeah, she's nice.'

'Do you think he might like her?'

'Sure, she's likable.'

'Seriously?' Danielle turned and looked at him, frustration written all over her face.

'What?' he asked, glancing at her.

She shook her head. 'Men. If the world relied on communication for the species' survival, it would be over long ago!'

Nate started to laugh, and Danielle grinned.

'I'll keep you posted,' he said with a nudge, and they left the troubled area. They drove past Nate's childhood home to check that it was still intact so he could report to his parents.

Chapter 16

T **hen...**

With the light off, Adam and Nate knelt beside the window in Nate's bedroom and lowered themselves so only the tops of their heads and eyes could be seen.

'Dad said there might be big trouble tonight, and maybe you shouldn't have stayed over,' Nate whispered.

'Why?' Adam asked alarmed.

'In case you get hurt,' Nate said. 'Dad said he'd have to look after mum, me, and you if anything happened.'

'I better go home to Audrey and look after her,' Adam said now decidedly, and Nate shook his head.

'No. Mum rang Audrey to invite her over, and Audrey said Charlie was there and your security guy would be outside our house all night. Mum was happy about that.'

'Oh yeah,' Adam exhaled with relief. 'Charlie's moved into the wing with the river view that Mum doesn't like because you can see the water. She'll look after Audrey.'

'She'll kick arse,' Nate agreed, using the term he'd learnt from the action videos the boys watched.

'Look!' Adam exclaimed.

In the distance, over the top of the rooftops, they could see smoke rising and hear horns blaring.

'It's because of the carnival,' Nate said. 'The people at the new estate want it gone.'

'It's not fair; *Carnival World* was here first. Besides, it's more fun than some dumb houses.'

'Yeah.'

The boys gasped as huge flames went up in the air.

'Look at that, it must be a house!' Adam exclaimed, and they heard the sound of sirens.

'Bet it's the firies and the cops,' Nate said.

They could hear Nate's parents talking, and Nate's mum was checking to make sure everything was locked.

'Are you all right, boys?' Nate's dad yelled up the stairs.

'Yes!' they replied in unison.

'Good, stay there unless I tell you to come down.'

'Yes, Dad.'

'Yes, Mr Delaney.'

'It's kind of cool,' Nate said, and Adam grinned.

'Yeah. I wish we were there. Wouldn't it be cool if the skeletons from the Carnival Ghost House visited the people who want it gone!'

'Wow, yeah,' Nate said and laughed. 'That would be really freaky. What if the horses from the merry-go-round took off, running away?'

'Freaky,' Adam agreed, grinning.

The boys watched in silence, listening as the sounds of a battle rumbled several blocks away.

Now:

'It's kind of freaky, isn't it?' Adam said as he and Nate sat in Nate's Audi on yet another surveillance night, studying the darkened street and *Dobrev's Carnival World*. The abandoned carnival looked sinister at night, a playground for ghosts, ghouls, and Stephen King tales.

'It's like the horses are about to take off, and the sign on the ghost house is going to topple,' Nate said, and the pair chuckled.

Nate had parked as close to the derelict grounds as he could, in a dark area where the pair could see the comings and goings—should there be any—at the carnival and in the surrounding street. They turned the interior light off and sat in silence, except for the occasional barking of a dog or a car driving by to break the stillness.

'Did you bring a thermos and biscuits?' Nate asked as he pushed back the driver's seat as far as it would go. He glanced in the back seat, answering his own question.

'No, have I ever? Did you?'

'Of course I did. It's our last night on surveillance, spending quality time watching the carnival, just the two of us,' he joked.

'You're making me misty-eyed,' Adam said, joining in the joke. 'Did you really?'

'Yeah. Audrey gave it to me as I was leaving. She's got sandwiches, cake, and coffee in there. I mentioned it this morning when I saw her collecting the paper near the gate as I went for my jog.'

'She'd see right through that,' Adam huffed with laughter.

'We're both happy playing our roles,' Nate smiled and reached into the back seat for Audrey's offerings. He opened a tin and offered a sandwich.

Adam was hungry; he hadn't eaten and took two with a paper serviette. He saw Nate's pleased look and rolled his eyes. 'Thanks.'

Nate helped himself, and they sat back, watching and eating.

'What's Jessica doing tonight?' Adam asked.

'She's got a hen's party, so she probably won't return to her own home until the early hours.'

They knew this routine well: no rush, no hurry to make conversation, but Nate usually made Adam think out loud.

'Righto, since you're going to spend the next hour in your head, let's talk about the case and anything else you want to talk about,' Nate said, glancing at Adam.

'Is this cheap therapy?' Adam asked.

'Can be if you want. I'm no psychologist, but no one knows you better than me,' Nate said and added, 'except for Audrey, maybe. But she doesn't know half the stupid things you used to get up to.'

Adam gave Nate a wry look, making him laugh, before turning his attention to the carnival. There was no movement or sound, so he took up Nate's offer to discuss the case.

'I've been thinking about the interview with Rayco Dobrev in his aged care home,' Adam started. 'From what Rayco said, neither his son nor wife are the sharpest knives in the drawer, but if there is no other will, and Gerry knows his entire inheritance is going back to the community unless he does something about it, he'd be out to right that.'

'You bet,' Nate nodded. 'He could create a will, but he would have to prove its validity, and I wonder if he knows what date Rayco wrote his will so he could supersede it.'

'I wouldn't put it past him to try and prove Rayco wasn't of sane mind when he drew up his will benefitting the community groups.'

Nate agreed. After a while, he said, 'The aged care home confirmed the only visitor Rayco has had in the last six months was his aged sister and her daughter, who brings her up to visit. So, Gerry's not putting the heavies on him. Truth be known, they've been estranged for years. Coffee?'

'Yeah, thanks.' Adam held the two cups while Nate found the thermos and poured.

'If Gerry is driving everyone out, like one of the neighbours, Karen, suggested to Danielle and me, he needs some allies to help him buy up big. Imagine the land he'd own.' Nate shook his head.

'Norman's helping him,' Adam said with a smile. 'Who the hell is Norman? Laura and I couldn't get an answer out of Rayco.'

'Dan and I had no luck finding a Norman in the neighbourhood,' he sighed. 'Maybe he's a former carnival worker or business associate of Gerry's – a fellow jailbird.'

That sat again in silence for a while. Nate packed up the cups, they grabbed a slice of cake and watched the carnival grounds.

'One of the residents said Gerry left the carnival grounds a few times with a small group,' Nate mused. 'Plotting, no doubt.'

'It would be great to get a photo of that group and see who we could identify.'

'Dan could do that,' Nate agreed. 'She loves a hunt. They might be hanger-on friends, or just maybe, some useful people are meeting here and plotting – a developer, town planner, legal eagle, builders, anyone who can make a dollar out of this, along with Gerry.'

As the hours passed, the lights in the neighbourhood went off, people turned in for the night, and the street became dark and deadly quiet.

'Do you think we should call Charlie and ask her for her memories of the time in question?' Adam asked.

Nate snapped to look at him. 'Yeah, of course. Why didn't I think of that?'

'Because I'm the brilliant one,' Adam offered, and Nate huffed.

'How often do you speak with her?'

'Twice a year. She rings on my birthday and I ring her at Christmas. I'll message her and get a time. She's living in the U.S., so I'll have to work out the time difference.'

'Great. Good cake,' Nate said, reaching for another piece. 'We'll leave about midnight if nothing happens. Is that okay with you?'

'Sure.'

'Staying the night?'

'Yeah,' Adam agreed.

'So, are you going to move home? You should.'

'I might,' Adam said. 'I'm just trying not to make any decisions right now.'

'You're not of sound mind,' Nate agreed.

'I'm always of sound mind,' Adam scoffed. 'I'm just... raw.'

'I know, I've been there. After divorcing Erin, I never thought I'd have another relationship. I thought, that's it. That's my quota. Moving out of my place and moving to your mansion was brilliant. It was fun; it really lifted me.'

Adam scoffed, 'Mansion.'

'Trust me, it is by normal standards.'

'Having you there is good for Audrey and the house too. It's nice to have the pool used and to have signs of life around the place. It's looking good.'

'Then move home. Rent your house out. You can keep it or sell it later down the track.'

'I love that house,' Adam said. 'It's just different now.'

'I get it,' Nate agreed. 'Heads up!'

The pair saw the torchlight simultaneously, weaving through the carnival grounds. Nate lowered his window enough to hear ambient noise, and Adam did the same.

'I'm counting about four or five people, all in black,' Adam said. 'Local kids?'

'Maybe.'

The pair could hear voices, the occasional whooping sound and laughter.

'I can't make out a word,' Nate whispered. 'Next time, I'm going in during the day, and I'm going to plant a camera and recording device.'

'Good idea,' Adam said, watching intently. 'Someone might talk about Laura's cold case.'

But then, the quiet, dark street came alive.

'Holy crap!' Nate exclaimed.

Horns blasted, carnival and car spotlights came on, and dark figures moved in and out of the houses, thumping on doors, pounding on windows, hitting cars and moving from one home to the other. There were a dozen or more figures, all in black. They must have quickly and quietly moved into place in the shadow of darkness, unseen by the two men.

'Don't move,' Nate hissed.

The shadowy figures didn't come as far as Nate's car, but residents' lights were coming on. Men and the occasional woman appeared from households carrying makeshift weapons – bats, spades, anything to protect the family. A siren wailed in the distance.

Then Nate, Adam, and the street residents were treated to the same freaky scene as last time.

'For the love of God,' Adam watched as the derelict Ferris Wheel and the vintage merry-go-round came to life.

The Ferris Wheel began to spin, with carriages precariously dangling off it. The merry-go-round with the terrified-looking horses did one round, and then, as if someone had turned off a switch, it all stopped. The noise, the lights, the figures in black, gone.

'That's just creepy; no wonder the locals are getting out. It's like a ghost carnival,' Nate said.

'I know, freaky, but well coordinated,' Adam admitted.

Several police cars raced around the corner, their sirens wailing. Officers alighted, hurrying to speak with householders in their driveways, following their directions of where the figures in black went. Burnsy was not amongst them. Nate started the car and departed while they could.

'The show's over,' he said. 'There is definitely a gang at work. If I could pick up some audio or find proof of an agreement, we'd be in business. And, if they spilled something about Alex Armstrong, even better.'

Across town, Laura Armstrong had turned in for the night just after 11.30pm. She was not one of those who went out late every Friday night, but she didn't mind a drink or two after work with friends. Earlier that night, a girlfriend's birthday dinner at a restaurant was a great way to end the week. Passing on the chance to go clubbing, Laura returned to her two-bedroom unit in a small brown brick six-pack block at Annerley, where she rented. Her flatmate, Becca, was rarely home, preferring to stay with her boyfriend. The arrangement suited Laura just fine – rent shared, place to herself. One day, she hoped to dip her foot into the property market, but it wouldn't be possible while working part-time for No Fears, No Tears.

She had secured a small sum of money from her father's life insurance policy when she turned 21, five years ago, but that was going towards her degree and paying for a private investigator to solve her dad's murder. On graduating, Laura had several offers but knew the hours would be demanding if she went to a commercial law firm. At No Fears, No Tears, she was a big fish in a small pond, and they understood her mission as she understood their needs. Besides, she liked the work; it made her feel like she was doing something useful with her life.

Laura wondered how the surveillance was going and was tempted to ring Nate but thought better of it. It would be dark and quiet on location, and a phone call would probably not be welcomed. Adam would be with him.

Adam.

Imagine him being dumped. Why? Was he too intense or too up himself? He seemed closed off. Ironically, her ex had said that about her; maybe she was projecting on Adam when he was really the life of the party and a sweet guy. She couldn't see it.

Make-up off, teeth brushed, and in bed, Laura finally turned off the lamp and sighed.

She sat bolt upright. Had someone said her name?

'Who's there?' Laura fumbled for the light, blinking as it came on, her eyes squinting as she scanned the room. Everything looked the same as it did when she turned the light off. A glance at the clock told her it was 1.30am. She had been asleep for two hours.

Laura rose, stuck her head outside her bedroom door, and watched and waited. All was as she had left it. She went to the front door and checked; it was locked. She quickly checked Becca's room – it was empty. The case spooked her; that was all she told herself, and she returned to her bedroom. She saw in every hour until the sun came up Saturday morning.

And then Laura discovered she hadn't imagined it.

Opening the curtains in her bedroom, she saw the words written on the window:

"Leave it alone. Leave the dead buried."

Laura stepped back in fright. All the time she had been asleep in her room, someone had been on the other side of the window.

Laura rang Nate.

Chapter 17

Adam awoke in his old bedroom, a more sophisticated version than in his childhood years, given he and Kelsey had moved in the week before his mother's wedding when his old security guard, Tom, was trying to manage everyone's safety. He was surprised he slept; he hadn't the first few days after Kelsey left. Maybe it was just exhaustion. He'd return to his place today; he had to bite the bullet and get on with life. She was getting on with hers with the archive guy.

A familiar pang of hurt and anger hit him, and he stopped his mind from going over it all again and tried to focus on what to do next; he tried to take some of the small steps he was always telling his patients to take. But he couldn't remember who he was before Kelsey. A weekend alone was a rarity, and given it was the first weekend since the break-up, Adam didn't know what to do. It had been several years since he was one instead of two. He thought he'd make a coffee; that was a start. Coming down the stairs in track pants and a T-shirt, he could hear voices talking.

'Jack!' Adam stopped dead.

'Son,' his stepfather, Jack Bernham, grinned, rising from the bench seat where he was talking with Audrey and Nate while Audrey prepared breakfast. He grabbed Adam in a bear hug.

'What are you doing here?'

'I heard. I'm here.'

'Really?' Adam asked amazed. He'd never had that kind of parental support except from Audrey. He ran a hand through his hair.

'You look worse for wear if you don't mind me saying,' Jack studied him.

'He always looks that bad first thing in the morning. Trust me, I know,' Nate said, prompting Adam to give him a smirk.

Jack laughed.

'Pour yourself a juice, darling,' Audrey said, 'bacon and eggs are almost ready. How is the toast coming, Nathanial?'

'Ready to roll, Audrey,' he said.

'You didn't have to come up,' Adam said.

'We're family. I was planning to come up and see the publicist, so I brought it forward. A couple of the boys from the band came with me; they'll see their mum while here. Speaking of which, your mum sends her love and will call you.'

'Thanks,' Adam said, unmoved. 'I'm fine, really. I look this bad from a late night of surveillance.'

'And yet I was there too, but I look like I've just stepped out of a catalogue,' Nate joked.

Adam flicked him with a tea towel as he put the juice back in the fridge and followed the small party to the breakfast table. He felt everyone was studying him, and there was no way of escaping it unless he put on a good face and started acting cheerier.

'We were thinking, but of course, it is your decision, darling,' Audrey began, 'why don't you move back here? If you do so this weekend, Jack will help you move.'

'I am an expert at moving,' Jack agreed. 'I've lugged more gear around the country than your average removalist.'

'I could help, too, after I meet Burnsy at Laura's house,' Nate said, his mouth full of scrambled eggs. 'Delicious!' he proclaimed.

'Thanks, I'll think about it.' Adam said, then realised what Nate had just said. 'What's happened?'

'She got a note left on her window last night telling her to butt out of the case.'

Adam made a knowing sound. 'Not surprising.'

'That poor girl,' Audrey said. 'We could invite her to stay here until the case is wrapped up and she feels safe again.'

Adam groaned. 'You wouldn't be setting me up, Audrey?'

'Me?' she asked, feigning surprise. Smiling, she passed him the toast. 'I do like that young lady. She's whip-smart, full of personality, and handsome.'

Jack laughed. 'Handsome. What does that mean?'

'Plain as an arrowroot biscuit,' Nate supplied.

'I don't think she's plain,' Adam said, all eyes turning to him. 'No. I'm not interested and not rebounding.'

They looked away, smiling.

'How do we know Laura?' Jack asked, reaching for more bacon. Audrey told how she knew Laura from different walks of life, and now she was Nate's client.

Jack nudged Adam with a hopeful look. 'She sounds like a good sort. There's Danielle, too. She's a great girl.'

'She's seeing Eric, the photographer,' Nate said.

'Yeah? Good for them,' Jack said.

Adam nipped it in the bud. 'No.'

'No, what?' Jack asked, topping up Adam's coffee. 'Drink this, you look like you need it.'

'No, I'm not interested. I know what you are doing, and it's too soon.'

'Of course it is,' Audrey said, giving him a sympathetic look.

'It's been less than a week,' Adam said.

'That long,' Jack said, shocked, and Adam smiled and shook his head. Jack continued. "So, where am I staying? Here or at your house?'

Adam brightened. 'Want to stay the night at my place?'

'Sure. We'll get a pizza and some beer and talk about everything.'

'Yeah, thanks.' Adam felt lighter and studied his family as they ate breakfast together; he knew he was lucky. They were right, though; he looked scruffy compared to Jack, who, even as a rock star, didn't have a hair out of place, and he was dressed like he was doing a magazine shoot – Winsome's influence, no doubt. Audrey looked glamorous in a crisp navy shirt, cream pants and deck shoes, and even Nate was shaved and wearing a clean-collared shirt and jeans.

'You won't be on the market for long,' Nate said, 'unless you keep looking like the poor son the cat dragged in.'

'I'm perfectly happy being single; it suits me and my lifestyle.'

Audrey sighed, and then Jack sighed, looking resigned. Adam looked at Nate, waiting for his sigh, but he smiled at his best friend.

'I just want to see you happy and with someone who loves and supports you as you deserve, Son,' Jack said. 'You're young, and you could have a family. Imagine kids running around here, causing terror.'

'Just like you and Nathanial when you were younger,' Audrey said, smiling at the memory.

'It's a great place for them to ride their bikes, play cricket, build ramps like we used to do, and swim,' Nate agreed as if it were an intervention they had planned before he came down for breakfast.

Audrey continued. 'You know, I'm only 79. I could live for another two decades and see them grow up.'

Their words threw Adam for a moment, and he turned his focus to the coffee in front of him.

'Just promise me, Adam darling, that you won't wallow,' Audrey said. 'Kelsey was a lovely girl, but there'll be a better fit for you somewhere out there. But until then, we're always here for you.'

'Thanks,' he said and glanced towards the exit. 'It's not my first break-up, and I am thirty now, not sixteen, but I appreciate the sentiment.'

'You won't go heavy on the alcohol, drugs or work to compensate?' Jack asked. 'I know that's an easy thing to do.'

'Well, that's my normal day,' Adam joked.

'Or have flings and get a young lady pregnant that you are then connected to forever when it was just a one-night stand and should never have been anything more. That happened to one of my friend's grandsons,' Audrey said, and Jack nodded as if it were a sad, universal truth.

'Audrey's right,' Nate said with a sly grin at Adam. 'This is the time to stay busy, hang out with your best friend and stepdad, and be open to meeting new people.'

'Shut up,' Adam said to him, making them laugh.

'I've got to meet the boys and our publicist at eleven,' Jack said. 'I'll come to your place late this afternoon. That work for you?'

'Perfect.' Adam's phone buzzed. A glance at the screen told him it was Danielle; she was going to the gym at ten and suggested he get his butt there.

Adam texted her back, *'Great, see you there.'*

'Something important?' Nate asked.

'I'm meeting Dan at the gym at ten.' He imagined their sigh of relief but none more so than himself, having escaped the scrutiny and sad looks of his nearest and dearest.

Sergeant Matt Burns showed more attention to Laura than most crime victims he dealt with, or so Nate thought, watching them interact. She looked sporty this morning in gym gear, showing off a fit figure; it suited her more than the corporate gear she usually appeared in.

'If you had somewhere else to stay until this is all over, it wouldn't be a bad idea,' Burnsy said to her.

'I could move back in with Mum and my stepdad, but I really don't want to, and I'll hear nothing but "I told you to let it lie" from Mum,' she said.

'Audrey's offered her place if you would feel safer staying with her. I live in a different wing, and Jessica is there every second day,' Nate said.

'A different wing?' Laura laughed. 'Goodness. That's very kind of Audrey. But no, I'll be okay here. I've asked my flatmate Becca and her boyfriend, Kai, to stay a few nights here rather than at his place, so I'll be fine.'

'What does he do for a living?' Burnsy asked.

'He's an accountant.'

Burnsy's lips thinned.

'He's tall and fit. Does triathlons and hiking, so he'll hold his own if needed.'

'Sounds like a good plan,' Burnsy said. 'Here's my number if you get any more nighttime visits or are frightened someone is outside.' He wrote it down for her, confirming Nate's early thought that there might be a spark of interest from the sergeant. He didn't see Laura reciprocating it. Nate berated himself; he would never have noticed before dating Jessica.

Now she had him bloody matchmaking and preparing for her inevitable questions.

Rejoining the conversation, Nate said, 'It's a shame he typed the message stuck on your window.'

'Yeah, but we could run it for prints. There are no footprints outside the window, but I'll see if your neighbours saw anything or have CCTV on their balconies. You never know your luck,' Burnsy said.

'I could have sworn whoever it was said my name. That's what startled me awake. I'm not saying they were in the room, but when it's dead quiet at night, they might have called from outside the window and then taken off,' Laura said with a glance at the window not far from her bed.

'It's a shame you're on the street level, not the second floor, just for safety. Have you got security locks?' Burnsy asked.

'On everything. While you are here, and thanks for coming,' Laura added quickly, 'could we talk about Dad's case? The original case. I'll make you both a cup of tea or coffee?' she bribed them with a hopeful smile, and Burnsy chuckled.

'Have you got a biscuit to go with it?' Nate joked.

'Yep!'

'Done deal,' Burnsy agreed, and they followed her to the old-fashioned kitchen, which looked colourful with Laura and Becca's vintage colour themes.

While she made them coffee and placed a plate of biscuits in front of the men—no Milk Arrowroots—Laura asked Burnsy what he knew of the original investigation. The two men sat at the kitchen table, looking out the window to the street.

'As I'm not on your case, so to speak,' Burnsy said, 'I have no grounds to open the files, but I did give a copy to Nate.'

'Thank you,' Laura said gratefully.

'No problem,' Burnsy continued, 'I sought out the police officer assigned to manage the neighbourhood riot eighteen years ago to get his take on it given the current trouble brewing – his name is Michael Lawson. He was in his late forties then but is still in the police service, close to retirement age, and doing more desk duties. He mentioned your father, but I'm sorry, his take was that it was an accident.'

'That's okay and not surprising, given it was never investigated. What was the police officer's impression of my father? Had he any dealings with him?'

'Yes,' Burnsy said. 'The area had been a hotbed for quite a while, and Mick had tried to broker the peace between your father's neighbourhood group and the Dobrev family. He said Rayco Dobrev was a decent fellow, had nothing good to say about the son, Gerry, and wasn't kind about your father.'

'I've heard as much. You won't shock or offend me, Sergeant. I've been on this case for a while,' Laura said, sipping her coffee. 'But, hearing your father was a bully is not easy.'

'It depends on who you talk with,' Nate offered sympathetically. 'I'm sure to many stressed homeowners, he was a great guy representing them.'

She smiled her thanks.

'I spoke with Mick as well,' Nate said. 'I haven't had a chance to update you since then. His account is not going to help our case.'

'Go on,' Laura said.

'Mick said there was not one witness at the time who saw anything untoward. They saw your father swinging and fighting; no one saw him falling, but then he was down. No one saw him pushed or hit in the head. No one who would own to it anyway.'

Laura inhaled sharply and exhaled slowly, calming herself. 'I'm not giving up on it. I still want justice for him. Someone must have seen something. It's been eighteen years; they mightn't be so scared to come forward now.'

'Except that the area is being terrorised again. An interesting coincidence with timing,' Burnsy said.

'Chicken or egg?' Nate asked Laura.

'Well, I did make it known I was starting the investigation. True crime and cold cases are very popular at the moment, so I took advantage of that, hoping someone might come forward with information,' she said, giving a small shrug as if maybe it hadn't been a good idea. 'So, I suspect I provided the perfect time to create a distraction for Gerry Dobrev. A good time to scare away anyone who might be open to helping me and to push through the sale of the dormant land for him.'

'Mick did have an interesting take on Gerry Dobrev,' Burnsy said.

'What's that?' Laura asked, leaning forward. 'Gerry's my number one suspect.'

'Then you won't want to hear this. He didn't think Gerry was responsible. Several people saw him at the other end of the street at the time your father was said to have hit his head.'

'But,' Nate added, 'Mick conceded that they might have said that for self-preservation.' Seeing her despondence, Nate added, 'Look, it just means we can't rely on material gathered from the first case. The focus was more on quelling the riots and cleaning it up quickly.'

Laura nodded. 'You'll tell me if you think I'm wasting my time, won't you?'

'Yes, no point throwing good money after bad. But, two things,' Nate said, finishing his coffee. 'I've taken your father's autopsy and asked a coroner to review it with fresh eyes. We're looking for anything that might have been missed or considered questionable.'

Laura brightened. 'Thanks, Nate, that's great.'

'That's my job,' he added.

'What's the second thing?' she asked.

'The fact that a threatening note was left on your window means someone is worried about the past becoming the present.'

'You're right, of course,' she said, snapping her fingers. 'We are back in business.'

'We never stopped,' Nate said. 'Have you seen today's newspaper?'

'Not yet.'

Nate nodded. 'There's a good write-up on last night's spookfest in Bougainvillea Street and Carnival Lane, in the Riverpark Estate. Adam and I were there to witness it.' He told them both what happened.

'I think you should move out,' Burnsy said again. 'Someone knows where you live, Laura and a number of players are involved in this, by the sound of it.'

She sighed. 'Thanks, Sergeant, I'll give it some thought.'

'I've just had an excellent idea...' Nate boasted, making her laugh at his confidence. 'Adam could use a flatmate, even a temporary one. If you're not keen to accept Audrey's offer or move home, move in with him. You'd have a hideout, and Adam would have some noise around the house, which might be good for him.'

'I doubt he would want that,' Laura said. 'We'd both be uncomfortable.'

'You'd be alive, and he'd be distracted,' Nate said. 'Just a thought. I'll mention it to him anyway.'

'If your flatmate and her boyfriend came home, that would work,' Burnsy said, and Nate read between the lines. He'd already lost Jessica to Nate, and maybe Burnsy wanted a shot at Laura.

'I confess, I find it rather exciting,' she said.

Nate smiled. 'How's that?'

'Well, I don't know whether I'm taking the fight to the enemy or the fight is coming to me, but I'm in it, and I'm going to get an outcome one way or the other.'

Chapter 18

'I can't believe I agreed to this,' Adam said under his breath, and Nate slapped him on the back.

'Consider it a good deed. Now you've got a crowded house for the weekend with Laura and Jack here.'

'Luckily, I have no life,' Adam said as Nate opened the boot of his Audi to reveal her luggage. He took the bags that Nate handed him. 'How long did you say she was staying?' He frowned at the three bags.

'A week or two. Depends on the case. If I solve it tomorrow—and we both know I'm brilliant—she could be gone by Monday.'

Laura pulled up next to Nate in Adam's driveway and alighted from her old white Peugeot. She grabbed her laptop and a beauty case from the back seat and locked the car.

'Wow, your place is beautiful; thank you for this,' she said to Adam.

'Sure, no problem,' he said, feeling Nate give him a side glance. He was hardly going to say otherwise. 'You can drive in and park next to my car in the garage. I'll give you a remote.'

'Thanks.'

A taxi pulled up, and Jack got out, thanking the driver. He removed a large duffel bag and a guitar from the boot before tapping on it to give the driver the all-clear to leave.

'It's my stepdad,' Adam said to Laura.

'Jack Bernham?' she said wide-eyed.

'Yeah, he's just staying the night. Hope that's okay?'

Laura laughed. 'It's your house. I'm lucky to be staying the night.'

Adam didn't argue with that.

'Ah, another freeloader,' Jack joked, seeing the bags, and Laura laughed as Nate did the introductions.

'Be careful with those bags, Son,' Jack said to Adam. 'You are supposed to be recovering.'

'What from?' Laura asked.

'He got stabbed by a patient,' Nate said.

'It was ages ago and in the leg. It's fine,' Adam said.

'Don't worry, he never pulls his weight anyway,' Nate threw in for good measure as he took the last of the bags and locked up his Audi.

'That it?' Adam asked with a small smile and a glance at Laura's Peugeot.

'Yes, for now,' she said with a grin. 'I didn't bring my cooking utensils, so I hope you've got a fully stocked kitchen. I love to cook.'

'Move in with me!' Nate said, changing his mind and pretending to return her bags to his car. The group laughed.

Adam led them inside. Laura and Jack admired Adam's classic Queenslander timber home, which had a sprawling verandah, polished timber floors, and high ceilings.

'Haven't you been here?' Adam asked, surprised, and Jack shook his head.

'Sadly, I've never been invited,' he said, winking at Laura.

'Jack normally stays with Audrey and Nate,' Adam added for Laura's benefit.

'His other favourite stepson,' Nate added of himself.

'You'd think he was family,' Adam joked, and Nate looked at Jack with a shocked expression.

'You mean you haven't told him I'm the love child?'

Adam rolled his eyes and ignored him, escorting his guests to their bedrooms.

'Jack, we'll share a bathroom if that's okay. Laura, you have the ensuite.'

'That's fine,' Jack said.

'This is lovely,' she said, entering the room with its large double bed topped with plush white pillows and quilts. Laura put her bags down. 'Thank you; this is so tasteful.'

'If you'd stayed at the mansion, you'd have your own bathroom,' Nate joked, hitting Jack on the back. 'Sadly, not every house has twelve rooms and twelve bathrooms.'

'Seriously?' Laura asked. 'I thought I would put Audrey out if I accepted her offer. I thought you were joking about living in a different wing.'

Nate shook his head. 'Nope, three wings, crazy.'

'You'd probably never see her,' Adam said, quite used to the shock his childhood home brought out in other people. He suggested they have a drink on the back deck; it was late afternoon, and the dusk light was welcoming.

'I'll just have one and then get going,' Nate said, 'Danielle and I are planting cameras and listening devices tonight if we can get into the carnival grounds without being seen.'

'I'd love to come,' Laura said, 'but I know you won't let me.'

'Correct,' Nate said, accepting a beer; Jack did the same, Laura requested a glass of white wine, and Adam took a beer. Jack brought his guitar with him and perched it near the outdoor seating.

Adam was pleased Laura had not been a fangirl; she seemed to take Jack's presence in her stride.

'If we find we have something to watch or have caught anything on audio, we'll tell you what we've found,' Nate assured her.

'We're speaking to my former security guard on Monday morning, too,' Adam said.

'Charlie?' Jack asked with a smile.

'Yeah, she will tell us what she remembers about the time. Gerta and Gerry threatened her.'

'Good grief, how frightening,' Laura said.

'Give her my best. She's an amazing lady,' Jack said.

'Speaking of which,' Nate said and cleared his throat. Adam knew what it meant; Nate was going to say something he didn't want to hear. 'Audrey thought we might need to hire security if things become a little hairier. I told her of the threatening message Laura received.'

'You're not going to suggest Tom Hartigan,' Adam said, and Jack chuckled.

'He's Adam's first security detail, and they got on like a house on fire,' Jack told Laura. Adam's expression indicated otherwise.

'No, we don't need to hire anyone yet, but just a thought,' Nate said.

'Is Audrey scared? If so, I'll hire someone right away.'

Nate grimaced. 'Hard to say with Audrey, she's very stoic, but I think she's uneasy.'

'The Dobrev family has always unnerved her.' Adam told them of the cemetery visit as a kid and again last week when Gerry Dobrev threatened them.

'Creepy,' Laura said, shaking her head. 'Is Gerta any good at fortune telling?'

'I couldn't tell you,' Adam said, 'but she always claimed to have a message for Audrey from my grandfather. That was enough to convince Audrey she was a fake as, apparently, Grandpa would be too busy on the other side to send a message to her.'

The thought brought on a round of laughs, and Adam realised he was feeling better and lighter for the first time in a week. He returned to Nate's suggestion.

'There's plenty of security people we could hire.'

Nate agreed, 'But if we want someone who can hit the ground running, knows us and the houses in question, and has set up the security cameras already, that's Tom. He's a free agent... just saying.'

'Think about it,' Jack said. 'So, are we ordering a pizza tonight?'

'Laura's a good cook and loves cooking,' Nate said.

She laughed. 'I could whip up something to earn my board if the fridge isn't empty. You could provide a free concert while I do,' she said with a nod to Jack.

'Do you play or sing?' he asked her.

'I sang in the school choir ten years ago. I haven't hit a note since,' Laura said.

Adam smiled, watching them and felt Nate watching him. Nate was right, not that he'd tell him that. It was good to have Jack and Laura around and he felt better for it. The house was alive again.

Nate parked closer to the carnival grounds than the night prior with Adam and turned off the ignition.

'We might have been better off doing this during the day,' Danielle said. 'Gerry Dobrev, his friends, or any neighbourhood punks probably wouldn't be hanging around in full light.'

'I thought about that but decided the neighbourhood watch was too good at the moment, and everyone was twitchy. When we came the other day, we were barely three steps from the car before curtains started moving and doors opening.'

'Yeah, that's true. Someone would have called us in for trespassing,' Danielle agreed.

'Let's just observe for about thirty minutes, make sure the coast is clear and then if we can't see anything happening, we'll jump the fence and head in. I figure we should be right if we're in and out before nine o'clock.'

'It's good it is a dark night,' Danielle said, looking skyward through the window for the moon and not seeing it. 'We'll drop in a few little bugs to grab some audio and stick in a few subtle cameras, and Bob's your uncle.'

They sat comfortably in silence, observing the area for a short while.

'Have you got an Uncle Bob?' Nate asked.

'Yes. Don't you?'

'No,' Nate said. 'I thought it was a stupid saying, but if you've got one, there's hope for us all.'

Danielle chuckled. 'How was Adam today? He was good at the gym this morning, not that he's the type to wear his heart on his sleeve.'

'Yeah, I thought he was fine, better. Having Jack stay over and Laura temporarily move in on a protection order, so to speak, was a brilliant idea of mine.'

'Of course it was.'

'Burnsy was checking her out.'

Danielle groaned. 'Poor Matt if he lucks out again. Still, there's someone for everyone.'

'Is it going well with Eric?'

'It's going great.'

That was the extent of Nate's interest in anything romantic, and so they sat in silence again as the clock neared 8.30pm.

'What do you really think is happening here?' Danielle asked.

Nate shrugged: 'It could be drug deals, gangs, a reminder to the original residents not to remember anything about Alex Armstrong's death, or Gerry Dobrev calling in favours from his friends to play ghost games on the neighbourhood he wants to revenge.'

'It could be all that,' she agreed. 'I think it is greed, pure and simple. Shall we?'

'Yeah, let's do it.' They quietly exited, and Nate winced as he looked at his Audi.

'She'll be all right,' Danielle whispered and grinned.

He sighed with frustration, and the pair hurried to the fencing at the back of the fairground, out of sight of the bordering houses. Nate found footing and hoisted himself over, turning back to help Danielle, but she was already beside him; she rarely needed help.

He nodded toward where he and Adam had seen figures milling around on their last surveillance shift and arriving near the Ferris Wheel; they stood back, waited and listened.

'Creepy as hell but all clear,' Danielle said. 'I'll stick a camera here and one on the merry-go-round.'

'I'll do the same with audio,' Nate said as the pair removed their equipment.

Nate placed his audio gear on a carriage roof, and Danielle put the first of her two small night vision cameras on one of the Ferris Wheel arms. She felt the satisfying stick of the magnet and checked its radius; it would project a 120-degree view and send the images to her phone. They moved stealthily to the dilapidated merry-go-round, and Danielle chose a horse that had seen better days; they all had. Nate did the same. Moving back, he felt like the horse's eyes were watching him, and he turned away, not looking too closely at the animal painted to appear like it was galloping. It looked frightened in its dark and broken surroundings, begging to be released from the carousel and set free.

'Done,' Nate said, and the pair hurried to find a carriage on the ride in a position best suited to capture audio and vision, and placed their wares.

'Let's get out of here,' Danielle said when finished.

The gate rattled as someone leapt over it, and Nate and Danielle dropped to the ground.

'The ghost train,' Nate whispered, and they hurried to hide behind its hoarding. A sign bearing an image of a ghoul and witch hanged precariously above their heads.

Nate swore under his breath. 'We were almost clear.'

'Should we make a run for it?'

'No. We don't know how many there are. Let's wait and listen, but if we need to, run like hell. You know where the spare car key is.'

'I'm not leaving without you,' Danielle hissed.

'If you need to, you will,' he ordered.

They stopped talking as three men approached, all dressed in black. Gerry Dobrev was amongst them, smaller than the other two men but tougher looking.

'I think we've got another one; we should get a good price for it,' one of the men said.

Gerry scoffed. 'We'll have them all running scared. Just need the old bastard to cark it.'

'There's ways to hurry that along,' the second man said.

'It's not that easy. You can't get in to see him without a letter of authorisation, and I'm not even on the list of guests.'

Nate nudged Danielle in the dark. 'That explains why he hasn't been to visit,' he said.

More voices could be heard, and two more men joined them, all undistinguishable in the dark, with their black clothing and most wearing baseball caps.

'Ready for spook night?' one said with a laugh.

'The cops will probably be waiting for us since our last raid made headlines.'

'What can they do?' Gerry asked. 'We're not hurting anyone. So, the kids made a bit of noise. Call it a street party; it finishes before it starts.'

'Yeah, your hires did a good job, and I don't think you can be arrested for scaring the shit out of anyone.'

They all laughed at that, egging each other on.

'What about the girl?' one of the men asked, his voice a little older and more refined than the others.

'What about her?'

'Do you want us to pay her a visit?'

'Nuh,' Gerry Dobrev answered, 'let her do her thing. It might work for us if people think the area's violent and going to be the subject of a murder case. She won't find anything on us.'

The group moved towards the ghost train, and Nate and Danielle froze.

'Move on,' Danielle willed them in a hushed voice.

'We need to finalise the plan,' the more mature man said.

'I agree, tonight's the last night I can get here before we do the big one.'

'Yeah, righto. We'll give the others ten more minutes, then we'll start.'

Nate hissed between his teeth. 'Move on for the love of God.'

As if they heard him, one of the men said, 'I'll wander down and see if they're waiting at the other gate.'

A few agreed to do the same at various locations, and for a short window of time, Nate and Danielle found themselves with just a couple of the men lurking nearby. He nudged her.

'Agreed,' she said, rising slowly.

They moved to the back of the ghost train wall, looking around and stopping every few moments to ensure Gerry's gang hadn't noticed them.

And then they took off toward the fence where they entered.

'Look there,' a voice called behind them, but the pair didn't turn around. Let them think they are neighbourhood kids, Nate thought as he hit the fence, finding his foothold in the wire with Danielle right behind him. They were up and over in seconds, rushing toward their car.

Behind them, they heard an almighty crash and laughter. Once in the car, Nate saw the signage from the ghost train that had crashed to the ground where they had been hiding only minutes earlier. He couldn't be sure whether they had caused that or that was what the men were looking at, but the pair didn't stick around long enough to find out.

Chapter 19

Monday morning and Adam had not stopped since he got up early, went for a jog, and returned to find that Laura had already left for work and Jack was dressed and ready to go back down south. Adam was stronger today, better than he was this time last week. Swinging by to pick up Jack's band buddies, he dropped them all at the airport, thanking his godfather for the impromptu visit.

'I don't want to be soppy, but it means a lot,' Adam said, and Jack slapped him in a hug.

'If you need to talk, you call me, okay?' Jack said and released Adam, pulling his luggage from the car's boot.

'Thanks, Jack. I'm blown away you came up,' Adam said, offering words that did not go close to conveying how touched he was by his godfather and now stepdad's thoughtfulness.

'I really like Laura,' Jack said with a raised eyebrow in Adam's direction, laughing as Adam shook his head. 'What? Unlike those *Godfather* movies, my role is not to be the head of the mafia but to offer mentorship and guidance. I looked it up when your dad offered me the job.'

'Yeah?' Adam said and laughed. 'You've excelled.'

'Thank you, Son,' Jack said. 'And remember, it's not your fault you weren't bookish enough for your last partner. Each to their own.'

'Get on the plane,' Adam said and laughed. He wasn't a library archivist, that's for sure, and never would be.

'But seriously,' Jack lingered, 'I liked Kelsey a lot, but what was the last thing you did together that was fun?'

'Isn't that your boarding call?' Adam asked, took a deep breath, and sighed like the question was all too hard.

But he knew Jack had a point, even if he chose to make it now when he's been around all weekend. Kelsey was often intense. She wasn't light-hearted, fun, or frivolous; neither was he, but they were more serious together. If they were drinking wine, Kelsey would have to know what it was and where it came from; if the pair were going to see a film, she'd research the director and make sure the film would be stimulating, and he didn't share her love of history; he spent most of his time trying to forget his own. Sometimes, he just wanted to be "in the now", go to the football, watch an action film. Maybe they weren't making each other happy but just co-existing. He knew one thing, though: he missed coming home to her.

'Someone with a sense of humour and who likes a bit of fun might lighten you up a bit,' Jack said while thumbing for his boarding pass on his phone screen. 'Right, got it.' He looked up at Adam. 'On that note, adios.'

'See you when you next tour this way.' He watched his stepdad-godfather until he entered the building, and with a final wave, Jack departed.

Adam then proceeded to jail for his prison therapy group. He wasn't sure what they served them for breakfast, but this morning, they were all fired up and full of opinions, most of it unhelpful; Baz was still waiting to have his epiphany. Next, to the office of *Delaney and Murphy*, Jessica had timed the coffee run to suit him, and he gratefully accepted the double shot flat white not long after entering.

'We should give you a pay rise,' he said, enjoying his first coffee for the day.

'You just did.'

'Excellent. I'm worth my weight in gold. Is Nate in?'

'Yep. You've got the phone call with Charlie at 11.30. I'll set up the iPad in the meeting room for you and Nate.'

'Oh right, thanks,' Adam said and glanced at the clock. Fifteen minutes away. He strode to his office, depositing his laptop, phone and car keys. Walking to the window, he took a minute to drink his coffee and watch the traffic and pedestrians down below on the streets of Stones Corner. It was a cool day, and the weather made everyone scurry just that little bit faster to be indoors or out of the shade of the buildings.

'Is Jack gone?' Nate asked, knocking on the open door and walking straight in.

'Yep, he'd be landed and home by now.'

'Is Laura okay?'

'Why wouldn't she be?'

Nate shrugged. 'No one followed her to your place and put a sign on the window?'

'Not that we noticed.'

Adam remembered Nate was on location last night. 'How did it go? Did you get any vision and audio?'

'Maybe. Dan's running it and coming in this afternoon if you want to sit in. Laura and Burnsy will be here, too. I think Jessica's put it on your calendar.'

'I'll see how I go, but you don't need me; I'm going to the asylum.' He still called it by the name the boys knew it by when they played within its boundaries and had a friend, Joe, within its wall. With a glance at the clock, Adam headed toward Nate in the doorway, saying, 'We'd better call Charlie', and Nate followed him to the meeting room.

'We had a close encounter of the people kind last night – Gerry and his mates,' Nate said as the men sat and Jessica set up the screen for Charlie's incoming call. She dialled the number.

'Did they see you?' Adam asked.

'I don't think so. There were at least half a dozen of them. They're planning something, a finale of sorts. I hope they elaborated after we left,' Nate said. 'I think Rayco Dobrev needs extra protection at his aged care home.'

'Oh?' Adam asked as the phone rang, and Jessica turned the screen so both men could see.

'Charlie!' Adam said, smiling at his childhood security officer.

'My first love,' Nate said, sighing and placing his hand on his heart, making her laugh.

'I'm his latest love,' Jessica said with a grin, introducing herself.

'Well, we know he has excellent taste in women, Jessica,' Charlie said with a laugh. She was nearing fifty and still fit and sporty, her hair peppered with grey and her neck and face reflecting her years.

'That I have,' Nate agreed, and Jessica excused herself, closing the door behind her.

The party made small talk for a while, and Charlie was openly affectionate to them, especially Adam.

'What is meant to be will be,' she told Adam of his breakup. 'I would love to see you as a husband and father, though.'

'You're sounding like Audrey now,' Adam teased.

'We were bound to rub off on each other after all those years,' Charlie laughed. 'You know, it was during the Dobrev riots that I moved into your house and stayed the next six years. I always intended to move out, but time flies… you know how it is.'

'I do. I'm thinking of moving back,' Adam said, 'but living in a different wing from Nate.'

'Yeah, we like each other, but we have our limits,' he agreed in jest.

'I think that's a brilliant idea. You can workout together and keep an eye on Audrey. It's a very safe house, too, with all that security.'

After a bit more small talk, Nate got down to business. 'Can you tell us what you remember of the Dobrev years?'

'I have given it considerable thought since your request to talk, so I'll tell you what I think are the salient facts.' Charlie took a sip of tea and began, remembering the day she spoke with James Murphy—Adams' dad—about the threat that was the Dobrev family.

Then…

James Murphy loved coming home; Winsome, however, did not. She made the trip twice a year, plus Christmas, reasoning that if Adam were in boarding school, she would only see him for the same period.

But James loved Brisbane's pace and relaxing with his son and mother. Audrey cooked, but Winsome did not. He enjoyed visiting the Brisbane newspaper office, keeping them on their toes and encouraging the young guns. One day, James hoped Adam would start working with the journalists and work his way up to manage the Murphy empire. He wouldn't find time to do all he planned on this trip, but his priority today was to get a briefing from Charlie on the *Dobrev Carnival World* debacle, which was close enough to cause concern. If Audrey felt threatened, there was something to be worried about, as he knew his mother had a steel backbone. Ironically, his father, Edward, made his fortune in steel and lived to see his eleventh wedding anniversary—the theme of steel—dying the year after. His father gave Audrey a Jaguar car that year, which she still owned. James sat in his home office with the two strong women – Audrey and Charlie.

'I'm thinking of withdrawing from the committee working with Rayco Dobrev,' Audrey told her son. 'Rayco is a lovely man, but his son's appearance to Charlie at the carnival and his veiled warnings worry me.'

'I think that's a good idea, Mum. How will Rayco take it?'

'He will be disappointed, but Rayco is a kind gentleman, and hopefully, he will understand. I will say it is due to my health rather than disparage his son.'

James agreed. 'For Rayco's safety and the community's best interests, I wish he would retire and sell the place to developers. He'd enjoy a lovely retirement on the funds even if the community groups missed out.'

'He's the right age,' Charlie agreed. 'If only his son were as obliging and diplomatic, but intimidation seems to be Gerry's strength.'

James sat back and webbed his fingers. 'Let's all take a family trip to Carnival World. I'd like to see it myself and meet Gerta if she dares approach. Charlie, you'll come with us?'

'Of course, Mr Murphy.'

'We won't take Nate. Let's reduce the risk and keep it to us,' Audrey suggested.

'Agreed. This afternoon when Adam gets home from school then,' James said. 'Who is the ringleader of the neighbourhood group that wants the carnival gone?'

'It's a man named Alex Armstrong,' Charlie said. 'He moved in six months ago with his wife and daughter.'

'The little girl is only six or so,' Audrey added.

'Yes, and he's got a bit of thuggery about him too,' Charlie said.

'Hmm. We might drive through that new estate on the way home. See just how noisy the carnival is for them at night.'

'Perhaps we should go in my car or your hire car, Mr Murphy. Let's not take the Jag,' Charlie said.

'Good idea. As soon as Adam gets changed from school, we'll depart.'

Now...

'I remember how excited I was,' Adam laughed as Charlie recounted her memories of the Dobrev family and Alex Armstrong. 'Dad never did anything with us, and here he was, staying four days and wanting to take me to the carnival! That was before Alex Armstrong died, and Gerry scared Audrey in the cemetery.'

'Your recollection of Alex Armstrong is interesting,' Nate said, 'we've heard he was a tough player, even a thug, from a few sources.'

'How is his daughter taking those sorts of character assassinations?' Charlie asked.

'She's not surprised,' Nate said. 'So, what happened at the carnival? All the fun of the fair?'

'And more,' Charlie said. 'Mr Murphy got the full picture that night. He met the whole family – Rayco, Gerta, and their son, Gerry. Rayco heard your dad was on the premises and came out to greet him. He was a lovely man and gave your family the tour. Do you remember, Adam?'

'I do because I wanted to go on the rides with Dad and not look at the land and see the plans Mr Dobrev had drawn up,' Adam said.

'Well, you got your wish. Your dad was keen to go on the Ferris Wheel to see how big the Riverpark Estate development was and how much the suburban sprawl encroached on *Dobrev's Carnival World.*'

'From memory, Gerry and Gerta didn't come near us,' Adam said.

'But when you and your dad got on the ride, they appeared at Audrey's side like slithering snakes. Gerry made a snide remark about the Murphy family having enough wealth without looking to distribute his rightful inheritance. Gerta implied that if she lost her family fortune, so would you. I don't know how she intended to do that.'

'She might have cursed the family,' Nate said, shrugging when Charlie and Adam looked at him. 'She was into all that tarot and witchery stuff. Who is to say she didn't have a doll she was sticking pins in? What was your dad's interest other than a good media story?'

Adam looked to Charlie for an answer.

'He was protecting his family, pure and simple,' she said. 'Audrey and Adam were alone in that big house and no match for Gerry Dobrev and his cronies. That's why I moved in. But you were in the right place up high in the Ferris Wheel when the fight broke out,' Charlie said to Adam.

'Not according to Dad, if I remember correctly,' Adam said.

Then...

The Ferris Wheel was not as big as the one at the yearly Brisbane Exhibition—The Ekka—but it was high enough to make you feel like falling would be scary. It gave the rider an expansive view over the neighbouring suburbs and the Brisbane River.

'I came on this ride with Charlie and Nate,' Adam told his dad. 'It's not as fun as the dodgems, but Charlie said we could eat our fairy floss and find our house.'

'There's our home,' James said, pointing it out to his son.

Adam pointed out Nate's house and Stuart's, then waved to Audrey and Charlie below. He kept glancing at his father; he rarely saw him in jeans and a shirt, with no jacket, and rarely got this close to him.

'They're a funny family. Mr Dobrev is very nice. Did the old lady who owns this place or anyone here say anything to you on your past visits?' James asked his son without making it sound like Adam was in trouble.

'Yeah. Mrs Dobrev said she had a message for Audrey from Grandpa.'

'Is that so? What did Audrey say?'

'That Grandpa knows where to find her.'

James laughed out loud. 'That's true.'

'You don't have to worry about Audrey, Dad. I'm looking after her,' Adam said, and James looked at his 12-year-old boy and smiled.

'That makes me feel a lot better. Thank you, Son.'

The wheel circled lower, giving a full view of the gates and the people entering – a mixture of families coming after school with the promise of a weekend ahead, young sweethearts, and teenagers keen to hang out somewhere away from their parents.

James continued, 'I don't want you to speak with the Dobrev family or go anywhere with them, Adam. You let Charlie know if they talk to you. Understand?'

'Sure, Dad. Look!' Adam exclaimed excitedly. 'That man just pushed the other one.'

James leaned forward in his seat in the carriage they shared. 'That's Gerry Dobrev, and I believe that is the neighbourhood group leader, Alex Armstrong.'

'Nate's dad said he's going too far with all his protest stuff.'

'Nate's dad is right.'

Several men stood with Gerry Dobrev and another couple with Alex Armstrong, and then a punch was swung.

The Ferris Wheel shuddered to a stop. James and Adam were in a carriage hanging near the top. James looked down and saw Gerta smiling up at him. She made a sign touching her right eye and pointing at him as if implying she was watching him. Before he could respond or whistle for his security, Charlie was at the woman's side, pushing her away and ordering the operator to start the wheel again. Gerta laughed, and James turned his attention to the fight again as the wheel began its rotation.

'Dad, it's getting wild!' Adam said, leaning over the edge of the carriage to watch; his father pulled him back.

'Arms in the carriage, Son.'

The fight had accelerated quickly; punches were thrown, and at least a dozen men had entered the fray. Parents with children were pulling them away from nearby rides, and James could see Rayco Dobrev running towards the commotion. More men rushed in to break up the fight, and a police siren wailed nearby as if they had been on standby, patrolling the neighbourhood and expecting trouble.

As they neared the bottom of the wheel, James Murphy ordered the driver, 'Let us out now, please.'

The operator pulled on the wheel, stopping it, and unhitched the chain across their carriage.

'I'm not supposed to do that,' the boy said.

'We appreciate it, thank you,' James said, reaching into his pocket, pulling out a few notes and tipping the young man more than he probably earned in his night shift.

'Thanks, Mister!' He smiled delightedly and started the ride again.

'Let's get out of here. I've seen all I need to see,' James said, his hand on Adam's shoulder. He hustled his group towards the carpark.

Adam was too excited by the action to be disappointed that his night at the carnival had ended early.

'What's going on?' Audrey asked as they entered the car. James locked the doors and drove away. 'We heard shouting but couldn't see a thing,' Audrey added.

'The neighbourhood group arrived and confronted Gerry Dobrev on his property,' James said. 'I suspect they are stirring up noise and drama just to prove the carnival is no longer suitable for the suburb.'

'Very sad,' Audrey sighed.

'Poor Rayco,' Charlie added.

'He may win yet,' James said.

Now...

'But he didn't,' Charlie said. 'Not long after Alex Armstrong died, the neighbourhood group disbanded, and the carnival continued, but it was never the same, and with their restricted hours and noise limits, I believe it was tough to make it a success.'

'I understand how Gerta might feel cheated of a very generous retirement, given that she worked there for years,' Adam said.

'Yes, I have some sympathy for her,' Charlie agreed.

'Was dad threatened?' Adam asked.

'Not to my knowledge,' Charlie said. 'Gerta and Gerry were frightening figures, but your father wasn't worried about the evil eye she gave him.'

'I would have been,' Nate shuddered.

'Me too,' Adam agreed. 'She was always scary.'

Nate grimaced. 'You're not going to like this, but I think Gerta is the person we need to speak with next.'

'Yeah, I don't like it,' Adam agreed and grinned. 'But I'm curious to see her.'

'Be careful,' Charlie warned, 'you don't have your hot security agent with you now,' she teased.

'Care to make a comeback?' Adam joked.

Chapter 20

Dane paced, unaware that his psychologist, Dr Adam Murphy, was watching him on CCTV in the River Centre for Mental Health office hub. Adam observed that anytime a male warden dealt with Dane, the boy adopted the persona of Trey, the model. Slightly flirty, vulnerable and his every move considered. Adam watched, intrigued. It was as if the boy was inviting the encounters he most feared and hated. That need to feel wanted even if the attention was unwanted.

When rejected or ignored by the male staff, Dane would revert to himself to act as the bodyguard and berate Trey for leading men on and accepting their attention as if Trey was disgusting. Seeing the boy's anguish was difficult; Dane needed to learn to deal with men again. The patient did not display the same behaviour with the female staff, which was not surprising, given his abusive record was at the hands of men.

Then, Dane began yelling for him. 'Adam! Adam! Adam!'

'He does that a lot,' Adele Warren, the senior manager on today's roster, said, looking over Adam's shoulder. In her fifties and wearing a faded uniform that fitted better a long time ago, she gave a small sigh of resignation. Adam met Adele over a decade ago, and they had regularly run into each other in psychology circles and conferences over the years.

'How long does it go on for?' Adam asked, concerned.

'Sometimes only a few minutes. The day we called you in, he had worked himself up to the point of collapse.'

Adam shook his head. 'This kid.'

'I know – so much potential. No one will ever pay for it, but I'd love to get some of the offenders, lock them in here, and let their poor victims go. I'm sure we could find some good treatments for them.'

Adam smiled at her. 'One of your revenge fantasies?'

'One of many,' she agreed with a grin.

'You're very scary, Adele,' Adam said and playfully shuddered.

She laughed. 'Good. I've been working on that for years.'

Dane continued to call out for Adam.

'Do you want to see him?' Adele asked.

Adam looked at the clock. 'If that's okay? I've got fifteen minutes before my next patient; I'll drop in now.'

'That would be good, thank you,' Adele said and departed for the counter to speak with a visitor who had just arrived and wished to sign in.

Adam made his way to Dane's room. He had only been in there a few times; they usually met in a meeting room, and with a knock on the door, he opened it and entered.

'You're here!' Dane said, looking surprised and delighted in equal measure.

'You called?'

'But how? Have you got a superpower?' Dane joked, and Adam laughed.

'Sadly, no. I'm here to see someone else.'

'Ah,' Dane nodded. 'You've got more than one psycho to visit in this place. Am I your favourite?'

Adam smiled. 'I haven't given it that much thought, but if you keep working yourself up by calling out my name, you're soon going to be the biggest pain in my arse.'

Dane's eyes widened in surprise at Adam's frankness, and then he laughed out loud. 'Yeah, love you too,' he said, shaking his head.

'What's going on?' Adam asked, sitting on the only chair in the room while Dane dropped onto the bed.

'Trey was being a dick and flirting with the male nurse.'

'Why?'

'Why what? Why was he flirting?' Dane shrugged. 'Probably thought he was cute and the nurse would want him.'

'Is Trey gay?'

'No way,' Dane shot back.

'It's not a big deal if he is.'

'He's not.

'Did Trey want attention, someone to notice him?'

'I'm here. Why would he want that?' Dane demanded.

'Maybe you need to tell him that he's all right. He doesn't need to worry that every man likes him or wants to be anything more than a friend. That's he got you.'

Dane scoffed, 'But they do want him.'

'No,' Adam said firmly. 'Maybe the men Trey met in the past wanted something from him, but that was in his modelling days. Those days are over now. The men he meets now are here to help him. You should tell him it's okay just to be himself. No one here wants anything from him.'

'Sam doesn't like you.'

'Sam's sporty, isn't he?' Adam asked, trying to remember the alter ego without having his notes present.

'Yeah. Sam says you're trying to take me away from him. Sam says it was a mistake to start seeing you, and I shouldn't see you anymore. He says I'm hanging out for your visits.'

Adam felt exhaustion riding him. He didn't need all this today. He wished he had let the boy keep yelling his name and checked on him after his other patient.

'Do you agree with Sam?' Adam asked.

'No. But Mum agrees with him. She came up to visit and said I'm just showing off. She said my self-esteem is so low that I've resorted to making up stuff to come in here and get attention.' Dane was working himself up now, and his hands were thumping the bed.

Adam knew this familiar track; a parent can't believe their partner—in this case, Dane's stepfather—is capable of the abuse and believes their child is lying.

'Dane,' Adam said in a very controlled voice, 'I don't care what your mum or Sam thinks. What you think is all that I'm interested in. It's natural to be scared of what's happening to you and to be nervous in here. But it's not a prison. It's a health facility to help you feel stronger and better about yourself.'

'What if he takes over my life and I can never come back?' Dane said in a low whisper.

'Who? Sam?'

Dane looked around and nodded.

'He won't. I know where you are and how to find you, Dane.'

'Yeah, yeah, you do. That's right,' Dane said and nodded, his breath expelling in a loud whoosh. 'That's right, I'm here. You know.'

'I know. I want you to do something for me now.'

'Okay, what?'

'I want you to do a mindfulness exercise for me. I want you to do this homework by the time we next meet, in a couple of days.'

'Okay,' Dane said, leaning forward and looking mildly interested.

Adam rose, found an exercise pad and neon pen, and asked, 'Can I write in this?'

'Sure.'

Adam found an empty page and proceeded to give Dane an exercise that suited his severe dissociative state. 'Okay, this homework requires you to start with mindfulness of your external world, not what's happening under your skin or in your head. Yeah?'

'Okay. So, like what do I have to do?'

'There are five headings,' Adam said, writing the words in columns, and Dane read them out loud as Adam wrote them.

'See... hear... touch... taste... and smell.'

'Right,' Adam said. 'Under each heading, you need to experience five things and write them up before we next meet.'

'What if I don't?' Dane said defiantly.

'Then there will be no gold star for you,' Adam joked, and Dane grinned. 'I'll have to cut our session short and leave you to do your homework.'

'I'll get it done by then,' Dane said.

'Get creative,' Adam said, 'you'd be good at that.'

Dane smiled and didn't say anything. Adam continued, 'For example, for the hearing category, don't just tell me you heard the sound of someone yelling. Big deal, so does everyone. Listen and be mindful. What can you hear that no one else is focussing on? Like the sound of running water or the wheels of a trolley. I take points off your score if you pick something lame.'

Dane smiled. 'I get it.'

'Five in each category; take your time, but have it done before my next visit. Yes?'

'Yes.'

'I'll leave you to it and see you very soon.'

'Sure,' Dane said, with the neon and pad in his hand, and as Adam left, he turned back to watch the boy and thought, sometimes, Nate's murder cases seemed easier.

Chapter 21

Adam found Nate pacing when he arrived at the office just after 2pm; it was another of Nate's annoying habits.

'You made it back in time! And, good news, Gerta will see us tonight,' Nate said.

'Why tonight? Does she want to take us on the ghost train?' Adam scoffed, entering the office and closing the door behind him.

Jessica cut in. 'Don't you guys ever say hello or goodbye to each other?'

'Oh, yeah, hi Adam,' Nate said formally.

'Hello, Nate,' Adam deadpanned, and Jessica laughed at how silly it sounded.

'Forget it,' she said, waving her hand. 'Dan and Burnsy are here; Laura just parked in the visitor's zone.'

'So,' Nate continued, 'Gerta, tonight, do you think she wants to spook us?'

'I wouldn't put it past her, the scary old—'

Danielle raced through the door in her usual fast fashion, startling both men. Burnsy followed her in, taking off his police cap.

'Sorry boys, a bit on edge, are we?' she grinned.

'We've got a date with Gerta,' Adam said.

'That'll do it,' she agreed. 'Can I come?'

'No,' they both said in unison.

'Thanks for coming in, Burnsy,' Nate said.

'No problem. Is Laura coming?' Burnsy asked.

'She's on her way up the stairs as we speak,' Jessica informed him.

'So, can you join us to catch up on this case?' Nate asked, looking at his phone, texting, and talking simultaneously. He stopped long enough to look up at Adam.

'Oh, you mean me?'

'Yeah, the rest of us are already in. It will probably be your most interesting meeting today,' Nate ribbed him.

'I did my monthly accounts earlier.'

'I stand corrected,' Nate said. 'Only if you have time for a brief overview before we meet with Gerta.'

Adam looked at Jessica, and she said, 'You're free; I did put it in your diary.'

'Bummer,' he joked. 'Let's do it.'

Jessica buzzed Laura in, who greeted everyone and assured Sergeant Matt Burns that she had received no more visitors or notes on her window since they last saw each other and since she had temporarily moved into Adam's home. They filed into the meeting room. Nate, Adam and Danielle sat in their usual seats, and Jessica offered to bring in coffee.

'Want to begin, Burnsy?' Nate asked.

'Yeah. We were called out twice on the weekend at night to Bougainvillea Street at the Riverpark Estate. It's fair to say the residents are spooked. There was quite a bit of damage to cars parked on the street, and the carousel coming to life is freaking the kids out, apparently. There are four houses up for sale now.'

'Despicable,' Laura said. 'Could I afford one?'

Burnsy chuckled. 'Hang out a bit longer; you might get one even cheaper.'

'We've got something on that,' Nate said. 'Dan and I were talking with the neighbours, and the resident at number 11 has already received an offer from Gerry Dobrev. She's a senior woman, and he made her feel it would be in her best interest to sell to him.'

'I bet he did the little creep,' Laura said.

Danielle picked up where Nate left off. 'While working the street, so to speak, I caught up with several residents about their memories; honestly, it was a waste of time. I suspect they told me what you've already got in your police reports, Burnsy. I think they were too scared to say much. The handful of residents living there 18 years ago said they locked themselves in then and are doing the same now. It's gone full circle.'

'Any surveillance footage or dashcam from the locals?' Adam asked.

'Still working on it,' Nate said. 'But no joy so far. I did score some security footage, but the camera faces the house's backyard, not the street. Let's stay in the present for a minute. We've got some audio to play that we captured over the weekend,' Nate told Burnsy.

Burnsy asked, in his police role, 'How did you get the audio? Did you go onto the carnival grounds?'

Nate looked at Danielle and back at Burnsy. 'We're taking the fifth.'

'Nice try,' Burnsy said. 'Can they get away with that?' he asked Laura in jest.

She shook her head in the negative. 'Sorry, guys. The Fifth Amendment only applies in the United States. However,' she said with a small smile at Nate, 'while there is no constitutional protection for the right to silence here in Australia, it is generally recognised as a common law right and part of the privilege against self-incrimination.'

'There you go. Handy to have my solicitor present,' Nate joked as Danielle set up the audio and vision to play.

'We found ourselves trapped after we'd planted the equipment,' Danielle said and told Laura about their escape.

'Oh my God, you were lucky you didn't get hit by the ghost train sign!' Laura exclaimed.

'It was never a very scary ghost train,' Adam said with a grin and a glance at Nate.

'Especially when Adam's security detail, Charlie, had her hand on our shoulders the whole time,' Nate agreed.

Everyone laughed at the image.

'Did anyone see you?' Laura asked, getting back to business.

'No, I don't think so; I think the falling signage probably gave us a clean getaway by diverting their attention.'

'Someone's on our side,' Danielle said.

'Maybe Dad is,' Laura said, not at all self-conscious in believing in the righteousness of her quest to find her father's murderer.

'Just remember it's still private property,' Burnsy added, leaving it at that.

'Don't worry; we're not storming the place to get in there,' Danielle said. 'Even by my standards, it's creepy, and I love a good horror film – the bloodier, the better. Okay, ready.' She nodded at Nate.

Nate looked at the projection and explained, 'Dan enhanced the footage. It's as sharp as it is going to get. Here's the people in dark clothes.' As the footage ran, they all squinted, trying to make out any detail that might help the case.

'This second lot of footage is from the next night, probably when your boys were called out, Burnsy,' Danielle said. 'You can see the people—we'll call them doorknockers—running up and down the street, waking people at midnight. We caught this footage from the Ferris Wheel camera. There's about half a dozen of them, and even though you can't see them very well, they are in ghost face masks.'

'What's a ghost face mask?' Adam interrupted, not seeing it clearly on the screen.

'I was wondering the same thing,' Burnsy said.

'C'mon Adam, Burnsy, get with the program,' Nate jokingly said.

'Do you know?' Laura asked Nate.

'Sure, it's a mask like a ghost,' he said and shrugged. Danielle rolled her eyes.

'I work for a team of clowns.' She opened her iPad, searched for an image and turned it around to show them the elongated face mask, like the figure in the painting *The Scream.*

Nate shuddered. 'Creepy. I hate masks; I hate clown masks more than anything.'

'Scaredy-cat,' Adam ribbed him.

'We made out a few sentences from the recorded dialogue.' Danielle played it for them and then read her transcription. 'They said:

"It's a memory… Wednesday, we'll bring what we have and compare… They deserve it… They deserve all they get".'

The team mulled over it briefly, and Danielle read the audio transcripts again.

'There's not much to go on,' Nate said, disappointed. 'Can you play the audio we definitely didn't get from entering the grounds?' Nate said with a quick smile at Burnsy, who shook his head.

'Sure,' Danielle said, finding the file. 'Here we go.'

'Friday. That's the day.'

'What about the woman?'

'Leave that with me. I've got a plan.'

'Does the daughter know anything about the agreement?'

'Nope, and who's going to tell her?'

'It's coming together, Gerry.'

'Yeah, I'd like to get three or four more.'

'Oh wow,' Laura said. 'I'm guessing the daughter mentioned is me.'

'We believe so,' Nate said. 'Do you know anything about an agreement?'

'No, nothing.'

'Well, that's it,' Nate said. 'So, Friday, what the hell will happen on Friday?' he tapped impatiently. 'It would be good if we could just focus on history and not have all this other stuff boiling away in the background.'

'Yeah, well, one thing is for sure: we need to get better security on old Mr Dobrev,' Danielle said. 'He's a sitting duck if Friday involves finishing him off.'

'I'll get some extra backup down there and around the neighbourhood just to be prepared,' Burnsy said, writing a note for himself. 'The comment about the agreement worries me – *"She knows nothing about the agreement"*. What is the agreement that no one is going to tell Laura about? Is it now or then?'

'Maybe it was an agreement to kill my father as the head of the neighbourhood group and the most vocal then,' Laura said.

'It might mean that,' Burnsy agreed. 'So, if there was an agreement to bump your dad off, then Gerry Dobrev ensured he was far enough away not to be incriminated, even if he was the ringleader.'

'He's as shifty as they come,' Nate said. 'I wouldn't put anything past him. As for the agreement, maybe Gerta will tell us. She likes to boast.'

'You're going to talk with her?' Laura asked, pleased and surprised.

'Tonight. She's agreed to see us,' Nate said. 'I'm hoping she'll get sentimental seeing Adam again.'

Adam scoffed. 'That's not the word I'd use for it.'

'Can I come?' Laura asked, and Nate winced and looked at Adam. Laura did the same, given that Nate had left the decision to him.

Adam thought for a moment. 'I think she'll find you a curiosity, but she's likely to clam up knowing you will be looking to incriminate her son in the murder. If it is just Nate and me, she might be inclined to reveal a little more.'

'Fair enough,' Laura said disappointed. 'At the end of the day, I want information, so if I have to bow out to get it, that's what I'll do.'

''I'm not expecting great insights from her,' Nate said, 'but she might spill something or give us one of those obscure tarot-type comments, like the sun and mercury were in the seventh house then, which explains it all.'

'Yeah, that old chestnut,' Adam played along.

'Nate, do you want back up tonight when you meet Gerta in case Gerry and his mates are there?' Burnsy offered.

'Thanks, but no,' Nate said.

'It's just a catch-up with old friends,' Adam smirked. 'Worst case scenario, we'll have our fortunes told.'

The group laughed, but Adam wouldn't put it past her. As the meeting ended, Adam asked Laura, 'Do you need a lift home? I'll be going in about an hour.'

'No, but thanks. I've got my car here.'

He realised he said "home" as if they were living together. Adam quickly said his goodbyes and headed to his office; Nate followed shortly after.

'Rob was looking for you before he left. He wants you to call so he can read your head.'

'I bet he does,' Adam sighed as he sat behind his desk.

'So, you're all right?' Nate asked.

'Sure,' Adam said.

'You look like something is bugging you.'

'Nope, I'm fine. Late night, early morning, full house over the weekend, and everyone is telling me that Kelsey and I weren't suited.' Adam realised he had said what was wrong with him.

'Ah, that,' Nate said, moving inside the doorway and leaning against it, arms crossed. 'People are quick to say that when you break up with someone. Everyone suddenly doesn't like them or finds fault with them. Call it loyalty.'

'So, did you think we were suited?' Adam asked.

'I liked her a lot.'

'Right. But... never mind.' Adam smiled, giving him a good impression of his *I'm in control face*.

'I'll leave you to it then,' Nate said and headed out with a backward glance.

Adam knew he couldn't get much past Nate, given that they had known each other since they were young boys. He picked up his phone and called his mentor, psychologist Rob. Getting the head reading over with sooner rather than later was best.

Chapter 22

The black Mercedes convertible made its way down Carnival Lane, Adam behind the wheel, and Nate in the passenger seat.

'I never knew the Dobrevs had a private house at the back of the carnival grounds,' Nate said.

'Me either. Wouldn't it be cool as a kid to have a carnival in your backyard?'

'Yeah, it's a bit like your house with the pool, tennis court, bike ramp, and big enough yard for a cricket pitch,' Nate mused.

Adam scoffed. 'I should have asked Mum for dodgem cars.' The house came into sight at the end of the lane. It was a sprawling brick home rendered white, with an imposing fence.

'Rayco spent a bit of money on their premises.'

'A man's home is his castle. I'm parking on her front porch,' Adam joked. 'There's no way I'm leaving my merc on the street even if no one is around. Tell me why we couldn't take your car again?'

'Because your car is darker and will blend in,' Nate gave him his illogical excuse, and Adam huffed. 'Fine, your insurance cover is better than mine.'

'Ah, makes sense,' Adam said.

The gate was open, so he drove in and parked in front of the closed garage door. A porch light was the only sign of life until the door opened, and Gerta appeared, looking conservative in dark pants, flat black shoes and a light blue cardigan.

'I've never seen her without her witchy robes,' Nate said under his breath as they exited the car. He and Adam had changed into jeans and shirts before arriving so as not to appear too officious.

'Come in,' she said as Adam locked the car, and they made their way to the porch. Adam carried a tin of biscuits that his grandmother insisted he take with him, and when Gerta was greeting him, he presented Audrey's offering.

'Ah, she remembered,' Gerta said, appearing genuinely delighted. 'Thank her for me. That's a nice surprise.'

'Your favourites?' Nate asked.

'Orehovki – little pecan cookies from my hometown in Bulgaria,' Gerta said, standing aside to let them enter and closing the door behind them. 'They are normally made at Christmas time and only available from a delicatessen in the city. Most thoughtful of Audrey.'

Adam didn't recognise the lady they were speaking with; it was as if she had taken off her tarot costume and become a sweet, senior woman.

'Have a seat; I will make tea. Try the biscuits,' she said, opening the tin for them. The men sat at a table covered by a white lace tablecloth, with tea cups, sugar, and spoons already placed for their arrival. She returned with a milk jug and then a teapot, sitting and pouring for them once the tea had drawn.

'I imagine I have not changed much in 18 years,' she said, stirring sugar into her tea. 'There is not much difference between a woman of 60 and 78, but to see you both as men – there is a big difference from a boy to a man,' she said, studying them.

'Yes,' Adam agreed with a smile. 'There's a big difference between 12 and 30.'

'I'm feeling it,' Nate joked and made her laugh.

'This is a beautiful home,' Adam said, admiring the tasteful room and ornamental architraves.

'I have always loved my home. So you can imagine why I am not willing to give it to the community,' she said with a flash of anger, bringing to light the woman they have always known her to be. Now, she focussed on Nate. 'What did you wish to ask me about? There's a lot you don't know.'

'Exactly. I want to know what you know,' Nate said, making her laugh again. He continued. 'Your husband is still determined to donate the land to the community?'

Adam knew that if she told them that much, she would reveal the true contents of her husband's will, and he watched her with interest.

'I am guessing your grandmother told you that?' she turned to Adam and continued without waiting for an answer. 'When the war began—the war to get us evicted from the neighbourhood, or at least that is what it felt like—Rayco showed his weakness. The carnival was our life work, and there he was, bending to their whims, offering to accommodate their demands. It debased us.'

'Surely not, if you simply closed the business a little earlier or reduced the noise from the spruiking and music,' Adam said.

'We were here long before the Riverpark Estate developers came. But it was more than meeting a few demands; Rayco met with your grandmother's community group and the others and told them his plans to create Dobrev Community Village one day. He was 65 then, and I thought we should have sold up and enjoyed our retirement, not give away our wealth. It would be like someone claiming your father and mother's money when it is rightfully yours.'

'No, it's different,' Adam said, seeing her defiant expression. 'I didn't earn my parents' wealth. On the other hand, you worked in the business with your husband and built that wealth.'

'Thank you,' she said, slightly taken aback by his support. 'Rayco said we would always have this house and the 800 square meters block it sat on, but the community would be built around us.'

'But at least you'd have a home and land,' Nate said.

'Where's my share in the business? This is our private home,' she said. 'And what of my son?'

Adam frowned. 'So, Gerry agrees that Mr Dobrev has no right to donate the land? Gerry doesn't live here?'

'Of course not. He's a grown man. Do you live with your mother? He lives near his work; he has a unit there. But the carnival sale would also give him a comfortable life; he's 46 now, and his job is very physical.'

'He's a baggage handler at the airport, isn't he?' Nate asked.

'You've done your research as expected.'

Nate nodded and tried again to find out what was in that final will, saying, 'So, when Mr Dobrev senior dies, the land will go to the community except for this block and your house, and Gerry is still trying to prevent that?'

Gerta saw right through him. 'I am not going to speak about family matters of that nature with you both. It has nothing to do with you,' she said, reaching for the teapot and topping up all three cups again. 'What do you want to know then?'

Adam looked to Nate; it was his case, and Nate stepped up.

'What do you know about Alex Armstrong's death?'

Gerta smiled. 'That's what I expected. I thought long and hard about revealing what I know about this, and I've decided to tell you what happened that night.'

Nate and Adam's expressions relayed their surprise, and neither said a word, not wishing to change her mind or detour Gerta from the subject.

'There is nothing to lose or gain now from telling you, and Gerry thought I should throw you some crumbs,' she said looking smug, a familiar expression. 'You can tell the girl that Gerry and I were working with her father. We were not enemies. You didn't expect that, did you?' She laughed at their shocked expressions.

'Gerry and Alex were on the same team?' Nate asked incredulously, pondering over Gerta's words.

Gerta nodded. 'As I said. That's why Gerry isn't guilty of killing Alex. He wanted him to succeed, and he even helped him. We all wanted the carnival shut down and the land sold, except for Rayco. I wanted us to retire, Gerry wanted to start another business, and Alex Armstrong wanted us gone. So, he and Gerry worked on a plan to create a vocal neighbourhood group and staged several riots and fights. Rayco never knew about our involvement, but then Alex got himself killed, and everything shut down. We were so close, too,' she said angrily. 'I did my best to scare off the community groups seeking a claim.'

'Yes,' Adam agreed. 'Audrey withdrew because she didn't want to put me in danger.'

'Very clever of her,' Gerta agreed. 'Gerry can be quite persuasive.'

'But if it was all staged, who was fighting who? I saw one of the fights; I was at the carnival with Dad,' Adam told her.

'Oh, those tiffs were over as quickly as they started. Gerry paid a few friends who he knew from his boxing and weights groups to come in and have a fake punch-up. They were more noise and aggression than action. Gerry told them not to do any real damage, especially since most of the neighbourhood men were not the fighting types. Alex Armstrong was different; he was a wall of a man.'

'So, who killed him?' Nate asked.

Gerta shrugged. 'He wasn't liked, so it could have been one of his neighbours, or he forgot it was fake fighting and struck too hard, then got the same back. For my money, I'd say he fell and hit his head, just like the coroner said. But it wasn't us.'

'Why is Gerry creating the riots now in the street? Are you trying to scare people out and buy up the area to create your own large community that you profit from instead of the not-for-profit sector getting it?' Adam asked.

'That's a good plan, isn't it?' Gerta said and laughed.

'Would it not be a good feeling to be the village matriarch?' Adam continued, prodding her ego. 'You would be cutting the ribbon to an estate named after you, the VIP guest, the one who can walk around the village like a generous benefactor sharing your life's work and profit, everyone knowing you are the queen of the community and your name immortalised here forever.'

For a moment, Gerta Dobrev preened as if she could see herself in that role.

'You are a lot like your grandmother,' she said, studying Adam with an intensity he did not like. 'You both work with people and help them. Interesting.'

While Nate asked another question, Adam thought about Gerta's observation. He had never considered that he took after Audrey. His ambitious grandfather made his fortune in steel, his father built a media empire, and his mother sought celebrity fame and achieved it. He was a disappointment to them; he knew it. But now, he saw he was like Audrey.

Why had that not occurred to him before? Was he too busy comparing himself to his parents and falling short?

Was it nature or nurture? Audrey raised him more or less. If he had spent more time with his parents, would he be more like them?

No. Adam remembered hating the modelling shoots when he was as young as five. That was nature, not nurture.

Aristotle, or maybe the Jesuits, said, "Give me the child until he is seven, and I will give you the man," so he realised his nature was different from the beginning.

Perhaps Gerta was right; he and Audrey were the compassionate side of the family, the humanitarians.

Nate caught his eye, and Adam vowed to think about it later.

'I don't know what Gerry is doing with the carnival,' Gerta was saying. 'It's his right to do as he sees fit with his family's business. There is nothing more I can tell you about that. But tell that girl she is wasting her time looking at my family. If she wants to pin her father's death on someone, look closer to home. And that's what the cards have told me, too.'

Adam knew she would work that in somewhere.

It all seemed a bit cosy, but as Nate promised to update Laura after seeing Gerta, and Laura was staying with Adam, Jessica and Laura suggested they cook a meal and meet at Adam's house when the boys returned.

Turning into his driveway, Adam liked seeing the house lights on inside, the warmth of someone being home. Not that he said that out loud to Nate, who was bound to read too much into it. Jessica's car sat in the driveway so that she and Nate could drive back to the mansion after dinner.

As Jessica welcomed Nate, Adam sized up Laura. She looked sporty in casual gear – black jogger pants, a long-sleeved grey T-shirt, and white runners. Kelsey never looked sporty.

'Just in time!' she exclaimed as the boys walked in.

'Something smells great,' Nate said as if he were coming home.

'Laura wasn't exaggerating,' Jessica said, 'she can cook!'

Laura laughed. 'I do it for stress relief; I've been very stressed over the past few years,' she joked.

'Our gain,' Nate said. 'Every time Adam has me over for dinner, he cooks—'

Jessica held up her hand to stop him, and Nate paused before finishing his sentence.

'We all know what men cook... pasta,' Jessica said with a roll of her eyes.

Adam laughed. 'True.'

'Oh, good. I've made spaghetti Bolognese! I'll serve it up,' Laura said and saw their faces drop. 'Just kidding. I figured you wouldn't have too many home-cooked roasts, so I've made roast pork with crispy crackling and apple sauce, accompanied by roast vegetables.'

'Fantastic,' Adam said, realising how hungry he was. He didn't think about food much these days but was slowly getting his appetite back. He dropped his keys and phone in the usual place and set about getting himself and Nate a drink and topping up the girls' wine glasses.

Laura continued, 'And for dessert—'

'There's dessert!' Nate exclaimed. He was known for his sweet tooth.

'There is. I've done a traditional apple crumble with ice cream and clotted cream.'

'Want to move into my place?' Nate asked. 'There's plenty of room.'

'Laura should stay here,' Adam said, 'you've got to watch your figure, and no one wants to hear you two going for it.'

'Eew,' Jessica said. 'That's something I'd expect Nate to say.'

Adam looked surprised. 'You're right; I've been hanging around him for too long.'

'I set the table,' Jessica said. 'That's my contribution.'

'Well set,' Nate agreed, looking over at the table and hugging her.

'How did it go?' Jessica cut to the chase.

'Surprisingly very good,' Nate said. 'We learnt something that you will want to hear,' he told Laura.

'Tell me when we're sitting down in case the shock is too much,' she joked as she started serving and issuing orders.

'I wish I had seen the carousel and Ferris wheel move at midnight,' Jessica said, plating the roast vegetables she had been assigned to serve.

'It was super creepy,' Laura said. 'Even sitting in the car away from it, I was freaked out.'

'Me too,' Adam agreed. 'Luckily, Nate was with us.'

The small party laughed.

'You needed Danielle with you,' Jessica said, 'she's great at security detail.'

'She's very attractive and sassy,' Laura said, handing the finished plates to each person to carry to the table.

'Not my type,' Nate said as they took their seats. 'She always had the hots for Adam.'

'Is that so?' Laura studied Adam momentarily before spooning apple sauce onto her plate and passing the jar on. 'Let's talk shop. What's the big news?'

'Alex and Gerry were in cahoots,' Nate cut to the chase.

'No!' Laura stopped, frozen.

'True story.' Nate told her what they had learned, and she slowly resumed eating. Adam picked up the story, and Nate continued with his meal.

Laura sat back and reached for her wine glass, twirling the stem in her hand.

'So, Gerry Dobrev didn't kill Dad. I'd believed he had for so long; it will take a bit for me to adjust my thinking,' she said quietly.

'Sleep on it,' Nate said.

'It creates an interesting problem,' Adam said. 'If it was not Gerry or his men that left that note for you on your window, then who is it warding you off? I'd rather the devil we know.'

'Me too,' Nate agreed. 'I'll let Burnsy know in the morning.'

They finished the meal, Laura receiving great acclaim, and once the dishwasher was packed, Nate and Jessica departed. Laura and Adam were alone, and he said, 'It's nearly the end of your first week here. Everything okay?'

Laura looked surprised that he thought to ask.

'Everything is fine. Thank you for letting me interrupt your life,' she said. 'I've got good company, a new friend, and a lift to work twice this week in a black Mercedes convertible. Sure, the roof down caused havoc with my hair, but it was a small price to pay.'

Adam laughed. 'You wanted it down. I find it too noisy in traffic, but I love it down when on the open road or in nature.'

The pair was becoming increasingly comfortable sharing the space. Adam made them both tea, and they moved to the lounge room. The house was quiet and peaceful.

'Oh,' Laura suddenly said. 'Is there an ulterior motive for your question? Are you asking how soon I can leave?'

'No, not at all. It's all good with me. Stay as long as you need,' he said. He hadn't felt that way last week, but he had started to feel comfortable with Laura and enjoyed someone being in the house, especially given that she was tidy and he barely registered she was there.

'You know, if you want to bring anyone here and want me to disappear, I can do that,' she told him. 'I can work back, come home later, and just slip into my room.'

'There's no one I'll be bringing home,' he said.

'Sounds like my love life,' she said and laughed.

'Too busy for romance?' Adam asked.

'Too stupid,' she said, and seeing his expression, she explained. 'My last romantic encounter was a dud... I met this guy who was nothing like me, which made him interesting. I am the most sensible person you will ever meet – I know about contraception, I know my legal rights, I know the consequences of my actions. I've always been a good girl.'

'But then you weren't?'

'Precisely. I met him at a conference in Sydney. He was an artist working on a mural in the hotel where I was staying, and he was a bit Boho, a cool guy. At the time, we both fell fast and partied hard. We were just so into each other, like nothing I've ever experienced. Living in separate states helped.'

'Sounds great,' Adam said.

'It was, but I fell pregnant. I don't know how.' Then she made a face, 'Well, I know how the conception part happened, but I'd had a bit of food poisoning, and I think my pill might not have been absorbed. Anyway, he deserted me, I miscarried, and it ended as fast as it began. I thought it was the ultimate love affair for the ages,' she laughed at how silly it sounded. 'That was a few years back; I was heartbroken but healed with time. So, since then, I focussed on my studies, work, and Dad's case.

Uncharacteristically, Adam shared his Kelsey story on how they had first met and were reunited, concluding, 'So much for fate and love at first sight.'

'I guess you've analysed yourself to death,' Laura said.

'Occupational hazard,' Adam agreed.

'People suck,' Laura said, and Adam looked at her and laughed.

'Lucky we're balanced and normal,' Adam said.

Laura raised her mug, 'Amen to that.'

Adam then realised this was dangerously good. He liked her. She was fun and intelligent, attractive and easy to hang out with. Laura was also energetic and open-minded; it had been a while since he had felt challenged. Adam had to backpedal before he found himself attracted to her and rebounding. They were friends. Nothing more.

Forty minutes later, the dishwasher unpacked, and after bidding each other good night, Adam had just pulled off his shirt when Laura screamed.

He grabbed it, ran towards her room, and saw Laura standing safely in the doorway. He shrugged his shirt back on.

Laura stood aside. Across two walls, painted in large red letters, were the words, "Stay out of it".

'I've definitely got someone worried,' she said, looking around.

'Stay here while I make sure we're alone,' he said, opening the walk-in wardrobe and ensuite door. 'It's all clear. Is everything still here?'

She tentatively moved further into the room. He went to the window and saw that the casement window had been jimmied up. He relocked it for what it was worth.

'Nothing is missing. My laptop, phone, and purse are all still here. I am so sorry, Adam. I'll get it repainted, of course.'

'Don't worry about it. I never liked that shade; it wasn't my pick. Windsor or Whitely Blue or something like that,' he said with a wave of his hand, remembering Kelsey picking it and loving it.

'Wedgewood Blue.'

'Yeah,' he said, surprised and turned to her. 'How do girls know that?'

She shrugged. 'Good taste, maybe.'

He made a less-than-convinced sound. 'I'd better drop you to Audrey's for the night.'

'I'll be fine here. The window still locks, doesn't it?'

'Yes, but they're old windows; it's an old Queenslander. You won't sleep for hearing noises,' Adam said. 'Take my room, and I'll sleep here.'

'I'll be fine,' she assured him. 'I have this.' Laura went to her luggage in the walk-in robe and reappeared with a rubber duck.

'Oh,' Adam grinned and nodded. 'He'll keep you safe. Phew, I'll sleep much better now.'

She laughed at his play-acting. 'It will quack! I'll put it right under the window, and if you hear a quack, come and help me.' She pressed the duck a few times so he would recognise the quack.

He shook his head. 'I'll be hearing quacks all night now.' Adam returned to his room, a smile ghosting his lips at the girl staying in his second bedroom and her yellow rubber ducky.

Chapter 23

Truth be known, Laura didn't remember much about *Dobrev's Carnival World*. She had been there once with her mother years after her father's death; he would never have allowed it while the feud was ongoing. It wasn't that memorable, but 18 years later, it looked like a broken dream in the mid-morning light.

Laura had thought about what Gerta Dobrev had told Nate. The words kept her awake all night and well into the early morning hours – that and the break-in – "look closer to home". Nate had laughed at Gerta's prediction. When Adam left for work, she found Gerta's number in the white pages online; the senior tarot reader still had a landline. And then, she rang Audrey.

'Of course I'll come with you, dear, if Gerta will see us. She's had a message for me for years from my deceased husband. I suppose I'd better collect it,' Audrey had said, making Laura laugh.

And Gerta agreed to see them both that morning. For some reason, Laura kept the visit close to her chest. She didn't tell Nate that Gerta would meet them at the carnival grounds. Maybe she feared he would want to come or talk her out of it, neither of which she wanted. But she needed to know more about Gerta's comments and it wouldn't be the first time she had her cards read.

Now, Laura was not so sure she did the right thing, especially if she had endangered Adam's grandmother. What if Gerry Dobrev was there?

After collecting Audrey from the mansion, she told her about last night's break-in.

'I wonder if I should just let the boys know we are here,' Laura said, her hands tensing on the steering wheel.

'Goodness no,' Audrey said. 'They'll want to ride in on their white chargers and lecture us. What's the worst that can happen? I'm already old, so I can check out any time, and as long as you can run fast, you should be fine, dear.'

Again, Laura laughed. 'I love your attitude to life, Audrey. I am going to adopt some of that outlook for myself.'

'It has served me well,' Audrey agreed. 'I think you and Adam should come and stay with me until this is all sorted. It's a very big home; you'll probably never see me.'

'Thank you, Audrey, but I'd hate to impose.'

'You wouldn't be. Perhaps you should see the house for yourself. I rarely ever see Nathanial, or Jessica when she visits. She's a lovely girl.'

Laura smiled. 'I love that you call him by his full name. It always sounds like he is in trouble.'

'He was that kind of boy,' she smiled, 'but a wonderful and loyal companion for Adam. They were both only children and as close as brothers.'

Laura parked just outside the carnival gates, they exited, and she locked the car. Dressed in jeans, a t-shirt, a jacket and runners, Laura looked smart casual, but Audrey, as always, looked elegant in black pants and shoes with a cream silk blouse.

'I'm glad Gerta wants to meet at the gates to the carnival grounds and not at her own home,' Laura said quietly to Audrey as they approached the gate. 'Adam said it was at the end of a road with no houses around.'

'Yes, I've seen it a few times. Oh look, we've been seen; that should satisfy the boys.'

Sure enough, neighbours were clocking their appearance. Audrey waved to a man watering his garden, and Laura saw a curtain twitch.

'Good, someone knows we're here,' Laura exhaled with relief.

As they approached, Gerta startled Laura, appearing at the gate as if she had been hiding behind the wall waiting for them.

'Mrs Dobrev, I'm Laura—'

'Yes, I know who you are,' Gerta cut her off. 'I've seen the stories. Hello. And hello to you, Audrey, it's been a while.'

'So it has, Gerta. You are looking well.'

'As are you. Thank you for the biscuits. A lovely memory,' Gerta said, removing the chain from the gate to let them in.

'My pleasure. It allowed me the opportunity to pick up my favourite shortbread biscuits at the same time.'

'Thank you for seeing me,' Laura suddenly added.

'I expected your call.'

The ladies entered, and Gerta closed the gate behind them.

'So, the private investigator told you we couldn't have killed your father since we were in partnership with him?'

Gerta locked the gate, and Laura glanced at the fence; she could scale it if she needed to get out, but Audrey wouldn't have a chance, and she would not desert her.

'Don't worry,' Gerta read her mind. 'I'm only locking it in case any of the neighbourhood kids think it's a lark to come in and go through the rides. They're decrepit and too dangerous now.'

'And they would if my grandson and his friend are anything to go by. I hate to think what mischief they got up to as boys,' Audrey said, and Gerta smiled.

'Gerry was the same. Into everything he shouldn't be. This way then,' she said, leading the way.

'Yes, to answer your earlier question,' Laura said. 'I was shocked to hear Dad had partnered with you. I'm sorry for my misplaced suspicion, but that doesn't mean his death was an accident.'

'That's true,' Gerta agreed.

'Couldn't you sell these old rides?' Laura asked, walking slowly beside the ladies in their seventies, past the ghost train with the signage on the ground nearby where it nearly clipped Nate and Danielle the other evening, and the carousel that must have been beautiful in its day.

Gerta shrugged. 'We'd probably get a dollar or two from someone wanting to do them up or sell them for parts. Gerry will manage all that.'

The tarot reader stopped in front of a small rotunda where a table was placed, draped in a red tablecloth, with three chairs that looked to be in good condition. It was a sunny, warm spot and would have been pleasant if not for the skeleton of derelict rides around them.

'This is where I used to work from when the carnival was open to the public. I could see all the comings and goings.'

'I remember,' Audrey said.

Laura followed Gerta's lead and took the offered seat; Audrey sat beside her. A very old, well-worn pack of tarot cards sat in the middle of the table.

'It's a great position,' Laura agreed, looking around and imagining what it was like in its heyday. Her eyes settled on the cards. 'Are you self-taught, or have you always had a connection with the spirit world?'

'My mother and grandmother were both clairvoyants; I'm a fortune teller, it fitted with the carnival theme, but I've grown up with the spirits; I never knew it wasn't normal to talk about the dead or to talk with them.'

'That's a beautiful design,' Audrey said, putting on her glasses hanging around her neck. She looked at the vintage design on the top tarot card.

'Yes. These were my grandmother's cards. There's lots of choices nowadays for cards, lots of pretty drawings, but my hands know these.'

Laura jumped at the sound of a door slamming and whirled around to see Gerry Dobrev approaching from a nearby building that bore the faded words "Office, staff only".

'Ah, here he is,' Gerta said. 'Gerry worked the night shift and is meeting some people here this morning. I mentioned you were visiting.'

He grinned, or rather, sneered on seeing them.

'Mr Dobrev,' Audrey said with her chin up and a smile.

'Mrs Murphy. Nice to see you again since our last visit to the cemetery. Although the first time with the whistle is still my favourite,' he grinned.

'Tell me, Mr Dobrev, what would you do if you were with your young grandson and feared you could not protect him?'

Gerry's face hardened. 'Whatever it took.'

'Precisely,' she agreed. 'I will make a fool of myself for love any day, and I love that boy.'

He gave a small huff and said, 'I'd never hurt a kid.'

'I wasn't to know that.'

Gerry turned to Laura. 'Mum told you that your dad and I were partners?'

'Yes.'

'So, I suppose you've got to start your investigation all over again?' he said smugly.

'I confess, you were my number one suspect, but you were never the private investigator's top pick.'

'That so?' Gerry gave a dry chuckle. 'Who would have thought? He was a bruiser, your dad.'

Laura suspected he was trying to get a rise from her; meanwhile, Gerta watched, not saying a word but smugly enjoying her son's stirring.

'I've heard that,' Laura agreed. 'It is disappointing, but I still want justice for him. Got any tips to help me?' Her reaction surprised him, and he sat back on the nearby rail inside the rotunda. Laura hoped it wouldn't hold him, and he'd topple off, but no such luck.

'Mum will help you with that; see what the cards say,' he said without any self-consciousness. He obviously believed in them, too. 'I'll give you some advice, though, if you want it?'

'Sure,' Laura said.

'If your dad was murdered, whoever did it has got away with it for a very long time. They won't be happy about you stirring things up, and if they had no qualms about knocking your dad off, they won't have any about bumping you off, either. Just saying.'

Laura nodded. 'Thanks. And, if you were going to bump me off, just saying you were in their mindset, how would you do it?'

Gerry let out a low whistle through his teeth as he thought. 'I'd scare you a bit at first, and if that didn't work, I'd be creative.'

Gerta laughed as if proud and encouraging of her son's predisposition to evil thinking.

Gerry continued. 'I'd string you up in here... you know, dangling from the Ferris Wheel or strapped to the horses.'

Laura looked horrified, and Audrey stepped in.

'Well, good to know you won't be doing that, Mr Dobrev, thank you.'

He laughed and looked up on hearing a whistle. Several men awaited him at the gate. 'Got to be going then. Might see you in the cemetery another time, Mrs Murphy,' he said with a grin.

'I look forward to that, Mr Dobrev. I believe you were visiting Laura's father's grave last time I saw you.'

Laura snapped to look at him, and he winked at her.

'A red herring they call that.' He leant down, kissed his mother on the cheek and departed with a swagger to meet the men waiting patiently by the gate.

'He's a good lad at heart,' Gerta said, convincing no one present.

'Are they Gerry's business partners?' Laura fished, knowing from the audio on the tapes that some sort of meeting was happening on Wednesday.

'Yes. We need to make plans for this site. The neighbourhood is being gentrified. I'd never heard that word before until recently,' Gerta admitted. 'There are interested developers and neighbours who want us gone, and we want to be going.' Gerta picked up the card pack, shuffled it, and placed it down again.

'It's ripe for gentrification,' Laura agreed. 'You would do well subdividing this and making it an estate of your own.' She fished, hoping Gerta would provide an insight into what the nightly fright sessions might be about.

'I don't know what Gerry has in mind. He's got a good mind for business; I leave it to him.'

Laura caught the slightly raised eyebrow that Audrey gave her. Both ladies quickly ascertained that Gerta was as sharp as a knife and most likely the brains of the outfit. But she hadn't managed to outsmart her husband.

Gerta tapped the tarot pile in the middle of the table and said to Laura, 'I read the cards and receive messages. Is there anything you don't want to hear?'

'Yes. Please don't tell me about any pending deaths.'

'I never do that. Let's begin. Think about what question you want to ask the Tarot. I am sure we all know what that is, but say it to yourself now, quietly and with meaning.'

Laura nodded, closed her eyes, and asked the question in her mind, 'Who killed my father?' She opened her eyes.

'Now shuffle the cards,' Gerta directed, 'put them down when you are ready and cut the deck.'

Laura picked up the smooth, worn cards and shuffled, following the instructions. Once she had done as requested, Gerta split the cards into past, present, and future, her hands moving quickly with the years of experience she had gained.

'Hmm,' she said, looking over the cards. 'The Two of Cups. You've got a potential love interest, not that you came here for that.' She looked upwards for a moment. 'I feel it is a man you will be friends with first, and then more will develop. He will be your great love.'

'I hope I know that man,' Audrey said. Laura looked at her and grinned.

'Would I be good enough for your "beloved boy"?' Laura asked, using the phrase Audrey so often did.

'A perfect match,' Audrey said, 'I could die happy.'

'Well, please don't do that for a long time yet,' Laura said, delighted with Audrey's endorsement. She returned her attention to Gerta, who was reading cards and moving them around, finally focussing on the cards on the left side of the table.

'It's the past you want to live in at the moment. The cards are telling me that your threat is close to home.' She tapped on a card. 'The justice card is timely, given that is what you seek.'

'How close to home?' Laura asked, and Gerta looked up at her and then returned to the cards. Laura saw the Hangman and grimaced. 'Should I be worried about that card?'

'No. He's looking at the world upside down... it means a change in perspective. Since you always believed my son was guilty, you are definitely changing your outlook now. It also means you must break old patterns, let go, stop waiting and sacrificing. Maybe you should get on with your own life,' Gerta said, but Laura didn't comment.

Gerta tapped another card and sat back.

'The Moon?' Laura asked.

'That is the card you need to be most worried about.'

'Why?'

'It is telling you everything is not as it seems. In your life, there's deception, dishonesty and false illusions. When you find the source, you will find your culprit. But be open-minded, not all is as it seems.'

Laura sat back and exhaled. She was no wiser or better off than before and now more wary of the danger she was in. Nevertheless, she thanked Gerta as expected.

'And you have a message for me from my husband, Edward, I believe?' Audrey asked.

Gerta chuckled. 'Good Lord. That was nearly two decades ago. Let me think; it was an odd message. It didn't come to me from the cards but when I shook your hand once. A transfer of energy. I shall let you know if I recall it.'

'There's no hurry,' Audrey said and they both agreed upon that.

As soon as they entered Laura's car, she locked the doors and asked, 'Are you in a hurry, Audrey? I need a minute to call Nate and let him know Gerry and his men are on the premises.'

'I am in no hurry, dear; take your time,' Audrey said, sitting back and relaxing.

Nate answered on the second ring.

'Hi, I'm in the car with Audrey outside the carnival grounds—'

'Why? What's happened?' Nate asked. 'Hello, Audrey.'

'Hello, Nathanial.'

'I'll explain all that later, but that Wednesday get-together we heard about on the audio recording is underway now, not this evening as you thought.'

Nate swore under his breath. 'Sorry, Audrey,' he added. 'Who is there?'

'Well, Gerry, for one and three other men we didn't see. I asked Gerta about it, but she pretended she didn't know what Gerry was doing and was leaving the business side of matters to him,' Laura scoffed.

'I need their photos. I'll head there now. You two leave immediately.'

She could hear him grabbing his keys and walking; he called out to Jessica to say he was heading to the carnival.

'I'll drop Audrey home and return. I won't get out of the car,' Laura assured him, 'but I'll snap a pic with my phone if I see them.'

'Too dangerous,' Nate said, and she heard his car door open.

'We'll both stay here,' Audrey spoke up. 'Our doors are locked. 'If they come out, I will pretend to be on my phone while Laura snaps some photos.'

Nate didn't say anything, and Laura could hear his mind churning.

'I'll get a few photos of the cars in the street while I wait, so you can run the regos and see who is visiting and who is a local,' Laura said.

'I don't like it,' he said. 'Especially after last night's incident. Adam told me this morning.'

Audrey soothed him, 'You need to convince Adam and Laura to move into our place, Nathanial, dear. Now, stop fretting. In the worst-case scenario, we won't take their photos; we'll just watch which cars they get into, and then your sergeant friend can help you with their registrations. Truly, they will not be too worried about a car with an old lady and a young girl in it.'

'Unless Gerry exits with them and sees you both,' Nate added.

'So, are you going to storm in and ask them what's going on?' Laura said, photographing the cars as she spoke to him.

'No. Given they're spooking the neighbours, I don't think they'll be friendly. But I'll grab the shots of them from a safe distance. If you've got the car photographs, you can go.'

'But they all might have come in one car,' Laura said.

'We'll just stay until you get here,' Audrey said, and Laura flashed a smile at her.

'We need to talk about putting yourself in danger,' Nate said.

'I agree that would be a good talk if I worked for you,' Laura said, reminding Nate that he was working for her.

'Fine. Stay on the line with me then until I get there. Tell me why you are there and what you've learnt,' he said, trying not to sound too authoritative but failing.

'Don't speed, young man,' Audrey said.

'No, Mrs Murphy,' he said, addressing her formally as he used to until he came of age, and she laughed.

Laura told him about being troubled by the warning on the wall and the idea that she had to look closer to home. She told him about requesting a tarot reading and how she had talked Audrey into coming along.

When finished, Nate said, 'I think Gerry Dobrev is right, and Lord knows I never thought those words would come out of my mouth, but I think what he is doing there has nothing to do with us or the case; we can probably eliminate him. I'll pass the information on to Burnsy, but we can walk away.'

They heard him slowing down and assumed he was turning off the major road and almost there.

'I'm five minutes away,' he confirmed. 'However, back to the case, the players back then might be the same players now. So, if you recognise any of those men, Laura, that might be your "close to home" threat.'

'That crossed my mind too,' she said.

'And if not?' Audrey asked.

'Then, Adam's not going to like it, but I think we should hire Tom to provide protection if he's available. Because, as Gerry said, if they got away with it once and have now threatened you with a letter at your home, and last night's graffiti, they will not let you flush them out.'

'I agree, Nathanial,' Audrey said.

Nate continued, 'Laura, you and Adam should both come home. If they know Adam is on the case, then he's a sitting duck, too.'

'Did he tell you about my rubber duck security?' Laura asked with a laugh in her voice.

'Yes. I've heard it all now. Nothing will ever surprise me again,' Nate said, making her laugh as she filled Audrey in.

They saw his car come into sight, and he drove past them to an area where he could see the exit to the carnival grounds and be a little hidden.

'I'm here now, you two go,' he said.

Laura started the car. 'Thanks for staying with me, Audrey.'

'A pleasure. The most exciting thing that's happened to me since Gerry threatened Adam and me in the cemetery.'

Nate groaned. 'Bye, you two.'

'Bye,' they said in unison, and Laura cut him off.

'Who's this Tom then?' Laura asked as they turned out of the estate.

'Ah,' Audrey said, 'let me tell you about Tom Hartigan and his relationship with Adam.'

Chapter 24

Adam looked at Nate with an incredulous look on his face. He had been doing reports only moments ago when Nate entered his office and filled him in on the photos they got and Audrey and Laura's irresponsible behaviour this morning. He saved the best—or worst—news for last, suggesting Tom Hartigan come on board for a brief period.

'There must be thousands of security people who could start work immediately and protect Laura and Audrey,' Adam said. 'Why do we need Hartigan?'

'Because he can hit the ground running. He installed the security cameras at the mansion,' Nate continued, ignoring Adam's wince at the term "mansion". 'He knows the dead spots, the lay of the land, and we don't have to bond with him.'

'You got that right,' Adam said. 'Doesn't Laura know anyone?'

'She's just finished studying. Why would she have any experience with security? That's your life; it's not normal for the rest of us.'

Adam sighed. 'Seriously, Tom Hartigan?'

Nate shrugged.

'Fine, but for the record, I don't want him on the job.'

'Noted, and I'll make sure he knows. He'll be so surprised,' Nate said drily, making Adam smirk.

'Can Laura afford him? I'll chip in with the—'

Nate cut him off. 'Audrey's insisting on paying. She says it is for her peace of mind, too, given the fight is in her neighbourhood and you have both been threatened.'

'That's good of her. So, Laura will stay with you and Audrey, and I don't need to see him.'

'About that...' Nate started.

'No.'

'If it's known that you're on the case as well as Laura and me, then you are at risk,' Nate argued. 'They already know where you live; if the rest of us have security, you're an easy target.'

'To be honest, Nate,' Adam said, using his best friend's name, which he rarely did, 'I don't care. If they want to bump me off, then get on with it. Stop leaving stupid signs on my wall and do something real.'

'Great,' Nate said, getting angry now. 'You're right. You won't be here to deal with the aftermath. Leave that to Audrey and me because neither of us will be affected.' He turned and strode out of Adam's office, fury coming off him in waves.

Adam sat back and sighed. 'See,' he muttered, 'Hartigan's causing problems, and he hasn't started work for us yet.' He shook his head. 'If I'm lucky, he'll be too busy to accept the job.'

Jessica could not help but laugh when she saw Laura's reaction. 'It's out there, isn't it?'

'Oh my God,' Laura said, driving through the gates of the Murphy estate with Jessica beside her in the passenger seat. Jessica had left her car at the office and would ride in with Nate in the morning.

'It's palatial,' Laura gasped, following Adam and Nate's cars as the gates closed behind her. She could not conceive of growing up in a place like this or wanting to move out if she did. An enormous fence sprawled around the estate, enclosing a large white mansion with three wings and expansive windows. The river peeked through the buildings and could be seen throughout the grounds. The gardens were manicured, and glorious large gum trees blocked the middle wing's river view, but the other two wings boasted water views.

'I thought Audrey had a four-bedroom home with maybe a granny flat that Nate stayed in. I didn't realise she had a mansion with three wings on acreage overlooking the river. And you're staying here too?'

'No. I only stay every second night or so with Nate. We're in that wing,' Jessica said, pointing. 'Audrey is in that one, and that's where Adam also stays. His mum and Jack stay in the middle wing when they visit. She doesn't like the water view.'

Laura huffed at the thought. 'Do they visit much?'

'Winsome never, except for the wedding, but Jack often comes up,' Jessica said. 'He's dreamy. Oh, and there's a 25-metre pool and tennis court, too, if you want to work out.'

Laura could see them across the estate. 'Seriously? This must be at least four or five blocks of land. Did Adam grow up here?'

Jessica nodded and lowered her voice as Laura cut the ignition, and they prepared to alight. 'I don't think he has a lot of happy childhood memories here; he's never keen to stay.'

'You'd feel safe having kids here,' Laura said, looking around. 'Look at the height of those fences and the gate.' They exited her white Peugeot, and Laura grabbed several bags off the back seat, closing and locking the car door.

'You travel light,' Jessica said with a laugh. 'I have that much for one night.'

Laura grinned. 'I find it's best to dress conservatively when working with not-for-profits.'

The ladies approached the men, and Audrey came out of the house to welcome them.

'It's good to have you here, dear, and to have you home, Adam,' Audrey said, and Nate slapped him on the back.

'It's great. So, you and Laura are staying in Audrey's wing and Tom's in mine unless you—'

'That's fine,' Adam said.

At the mention of Tom, a car appeared outside the gates, and Laura was surprised to find herself bracing; maybe she was more on edge than she thought.

'It's Tom, the security guy,' Jessica said quietly to Laura, sensing her apprehension.

'Audrey told me about his connection to the family,' Laura said as the gate opened and a grey Ford Mustang entered the grounds. Tom would stay on the premises until the matter came to a head.

'This will be interesting,' Jessica said.

Adam did his best not to roll his eyes at the sight of Tom driving up the long driveway in his Ford Mustang, but it took a superhuman effort.

'How fortunate he was available,' he said, and Nate laughed.

'I know, right? What good luck.'

Tom pulled up in the garage near Nate's car as if he belonged there. Exiting, he grabbed his bag out of the car and approached them. He greeted everyone warmly, shook hands with Laura, and came to Adam last.

'Adam.'

'Tom.'

'This reunion is making me teary,' Nate said, and Jessica hid her laugh, ribbing him with her elbow.

'Why don't we get settled and meet at the gazebo for dinner and drinks on the hour?' Audrey suggested.

Nate took off with Jessica and Tom, who kept looking around to ensure all his cameras were still in place, while Adam and Laura followed Audrey inside. Her rooms were on the lower floor, and Adam and Laura headed to the second floor, where each had their own bedroom, bathroom, and a shared sitting room in the middle.

'Unbelievable,' Laura said, looking out the window at the river and watching a group of rowers glide past. She mused about how the other half lived.

Forty minutes later, joining the group, Adam coached himself to keep his cool. Nate was working the barbeque, and Tom was roaming around the fence line checking on security. The ladies were setting the table and bringing out salads.

'I'll do drinks,' Adam said.

'You need to ease up on Tom this time around; he's no longer the young SAS officer who used to look after you,' Nate said, and Adam scoffed.

'Unless he's had a personality transplant, I'm not expecting him to be any different than he was at the wedding last year. If he stays away from me, we'll get on just fine.'

'Everything seems to be in order,' Tom said, joining them and accepting a drink from Adam. 'So, who is the threat?'

'Laura will brief you on the background. She's the boss, and I'm working on her case,' Nate said. 'But tell Tom what threats we've had so far.'

Adam filled Tom in on the window sign, the break-in, and that the original suspect, Gerry Dobrev, was probably out of the picture.

'I'll be the judge of that,' Tom said.

'Right, thanks. I forgot that you're the expert,' Adam retorted.

'Isn't this nice?' Nate said as the ladies joined them. 'We've only been in each other's company an hour, and we're straight back into the swing of things.'

'Some people just bring out the worst in others,' Laura said.

Everyone looked at her.

'There's no point fighting it,' she continued with a shrug. 'If you guys don't get on, that's fine. We'll all play our roles, and it will soon be over.'

Audrey smiled. 'Well said, young lady.'

'If you can all do what is required to keep you safe, it will make my job easier,' Tom said.

'No,' Laura said, and Adam snapped to look at her. His respect for her had just gone up one hundred per cent. 'I need to do a job, as do Nate and Adam, so we need security to let us do our jobs and keep us safe while doing them.'

'Same thing,' Tom muttered, keeping face. 'Since I'm protecting several of you, I need you all to stay in constant communication and follow instructions if danger presents itself.'

'We can do that,' Laura said with a sweeping glance at the group for consensus. Audrey, Nate and Jessica agreed.

Tom looked at Adam. 'I'm serious, Adam.'

'Of course you are.'

'You're not a kid anymore, and I can't spend my life making amends to you or rescuing you if Laura—the principal client—needs help.'

Adam shot back: 'Absolutely agreed. No need to make amends to me for anything, and if you just focus on Laura and Audrey, I'm sure I can look after myself.'

'The brief is for protection for all of us,' Laura said. 'If you two can put your digs at each on hold, at least for dinner, I'll fill you in on what's been happening, Tom.'

'Sure,' Tom said as Nate pronounced the barbeque ready.

Adam saw Laura looking at him, and he smiled. 'I'll do my best,' he agreed, pissed off to be put in place in his own home, but he couldn't help admiring her as well despite the strong desire to impale Tom Hartigan on the barbeque tongs.

Chapter 25

On Thursday morning, Nate paced the length of his office while Danielle sat in the windowsill seat, looking down at a carpark below and the green parklands. A cyclist sped along the bike path, and a lady with a dog sidestepped to avoid him. Nate stopped near the door as Jessica appeared.

'Burnsy just rang.'

'Why doesn't he call me on my mobile?' Nate asked, frustrated.

'Because he wants to talk with Jessica first,' Danielle said, stating the obvious, and Nate huffed.

Jessica smiled sweetly. 'He is in the area and has the names from the rego plates. He said you would find them very interesting. He's on his way but wanted to check you were in.'

'Well, if he called me on my mobile, I would have told him I was,' Nate said.

'He probably assumes you are very busy and important, so rings your office manager instead,' Jessica said in a pacifying voice as if brokering peace. She headed to her desk.

'Makes sense,' Nate agreed.

'Here he is now,' Jessica called as her door alarm buzzed, and she let him in.

'Is there anything I'm not supposed to say to him?' Danielle whispered.

'Yeah, avoid mentioning anything illegal we've done,' Nate joked. 'We got away with jumping the carnival fence the other day. Here he is; hi Burnsy,' Nate said with a smile.

Sgt Matt Burns narrowed his eyes as he entered the office; Nate wasn't usually that pleased to see him.

'Nate. Hi Dan, Jess. What are you up to?'

'Me? Nothing,' Nate feigned surprise and Danielle shook her head.

'Waiting for you,' she said.

He made a sound that said he was unconvinced and followed them into the meeting room.

Once seated, Nate said, 'Given you're usually sharing with us, we'll go first and share with you.' He mentioned that Tom Hartigan was coming on board for a couple of weeks or as needed. He avoided looking at Danielle, given she had a short and unhappy affair with the security officer. Nate updated Burnsy on the meeting with Gerta and the admission by Gerta and Gerry that they were partnered with Alex Armstrong, concluding, 'We can probably assume that the "agreement" mentioned in the recording related to this.'

Danielle continued. 'Also, we've assigned additional security to Rayco Dobrev. His sister, who is a little confused herself, agreed it would be a good idea. A private donor is footing the bill for security agents to act as caregivers so that no one will be suspicious at the aged care home.'

'So if anyone intends to bump off poor old Rayco, we'll be ready for them, or rather, the caregiver security dude will be,' Nate said.

'A private donor? Who would pay for that?' Burnsy asked, surprised.

'Keep it to yourself, but it was Audrey,' Nate answered without hesitating. 'She has a lot of respect for the old guy. Tom's coordinating it.'

'I hope she's not spending all Adam's inheritance,' Burnsy joked.

Nate glanced out to the hallway and lowered his voice. 'Apparently, Adam's grandfather was in the steel business, and Audrey has more money than she can spend in two lifetimes.'

Burnsy shook his head. 'I can't imagine it.'

'Can't imagine what?' Adam asked, tapping on the door and wandering in.

'Um, someone wanting to hurt Rayco Dobrev,' Danielle said quickly.

'Are you free to join us?' Nate asked with a grateful look at Danielle.

'Yeah, I've been thinking, just a wild thought,' Adam said.

'Uh oh,' Danielle said.

Adam smiled, sitting beside her. 'I was thinking back on what Rayco said to Laura about his son partnering with this Norman guy.'

'We haven't come across a Norman yet,' Danielle said, looking at Burnsy, who shook his head.

Burnsy produced the registration numbers and corresponding names from a file and scanned them for a "Norman".

'Nope, there's no Norman amongst this lot.' Adam's train of thought was forgotten as the police sergeant continued. 'The registration plate owners are Gerry Dobrev, Cameron Keeper, aged 46, a freelance town planner who used to work for the local council, and Phillip Tansley, 42, a solicitor specialising in conveyancing.'

The group exchanged looks.

'Gerry's getting his ducks in a row,' Adam said.

'A good team for a new estate development,' Nate agreed, eyes narrowing. 'I wonder what share they're all getting if Gerry inherits the land.'

'Is there anything new from the audio and video that I'm pretending you didn't break and enter the carnival grounds to plant?' Burnsy joked.

Danielle grinned, 'We have no idea what you're talking about, Burnsy, and if we did enter, we didn't break. However, I do have some audio that has fallen in my lap...'

Burnsy scoffed, and Danielle continued, 'It's from their Wednesday meeting, and it's not great because they met further away from where we would have planted the bugs if we had planted bugs.'

'Probably because Gerta was on the grounds reading Laura's palm,' Nate said, frustrated.

'Regardless, we picked up a bit of audio and vision,' Danielle said, ignoring Nate. 'If we can match audio with faces, we'll get a better idea of what they are up to and then see if Laura recognises any of them.'

'Now that we have names, we can look for their ugly faces online,' Nate said, and Danielle pushed the laptop to him while she found the audio bites she wanted the men to hear.

'Okay, first sound bite.... hear that? That's Gerry,' Danielle said. He swallows his g's—goin', fightin', acting the tough guy.'

'I'm not sure it's acting. I wouldn't want to meet him in a dark alley,' Nate said, nodding for her to continue. Danielle played the next audio clip.

'Stop!' Nate said. 'I know that guy's voice.' He looked at Danielle. 'Remember the huge, bald guy we interviewed when we were casing the street to find out who lived there eighteen years ago? I'd put money on that being him.'

'I've interviewed everyone in the street about the recent riots,' Burnsy said. 'I remember that guy, but I couldn't be sure that's his voice. How do you know?'

'He called Gerry "Gere", which he just did in that audio grab. I'd have to review my notes to get his name, but I bet it's him.'

'It's interesting he's involved,' Adam mused. 'He's a current homeowner, so what's his angle? Maybe he doesn't want Rayco Dobrev's dream village built.'

'Why wouldn't he?' Danielle asked.

'Because Rayco is planning on building lower socio-economic housing. That's going to bring down the value of an area and make gentrification impossible,' Adam said. 'Some of the existing homeowners won't like it.'

'True,' Burnsy agreed. 'So, the other two voices must be Cameron Keeper and Phillip Tansley.'

'They both sounded educated, not like Gerry,' Danielle said, playing the audio bites while Nate found their profiles online.

'Yeah, well, one is a town planner and the other a solicitor,' Nate said with a shrug.

'Nate, have you got the list of houses sold recently in the area?' Adam asked.

'Yeah, why?' He waded through a folder, looking for it.

'I'm wondering how long this big bald guy has been in the area or if he just moved in to help Gerry out and was given the first bite at a bargain property,' Adam said.

'Yeah, good thought,' Burnsy said.

'What was your wild thought you were going to tell us?' Nate said, finding the paper he sought with the homeowners' names and street numbers.

'Oh yeah. Sorry,' Burnsy said.

Adam downplayed it. 'That huge, bald guy, what's his name and house number?'

Nate glanced at the list. 'He was right next to the fairground on the corner, so any development would impact him more than most. This is him, number thirty-four, and, look at that... he just bought it for a really good price,' Nate exhaled. 'The sellers were keen to get out.'

'Any chance his name is Norman?'

All eyes turned to Nate; their breaths hitched.

'No. It's Wade Sampson,' Nate said, disappointed, and everyone slumped slightly. 'You were hoping it was the Norman plotting with Gerry, according to Rayco?'

'I was, but I bet there is no Norman,' Adam said.

'But Rayco named a "Norman", according to Laura, and you were sure of it too,' Danielle said. 'But I guess he has dementia and could have been confused.'

'Rayco was not confused about that,' Adam said. 'Rayco said Gerry was against the plan to donate the land for social housing and was buying up the land all around with Norman. He was angry and slurring – but it's not Norman, I think it's the *foreman.*'

'Foreman!' Nate said, inhaling. Hang on.' He searched for Wade Sampson online. 'Here he is; there's no mistaking that ugly mug.' Nate smiled. 'You're right, Adam. He's a construction foreman.'

Like a Mexican wave, relief crossed all of their faces.

Danielle shook her head. 'He's in up to his neck. He's buying property cheaply, and now he's working with Gerry to build the future village. We have his voice on tape to prove it.'

Nate clapped Adam on the back. 'You are not just a pretty face.'

'It's been said,' Adam agreed with a smile.

'We are on a roll,' Nate rubbed his hands together happily. 'Top that, Burnsy!'

'Fair enough, you've done well,' Burnsy grinned. 'Nice to get something back from you for a change.' He laughed at Nate's smirk. 'Our team believe if Friday is the day as we heard in your audio, then we suspect there is going to be a major assault on the street.'

'We need to be sure we're vigilant at Mr Dobrev's aged care residence that day and night,' Adam said, unaware of his grandmother's actions.

'Audrey and Tom have already seen to it,' Nate said, and Adam looked surprised.

'I'll also have a patrol near the aged care residence, and we'll have a reasonable size task force on-site at the Riverpark Estate, waiting to move in,' Burnsy said. 'Laura needs to be somewhere safe, just in case.'

'We'll sort that,' Nate said, wrapping up the meeting. 'Thanks again for the rego info. We'll see if Laura knows any of those men or recognises their names.'

Burnsy thanked them and rose. 'We're running out of time.'

'Yes, and hopefully, we're also applying pressure to them. That's when desperate people do desperate things,' Nate said, looking fired up.

Susan Armstrong suggested meeting at a café near her daughter Laura's office; she didn't want her late first husband's case brought into the house. Mid-afternoon suited them all.

'I suppose you think it's odd that I don't want to re-open the case,' Susan said to Nate. 'But we all went through a lot at the time, and I don't want it invading my home life again. My husband is also not keen on Laura's investigation.'

'I completely understand,' Nate said, ignoring Laura's frustrated expression. 'And a café is fine by me; I'd never say no to a good coffee.'

He thanked the waiter as three coffees were placed before them. He could see Laura in her mother; they shared a square jaw, full lips and sandy-coloured hair, except her mother wore her hair cut in an angular bob. It looked stylish, and Nate put her in her early forties.

'So, how can I help the investigation?' Susan asked.

Nate also recalled Laura saying her mother worked in administration, hence getting straight to the point.

'Can I ask you some questions about that time and what you can remember?'

'Fire away.'

'Were you aware that Alex had partnered with Gerry and Gerta Dobrev against Rayco to get the carnival closed?'

'No. I couldn't believe it when Laura told me. I supported Rayco. I didn't think he should have to shut down or be driven out, and I thought he was most compromising.'

'Did your husband know that?' Nate asked.

Susan scoffed. 'Absolutely not. Alex was a hot head.' She turned to Laura, 'Sorry dear, but it was a shotgun wedding, and I didn't know his true personality until after we were married.' She returned her attention to Nate. 'He frightened me, and I had a young child; Laura was six. I just kept a low profile back then.'

'Makes good sense,' Nate agreed. 'Did he have much support from the neighbours?'

'Alex started the group, and most of the supporters were of the same thinking – they were more interested in a bit of biff than the harmony of the community.'

'Would anyone in that group have bumped him off?'

'No. They thought the sun shone out of him. When he died, the group fell apart, but every time I saw them around the neighbourhood, they spoke of him as if he were a local hero. Mr Dobrev, the owner, not the son, came to see me after the funeral and insisted on setting up a scholarship to pay for Laura's education. I turned him down and told him we would be okay, but he insisted. That shows the decency of the man.'

'I didn't know that,' Laura said.

'I didn't want you to feel different from the other kids in the neighbourhood, but Mr Dobrev made a payment every single year towards your school fees, books and uniform, even long after I remarried. He was a better man than your father,' Susan said. 'That's why I don't know why you bother with this case. Your father lived by the sword and died by the sword.'

Nate noticed she did not care about disparaging her deceased husband even though he was Laura's father.

'There must have been something you once loved about Dad,' Laura said. 'I would have liked to have had him around when I was growing up.'

Susan softened and squeezed her daughter's hand. 'The best thing about your father—and I confess, it surprised me—was that he became a family man once you were born. He loved you like crazy.'

Laura's eyes welled with tears, and she quickly blinked them away, saying, 'Thanks, Mum.'

Nate, keen to get the interview over with, continued. 'So, Alex would have been very protective of Laura. Were you threatened at all back then or now?'

Susan shook her head in the negative. 'I don't think anyone would have been game to threaten Alex, and no, I've had no threats since Laura re-opened her father's case, thank goodness. I have two other daughters—Laura's step-sisters Casey and Angie—and I must consider their safety.'

'Of course,' Nate agreed and asked, 'Away from the neighbourhood tension back then, was Alex involved in any other business that might have put his life at risk?'

'You are thinking if someone wanted to bump him off, they could have joined the riot, done the deed, and no one would be the wiser?' Susan asked.

'Just a theory.'

'It's a good one.' Susan shook her head. 'I don't recall him being embroiled in anything. He worked in his father's construction business, so he didn't have an employer to answer to as such. He was a good builder, and the company had won some awards. He got on with his extended family; they were tight, and he had good mates with whom he regularly went to the football. All in all, Alex was a happy, easy-going, fun guy when he was in a good mood. That's what attracted me to him.'

'I've never heard you describe him like that,' Laura said and smiled.

'I guess because the last months of his life were full of the stupid neighbourhood fight, and he died a violent death. It overshadowed everything.'

Nate finished his coffee. 'That's about it, thank you. Is there anything you would like to tell me?'

'Yes,' Susan said decisively. 'As I said to Laura, I would let this go. Let his memory rest.'

'Someone wants us to as well, Mum. Doesn't that tell you something?' Laura asked.

'Yes. To let it go.'

Nate thanked Susan, and Laura walked her out, returning and dropping into the seat opposite him.

'I'm not due back for another thirty minutes. Have you got time to update me on your morning meeting with the sergeant?' she asked.

'Yep, I'm on your case all afternoon, so my time is yours,' Nate said, filling her in on the men they identified by their car registrations and showing her the printed coloured photos of their faces that Jessica had organised.

She studied them and shook her head. 'I don't know any of them.'

Nate suppressed a groan; that was a waste of time. After leaving Laura, he drove home. It was nearing four o'clock, and he wanted to do laps in the pool; it always helped him think.

Hurriedly changing and hitting the water, he reviewed the case; there was little of anything to go on. Gerry Dobrev could be ruled out, given he and Alex were in partnership. Alex was a folklore hero in the neighbourhood and had no enemies or no more than any other guy. The coroner's report that he received back with an updated professional analysis read the same as it did then – inconclusive and the result of a fall and strike to the head. He had left Laura with a copy and warned her it might be distressing.

He had nothing.

Turn, back the same way, follow the black line.

Nothing.

Look closer to home, Gerta had said. Good Lord, was he going to go with card readings now? Enough already.

Turn, another lap, follow the black line.

He had never given up a case without a result and wasn't about to do so now. But...

Another lap. Turn.

Nope, nothing.

Chapter 26

Adam drove into the grounds of the riverside mansion—his house—and saw the garages were full of cars. Surprisingly, it felt good to have the place used. Nate's Audi, Laura's Peugeot, Audrey's Jaguar, and Tom's Monaro were there. He parked his Mercedes next to Laura's car in their wing and went upstairs.

'Hey!' he said, surprised and somewhat pleased to find her sitting on the couch in the shared living room, looking out the window. She was still in business attire – a black jacket, skirt, heels, and white business shirt. She jumped, startled.

'Sorry.' Adam held up his hands.

'No, I was miles away. Hello!'

Adam took his tie off as he approached her to see what she was looking at. A team of rowers was going past on the river, leaving their trail like ducks gliding on the surface.

'I could look at this view all day,' she said.

'Me too. Mum hates the water view and won't stay in this wing.'

'My Mum hates a city view,' Laura offered. 'She's a country girl at heart and feels the buildings press in on her. Odd that.'

'Weird, our parents,' Adam agreed.

'Nothing like us,' Laura joked.

He sat on the couch opposite and leaned back with a sigh, relaxing in her company; he found it easy to do so. 'You looked a little despondent – a friendly, not professional observation. Is everything okay?'

'Right on both counts – professional and friendly,' she said. 'I've had my three things go wrong for the day, so the rest of the evening should be fine.' She smiled, but it did not reflect how she felt. 'Nate got my Dad's autopsy reviewed, and he gave me the returned paperwork today. Nothing new, same conclusion.' She sighed.

Adam studied her. 'That would have made for brutal reading.'

'It did; thank you for understanding that. I hope, like everyone who has lost a loved one, that he went quickly. If Dad didn't, I don't want to know; there are probably secrets we shouldn't uncover,' she mused.

'I've got several large filing cabinets in Dad's office that I haven't looked at yet, ' he said, indicating the direction of the office. I suspect most of it will be ready for the bin, and I'm sure there's a discovery or two in there I could do without.'

'You have to wonder why we would do it to ourselves,' Laura agreed. 'I have been thinking that maybe Dad just hit his head and died.' She looked back out the window.

'Maybe he did, but something made him fall or lose his balance to strike his head. Was he swinging a punch, or was he being attacked? It was a street riot, but no one came forward to say they witnessed his demise. That's a little odd.'

'That's what bugs me. But I'm pretty sure Nate thinks it's time to close the case.'

'Did he say that?' Adam asked, surprised. 'He's never given up on a case before.'

'Not in as many words, but he said we're back to square one, and he's been swimming for the last hour. I'm reading between the lines.'

Adam stood and looked out another window with a view to the pool. 'I'd better go get him out. He stayed in there for two hours once looking for a solution to a case and couldn't move his arms the next day.'

Laura laughed. He liked that she wasn't the maudlin type and he turned and smiled at her. There was a spark, but he wasn't going there. Still, she was clever, interesting, and light-hearted. She had an infectious energy about her.

'What was the second thing?' Adam asked, sitting in the large window frame seat.

'My client lost their case. It's hard to get a rape conviction to stick when your client is terrified and browbeaten in court and made to look like she wanted it. I know every case is different, but trust me, this young girl did not want it.'

'That's as heartbreaking as seeing some of my clients institutionalised when their attackers, often a family member, should be locked up.'

'Yes, and given a taste of their own medicine while locked up,' she agreed.

He realised their lives ran parallel. Although they could work for corporations earning big dollars, they chose the not-for-profit sector or community work.

'It's cold comfort, but I'm sure you did all you could,' Adam said.

'It still feels like I failed her. But you are right; I don't think I could have done anything more.' She put her chin up and smiled. 'And number three...' Laura gave a small drum roll with her fingers on her knees.

'Give it to me,' Adam smiled.

'I have to find a new flatmate. Becca is moving in with her boyfriend, Kai.' Laura shrugged. 'I knew it was coming; she spends more time there than at home. But I could do without the flatmate auditions right now.'

'When's the lease up?' Adam asked.

'In six weeks. But I'm very particular,' she grinned.

'No?' Adam acted surprised, and Laura laughed again.

'I'm a bit of a home dweller; I don't go out much, so I need someone happy to share the remote, who is not hoping to have the house to themselves a lot, and doesn't have a girlfriend or boyfriend visiting all the time.'

'I get that,' Adam agreed. 'I'm a bit the same.'

'Who have you lived with before?' Laura asked, and Adam felt her studying him more closely.

'Just my ex-wife. Before that, I lived here.'

'You and Nate have never flatted together?' Laura asked, surprised.

'No. He lived with another cop for a while in an apartment near his work, and then he married Erin, and they bought the house he now rents out. He has custody of Tilly—Matilda—every second weekend.'

'Does she come here?' Laura asked, surprised.

'Yeah, he lives here,' Adam said with a grin. 'Audrey and I don't make him move out when Tilly visits.'

She laughed. 'Of course not.' She glanced out the window again. 'You might never run into anyone here anyway; it's huge.'

'That's what I'm hoping with Tom.'

She gave him a wry look, and he smiled.

'Old enemies. So, are there any other flatmate terms and conditions?' Adam asked, seeing Nate turn and start another lap.

'You bet.' She rose and stood by the window closest to the pool, watching Nate. 'I need a private bathroom and a bathtub, proximity to a good running area, and close to work for public transport. And, preferably, if it's a guy, I hope he's not good-looking.'

Adam looked surprised.

'I know, said no woman ever!' she agreed, 'But I'd much prefer a down-to-earth, respectable, average-looking guy to share a house with platonically. No charmers, no playboys, no way.'

'You're right. You are particular.' He mused for a short while. 'Just a thought, but Nate's rented his house to Dan – you know, Danielle from the office? She might like a flatmate since she's living there alone. Or,' he added hesitantly, 'we flatted pretty well together for the week you were at my place. We could talk about whether we make that a permanent arrangement.'

Laura's eyes widened with interest. 'I would have my own bathroom and a bath, and Lord knows you're unattractive.' She grinned, and Adam laughed, having never been called that in his life. 'It's none of my business, but why wouldn't you stay here? Forgive me for saying this, but that seems crazy. It has everything.'

'Yeah, but I like my place. Even if I decide to stay here, I'd rent my house out anyway.'

'Well, thanks for the offer, but it sounds like you've got to make a few decisions about where you're living first. I've got six weeks, let's talk again.'

'Done,' Adam agreed, rising from the large window frame seat where he had been perched. 'I'd better drag Nate from the pool.' He took off his jacket and threw it, along with his tie, onto a large leather chair inside the door of an adjoining room with a river view as the rowers fleetingly passed by in the floor-to-ceiling glass door. Adam headed down the stairs to the pool, leaving Laura watching from the window.

What the hell did I just do? He asked himself, thinking about the flatmate's invitation, but found, surprisingly, he wasn't too worried about the outcome.

Chapter 27

Nate felt lost and unable to sit around all night—or swim—so he took himself off on surveillance.

'You don't need to come,' he told Adam and looked to Jessica, 'And don't call Danielle to join me.'

'Can I come?' Laura asked, and Nate and Tom said no in unison. She rolled her eyes.

Nate explained, 'I'm just going to stay in the car and watch. Listen to the recordings again and see if some inspiration hits me.'

'Will Burnsy be in the neighbourhood?' Jessica asked.

'He might be. I'll flag him down if he is,' Nate said.

'I'll be doing rounds too,' Tom said, 'So ignore me if you see me unless you need me.'

Nate agreed and apologised to Jessica for leaving her on their night together, but she seemed comfortable in the company of Laura and Adam. Audrey was at her card night, and Tom was around, mainly when Adam wasn't.

Heading out in his Audi, it was a short drive from the Murphy mansion to the Riverside Park Estate. Nate parked, killed the lights and sat quietly.

'Look close to home,' he muttered and shook his head, thinking about Gerta's words to Laura. He had spoken with everyone he could find on the neighbourhood protest group eighteen years ago, and the few men near Alex Armstrong that night were too busy minding their own backs to see

Alex fall. The men fighting were hired by Gerry and told not to harm Alex or his neighbourhood group because they were secretly partnered. No one was hurt; it was all superficial and over in no time. Except Alex Armstrong was dead.

An hour passed, and Nate grabbed his phone to play the audio grabs again in case he missed something. He turned it up as loud as it would go and listened with a new concentration level born from desperation. It was the first piece of audio that niggled at him, and he played it again and again, and then he froze. That was odd. Nate replayed the piece.

Got it! Nate grabbed his phone and dialled Adam.

'What?' Adam answered, and Nate looked at the time.

'You were asleep?'

'It's 11.30.'

'Right. Can you talk then?'

'I'm awake, aren't I?'

'Great, thanks,' Nate said. 'Listen to this.' He played the audio for Adam.

'Notice anything?' Nate asked

'Play it again,' Adam requested.

'I'm onto something, I know it,' Nate said as he queued the audio and played it for Adam a second time.

'Wow,' Adam said, 'subtle, but...'

'Exactly!' Nate agreed, pleased they were on the same page.

Adam exhaled. 'You've been set up, I'd say.'

'Thanks, but yeah, it sounds like it,' Nate agreed.

'Hard to pick,' Adam assured him.

Nate exhaled, frustrated. The voices on the tape had varied. Nate had been too busy listening for clues and trying to work out who was speaking to realise they were all low, all talking about bringing it to a head, about the final strike, but when they said the action would take place on Friday, it was slightly louder. Louder, as if someone were making sure he would hear it. Then, very faintly in the background was laughter, and moments later, a different voice said, 'Catch you Saturday then.' Barely audible. The action wasn't going to happen Friday; it was going down Saturday night.

'Why didn't I hear that before,' Nate said, swearing under his breath. 'You should have listened to the audio earlier.'

'I haven't listened to it at all. I didn't know that was part of my role.'

'It isn't, whatever,' Nate said, angry at himself. 'I'll call Burnsy,' Nate said, then uttered, 'Uh oh.'

'What's wrong?' he heard Adam's sudden alertness.

'There's a woman. She's just come running out of the carnival grounds looking freaked out.'

'Wait up, this could be a trap,' Adam warned.

'I know. Her dress is torn, and she looks terrified. She keeps glancing behind her. Damn it,' Nate hissed between clenched teeth. 'I'll have to help.'

'Call me straight back,' Adam said. 'I'll get Tom.'

Nate hung up. He had been caught in a similar no-win situation as a young cop. He stopped one night to help a woman standing alone at the edge of the road, only to find the woman was a store mannequin. His partner threw the mannequin in the back of their patrol car, and after a quick look around, they left, to his relief. He didn't want anyone else stopping, and he was sure it was a trap – someone was hiding, waiting to strike at him or steal the car. Was this the same?

She was getting closer to his car now.

Break cover and help, or ignore her and live with the guilt?

How can I ignore it?

Nate opened the car door and raced to help her. She looked relieved to see him and grabbed at Nate.

'You're okay. Get in the car, and then you can tell me what happened,' he assured her.

She looked up at Nate and smiled at him, and then three men stepped out of the shadows.

Adam rose and hurriedly dressed. There was no return call from Nate, so he rang Nate's phone. It rang out. He tried again. No luck.

Adam hurried out of his room and ran into Laura in the shared living area.

'What's happening? I heard the late phone call?' she asked, alarmed.

'Nate's in a trap, I think. I'll get Tom and go there.'

'I'm coming, and don't say no,' she said before he could open his mouth to say so. She was dressed in leisure wear and raced into her room to grab some running shoes, then followed him down the stairs.

Waking Tom woke Jessica, and Adam quickly ran through the story. Tom took his car; Laura went with Adam, who instructed Jessica to wait behind and keep calling Nate.

'Thank God it's close by,' Laura said as Adam drove at a speed to attract police attention, but there was no patrol around when he needed it.

Then, the deserted carnival came into sight, looking dark and eerie. They parked near Nate's car; it was empty and unlocked.

Nate took some comfort in the fact that the three assailants used their fists instead of a knife.

'What are you doing here?' One of them asked as they pushed him into a dilapidated shed near the carousel – their office.

'Surveillance,' he said.

'For who and what?' another sneered.

'For Gerry,' Nate lied. 'Where is he?'

'Who the fuck is Gerry?' the leader of the group asked, and the others snickered. That answered Nate's question. This group had nothing to do with Gerry and appeared to be using the carnival grounds to swap drugs and women, given several females were draping themselves over large guys with tattoo sleeves.

'Hide the bloody stuff in case he's a cop,' he heard one saying.

'Bit late now then, isn't it?' another said.

'I'm not a cop,' Nate said, and they fired question after question at him.

'What do you want then?' one of the women asked and was told to shut up by a heavily tattooed guy.

'Who are you with, asshole?'

'Who's this Gerry guy? Does he want a cut, or is he planning on moving in on our territory?'

'We'll find out, so put yourself out of your misery and tell us.'

'If you think you're cutting in, you're dreaming!'

Nate was a reasonable fighter; he could hold his own but not against four guys keen for a fight. He gasped as the first punch took his breath away and remembered being shoved around, taking several hits to the face and ribs before hitting the ground. Clutching his side, Nate was fairly sure he had put one out of action. He had one chance of getting out of this without every bone being broken, and that was to run.

Luck was on his side. Tom called out his name, and like a shot, Nate was up and gone, running into the dark carousel ride, hiding behind two of the broken horses that had collapsed onto a carriage. He heard the men packing up their stashes and swearing at each other. He hoped Tom wouldn't be their next victim. He glanced up and around when he could no longer hear their voices. Nothing. They were done, and the girl he was tricked into saving was gone. Staying low, he stumbled back towards his car, climbed in and locked the doors.

Adam grabbed Laura's hand and tugged her into the derelict ghost train as a group of men and several women thundered past them.

'Oh my God, do you think Nate faced all of them?' she whispered.

'I hope not,' Adam said, pressing back against the wall.

'I'm a good runner, how about you?' she asked.

'Even faster with a group of weight lifters chasing me,' Adam said and even terrified, she managed a huff of laughter. 'Tom calling out is probably helping drive them away.'

'I saw him come this way,' a gravelly voice said, and Laura's heart stopped. Adam pulled her further into the ghost train.

'If they find us, I'll step forward. You get out of here as soon as you can,' Adam whispered.

She turned her head to whisper in his ear, her lips brushing his skin. 'No.'

'Laura,' he hissed. 'What they might do to you... no arguments.'

She felt a wave of terror overtake her.

'Okay?' Adam said, his lips now close to her ear, his breath warm.

'Yes,' she agreed, terrified she was breathing too loudly.

'Where's Nate?' she whispered.

'I don't know. Hopefully, he's hiding somewhere too.'

'Come out, come out, wherever you are,' one of the men said in a sing-song voice and laughed.

'Forget it, let's go,' another said.

'He saw us. We need to find out who he is in case he's going straight to the cops.' The voices were getting closer, and Laura stiffened, controlling her breathing.

'I'm going. Cops could be on their way. Let's go.'

She heard one of the men striding out of the dark ghost train, but the other had not followed yet. Adam squeezed her hand; she guessed it was his way of saying stay quiet and still, so she squeezed back.

They waited for what seemed like an eternity. Then a voice nearby whispered, 'I see you, Laura. Come on out, Daddy's home.'

Chapter 28

The silence was splintered by Laura screaming as she flew towards the voice that had spoken, her hand pulling out of Adam's before he could stop her. Someone hit the ground with a thump as Adam fumbled for his phone and lit the area with the torch app. Laura was on the ground, on top of some guy. Tom raced in, pulled Laura up and hauled her behind him.

'Are you all right?' he asked Adam first, old habits dying hard.

'Fine. So is Laura,' Adam pointed out.

The man laughed and slowly got to his feet.

'You!' Laura said angrily.

'I'm just having a bit of fun; keep your hair on,' Gerry Dobrev said.

'Mate, you'd be a riot at a party,' Adam said angrily.

'You're a nasty piece of work, aren't you?' Laura said, glaring at him as she brushed off her jeans.

Gerry sneered. 'What are you doing here? You should leave the dead buried.'

'Nate saw half a dozen guys and a woman on the grounds; he was on surveillance,' Adam said.

Gerry swore. 'I've had them moved on a few times, but I'm not here often enough to enforce it. Bloody kids.'

'They weren't kids. Try huge guys with tattoos and drugs,' Laura told him. 'Have you seen him, Nate?'

'Nuh. Can't say I have.'

Adam's phone rang. 'It's Nate,' he announced, answering it and moving away.

'Let's go,' Tom said.

'Wait,' she snapped.

'He's all right,' Adam said, hanging up. 'He's waiting in his car. Come on.'

Gerry Dobrev put out his hand to stop Laura. 'Hey, I'm sorry, it was just a joke. I knew your dad, you know? He was alright.'

Laura nodded.

'You look nothing like him,' he added, and Laura smiled.

'I'm much better looking.'

'You got that right,' Gerry said with a grin as if he was charmed by her.

Adam was amazed she could smile at Gerry Dobrev after that ordeal. As they moved out into the grounds, they saw the police cars, and Gerry took off to talk with them about the break-in at his carnival grounds.

Blue and red flashes from their cars lit the three as Adam handed Laura his keys. 'Head home. Jessica will be worried, and Audrey too, if she's home. I'll deal with the police and drive back with Nate. We'll be there soon.'

'Okay, but what if Nate's in more trouble than you think?' she asked with a glance around assessing the scene.

'He said he's taken a few blows, but he'll be fine,' Adam bluffed, more worried about his friend than he wanted to let on. 'Head off, and we'll be there soon.'

She looked at the keys and then at him, 'I'll drive carefully.'

Adam nodded his thanks and tried to keep the pained expression off his face. He didn't like anyone driving his car. 'I'd better walk you there.'

'I'll see her there,' Tom said, and they departed. Adam straightened as one of the police officers approached.

'What are you doing here?' the cocky young officer asked.

'We're on surveillance, security. I'll call Sergeant Burns tomorrow and report what we saw,' Adam said, and the younger office agreed, recognising the name of the Sergeant and stepping back.

Adam took off, running down the street to Nate's Audi.

Unconscious for a brief time, Nate woke, his heart pounding. He had dreamt that he had rushed out of the car to save Jessica, but it wasn't her; it was a trap. He was drifting again and tried to stay awake.

Calm down.

Breathe in, breathe out.

He used the techniques taught in his police training.

A sharp rap on his car window startled him.

'Unlock the car,' Adam ordered.

Nate tried to focus and pressed the button to unlock the car doors. Adam opened the driver's side door and knelt beside him, a look of alarm on his face seeing the blood on Nate's face.

'How bad is it?'

'It's nothing, no weapons. It was just punches and kicks,' Nate's words slurred.

'And a concussion by the sound of it. We'll go to emergency.'

'No,' Nate winced.

Adam raised Nate's shirt. 'Holy shit. What else?'

'Just punches... ribs, head, you know.'

'No, I don't. Tell me,' Adam insisted as Nate was struggling to stay alert. 'Stay with me, C'mon, help me get you to the passenger side.'

Adam pulled Nate out of the driver's seat and dodged as Nate swung at him—instinct and pain, a fine line—before settling his arm around Adam's shoulder.

'Sorry. You'd better help me,' Nate mumbled.

'Come on.'

Nate pulled away. 'Stop,' he demanded and leant over, vomiting and missing Adam's shoes by centimetres.

'Sorry,' he said again.

'At least it wasn't in the car.' Adam grunted, half-carrying Nate around to the other side of the car. Opening the passenger door, Nate slumped in, hissing a few colourful words as Adam closed the door, raced around, got behind the wheel, and, finding Tom's number, dialled it while speeding off in the Audi.

'Is he all right?' Tom answered.

'He's been beaten up, hard to tell the damage.' Adam gave him the abridged version and then poked Nate, who must have drifted off because the sharp pain brought him around.

'For the love of God,' he gasped.

'Sorry, mate, but you can't sleep yet. Concussion,' he added for Tom's benefit.

'If you're listening, Nate,' Tom snapped, 'we'll talk about being bloody reckless and reporting to me when you're going to do something off the grid like getting out of the car.'

'Yeah, I'm sure he'll look forward to that,' Adam said. 'He needs to go to the emergency at the hospital.'

Nate interrupted to say no again, and Adam sighed. 'Do you know anyone handy with first aid?' he asked Tom.

'Me. I'm a trained Special Operations Combat Medic. Get him home.'

Adam hung up and pocketed his phone. 'Tom can fix you, allegedly.'

'Never thought I'd see the day that you voluntarily called Tom for anything,' Nate slurred with a smile.

'I wanted an ally to agree you should go to the hospital.'

Within five minutes, they were home, and Adam spun the car into the driveway. Tom, Jessica, and Laura stood waiting; Adam was pleased Audrey was home but had not stirred.

Nate winced as Tom assisted him out of the car and issued orders like a medic on a hospital ramping platform.

'Your bedside manner needs work,' Nate groaned amongst other rantings.

Adam had to give Tom his due; his SAS medical training was thorough. Despite Nate's groans, protestations, and confusion, he was soon asleep and would pay the price tomorrow.

Chapter 29

I t was a beautiful day; Nate didn't notice. He lowered himself into the office chair with a few choice words; his ribs were aching, his head throbbed, and even his breathing caused him grief.

'I can't believe you fell for that old trick,' Sergeant Matt Burns said, sitting opposite and looking to Laura for agreement.

'I think it was very noble of you to try and save that girl,' Laura told Nate, 'Although you should have stayed in bed today.'

'I'll be all right,' he assured her and added for Burnsy's benefit, 'The woman looked distraught, and the deserted carnival is the perfect place to take a date and take advantage.'

'If it were me, I'd want someone to stop and help,' Laura agreed and asked sympathetically, 'Where does it hurt the most?'

'I ache in so many places I can't distinguish which is the worst,' Nate said. 'Every part of me is making itself known like a long-lost acquaintance.'

Laura and Burnsy did their best not to smile at Nate's dramatic description.

'It looks painful; you'll scare kids,' Burnsy said, studying Nate's bruised face and swollen eye.

'He's been doing that for years,' Adam said, entering the room in time to hear Burnsy's barb.

'Stop it, both of you. The sympathy is killing me,' Nate said drily. 'But two good things came out of it.'

Laura leaned forward in her chair, 'What?'

'Firstly,' Nate said, looking at Burnsy, 'the raid on the neighbourhood is not tomorrow.'

'What?' Burnsy said. 'I've got all the resources lined up to go.'

'They want us to think it's Friday; that's why we heard it so loud and clear in the audio. It's Saturday.'

'Can I hear it for myself before I pull everyone out and change days?' Burnsy asked suspiciously.

'Knock yourself out,' Nate said, 'or have people on standby both nights.'

'You were a cop once,' Burnsy smirked at him. 'Remember the budgets?'

'Yeah, fair enough,' Nate said.

'Why are they doing that? I don't get it?' Laura said.

'I suspect they're bringing something to a head,' Nate said. 'It's not against the law to run their broken-down carousel and merry-go-round given it's on their own land, and if it spooks someone in the process, all the better for them.'

'It's against the law to be a public nuisance though,' Burnsy said, 'up to six months in prison.'

'But, depending on who they've got on their side, it might just be a street party that goes wrong,' Nate said. 'Suddenly, it's a riot, and residents are getting out, and maybe something will happen to Rayco Dobrev as well. Nice and neat, and decent money to be made.'

'It worries me you always think like a criminal,' Adam said, and Nate laughed and winced.

'Don't make me laugh, but thanks. That's the nicest thing you've ever said to me,' Nate joked.

'What's the second thing that came out of last night?' Laura brought him back on topic.

'Ah, yes, that involves you, Laura,' Nate said. 'Adam told me this morning that Gerry was taunting you before he decided to apologise and play nice guy,' Nate said, and Laura scoffed.

'Yeah. I thought for a moment he was going to ask me to partner with him like my dad did to get the carnival out of the neighbourhood.'

'It wouldn't have surprised me. Adam told me Gerry said the exact same words to you that were on the note taped to your window, "Leave the dead buried". Remember?'

Laura snapped to look at Adam. 'He did! I didn't even notice I was so busy freaking out. So, do you think he put the warning sign on my window? And if he did, he's worried and doesn't want me digging around.'

'But why, when he's already told Laura he was partnered with her father?' Burnsy asked.

'Well, according to our resident psychologist, it might not be about him,' Nate said, and all eyes turned to Adam.

'He might be trying to protect someone close to him,' Adam said.

'Look closer to home,' Laura thought out loud. 'Gerta said that, but I don't think she meant her own home; I assumed she meant mine, and she told me not all is as it seems.'

'She would,' Nate huffed. 'We could check the sign on your window for fingerprints and see if Gerry's prints come up.'

'You could,' Burnsy agreed, 'but it would cost you. And what if they are on there?'

'It means he's threatening me and wants me off the case. It doesn't mean he murdered Dad,' Laura said.

Adam agreed. 'But consider whom he might be protecting. From what I've observed of Gerry Dobrev, there are very few people he cares about or would go out of his way to protect.'

Laura gasped. 'Do you think Gerta killed Dad? He'd protect his mother.'

Nate shook his head. 'There's no witnesses to that, even if she did. But there's someone who might accidentally tell us.'

Laura looked slightly confused, and then Adam clarified where he and Nate were going with this train of thought.

'I think Audrey and I should visit Rayco Dobrev and take a trip down memory lane.'

Nothing happened Friday night. After visiting her mother for an hour on Saturday morning at the now tired Riverside Park Estate and hearing all the reasons why she shouldn't have opened the cold case, Laura returned to the Murphy Mansion, which she, like everyone else, assumed belonged to Audrey. Only Nate knew it was Adam's place.

She was surprised to find Sergeant Matt Burns visiting, working on her case with Nate, Adam, Jessica, Danielle, and Tom.

She accepted a coffee from Adam and joined them in Nate's living area.

'Rayco's sister has permitted Audrey and I to visit Rayco tomorrow morning after Audrey goes to church,' Adam said.

'Assuming nothing happens to him tonight,' Nate said.

'Our security is tight,' Tom told them. 'They'd have to storm the place to get to him, and I doubt they'd get far then. I can also report that there have been no threats here or unusual activity the last few days or at your unit, Laura, or Adam's house.'

'Thank you, Tom,' Laura said relieved.

'Thank God you picked that we had the wrong day, Nate,' Burnsy said. 'I would have had serious egg on my face.'

'And never worked with me again,' Nate said. 'Perish the thought.'

The group chuckled, but Sgt Matt Burns was a good contact for them, not one Nate wanted to blow off.

'They'll know we are onto them; they are one up on us,' Nate said. 'Either Gerry has his own cameras and saw us planting ours, or someone was on site watching Dan and me that night.'

'I'm going with the latter since you wouldn't bother installing security in the dump,' Tom said.

'Either way, they deliberately left us that clue because they suspected we'd be listening in, so they will be wary as to why the police weren't around the suburb in big numbers last night.'

'Maybe,' Burnsy agreed. 'But will they expect us back tonight?'

'Speaking of which, Mum's hunkering in for the night, so I'm going to stay with her,' Laura told the group.

'No way,' Tom said. 'Get your family out of there. It's just for the night.'

'Bring them here if you like,' Adam offered, and Laura shook her head.

'Thanks, but I've already suggested she evacuate. My stepdad's away... he's a FIFO—fly-in fly-out worker—and not due to fly back in for another week. My stepsisters won't be there; one's at camp, and the other has a sleepover. But Mum's invited one of her neighbours, Gavin, to come over. He's wheelchair bound, and she's worried if he stays at home, he might be vulnerable to attack.'

'I'm sorry, but you can't stay there, that's crazy,' Tom said. 'Two women and a guy in a wheelchair, you're easy pickings.'

'Mum said she won't be frightened out of her house, and she had already paid the price with Dad's death.'

'Did you suggest she's putting you at risk?' Tom asked.

Laura chuckled. 'Yes, actually. But she said that was on me, which was fair enough.'

'What do we know about this Gavin guy?' Tom asked.

'Not much. He lives a street away from Mum; she's met him a few times while walking. Apparently, he has a nice rose garden, and they've spoken of it.'

'I don't like it,' Tom said again.

'Someone might think the best way to warn you away, Laura, is to harm your mother,' Burnsy said, 'it's a risk.'

'I'll stay with Laura,' Nate said, looking at Tom. 'Are you good with that?'

'No, I'll stay with Laura; she's my client. Adam, will you stay here with Audrey?'

'Okay, if you think that will be enough security on my grandmother, given she's been threatened on our trip to the cemetery.'

Laura held up her hand. 'Can I pull rank as the client? Nate, will you come with me? Tom, please stay here with Audrey. I couldn't live with myself if she were threatened or injured. Mum and I are both fit and capable of screaming and running.'

Adam gave her an appreciative smile but shook his head. 'No, Tom's right.'

'Never thought I'd see the day,' Tom said incredulously.

'It shocked me, too,' Adam retorted.

'The action will be in your neighbourhood, not here. If Adam thinks there is a threat, he can call me, and I will be here in minutes,' Tom said. 'Seriously, I know this is your case, but leave the security to me.'

Laura nodded, and Adam agreed. Must be killing him, Laura thought, watching Adam.

Burnsy spoke up. 'If you're going to be there, Nate, no reverting to your former career. I don't want to see you out in the street fighting or getting involved.'

'If I wasn't so sore and sorry, I might be tempted to be part of the action,' Nate said honestly. 'But I'll just bide my time with Laura and Susan and keep a low profile.'

'If tonight is their "showstopper", they will be expecting results,' Laura said.

'Yep,' Nate agreed. 'It might be their last chance to buy up a lot of the properties cheaply, then Gerry produces his will, saying he's inherited Carnival World, and they are sitting on a goldmine. They can sell the houses they bought cheaply at a higher price to tide them over while they build the new estate and then make a killing on it. Every player wins a prize.' He looked at Adam as he said the words and the pair exchanged a smile.

'What? What are you remembering?' Jessica asked, looking from one to the other.

'Just a pink panda bear,' Adam said and laughed as Nate told the story.

Then...

Nate was desperate to win Adam's security officer, Charlie, a teddy bear, and the sign said, "Every player wins a prize".

'I bet those tins are glued on, so you can't knock them all off,' Adam whispered to Nate as the determined 12-year-old stood, ball in hand, eyeing the tins set up in a pyramid.

'Do you think?' Nate asked, now worried. 'Nah, that guy before knocked two off.'

'Yeah, but I bet the bottom row is glued on,' Adam said with a nod as if he was sure of the fact.

As the carnival worker approached them again, Nate blurted out, 'Have you ever knocked them all off?'

'Sure.'

'Can you show us how?' Nate asked, and the guy grinned as if he was being asked to show his special technique.

'Yeah, can you?' A girl about their age joined in as she stood with her mother, ball in hand.

'Hmm,' the carnival worker said as he rocked on his heels, pushed his baseball cap back slightly on his shoulder-length hair and thought about it. His clothes were fitted to show his muscly arms and a tight midriff, and his jeans sat snugly on his hips. He had been flirting with two girls in the corner who smiled at him now, ready to see his prowess.

'Sure. Why not?'

Nate and Adam grinned, and the young girl looked at her mother excitedly.

The carnival worker came from behind the counter and joined them, bringing the three allocated balls per throw.

'The trick is aiming at the right spot, but don't tell the boss I told you so,' he said with a wink, making the girls in the corner titter. An audience was gathering, including more attractive girls his age, and the carnival worker played up to them. 'So, see that spot in the middle of the pyramid? That's what you are aiming for. That's the weak spot; if you hit it, they'll all tumble. But you've got to really concentrate.'

He was under pressure now to show he could do it, not that he probably cared if he failed in front of the two young boys, the girl and her mother, but the audience of admirers was expanding. He took a deep breath, raised his hand, aimed the ball to the centre, and threw fast and hard. The tins fell over with a satisfying clang, and a roar rose from his small crowd.

'See, it can be done,' Nate said excitedly. 'Thanks, Mister. If I knock them over, can I win one of those bears on the top shelf?' he asked as the crowd dispersed, and the young girl next to them threw her first of three balls and missed.

'Is it for a girlfriend?' the worker asked with a sly smile, teasing Nate, who looked embarrassed by the question.

'Yeah,' he mumbled, glancing around and seeing Charlie standing behind them. She was talking on the phone with Adam's dad and watching the boys at the same time.

'Well, in that case, you can pick any bear you like if you win.'

'Thanks!' Nate said, grinning like he had already won.

The carnival worker re-entered the counter area to collect the balls the young girl threw and missed, giving her the consolation prize of a keyring with a fuzzy toy on it. He took the money from another young couple who wanted to try, gave them three balls, and returned to the two boys.

Nate's concentration was palpable. Adam held his breath, and Nate threw the ball, aiming for the space in the middle of the pyramid. All those summer months of cricket pitching paid off, and the tins skittled, leaving the bare space they once sat upon.

It was as if the boys had won a grand final; they cheered and whooped, and Nate selected a stuffed toy resembling a pink panda bear.

'That was amazing,' Adam said.

'It was like slow motion, and wham, they were gone!' Nate agreed, grinning.

'What's your girlfriend's name?' the carnival worker asked, reaching for it.

'Charlie,' Nate said hopefully.

'She's going to love you,' the carnival worker handed over the bear.

'Thanks for the tips,' Nate said and nudged Adam, 'let's go.'

As they approached Charlie, her eyes narrowed, and she hung up from her phone call.

'Who gave you that?' she asked worriedly.

'I just won it for—'

'Is that him there, with the greasy hair?' she asked, and both boys turned to see if it was the carnival worker they had just been talking with; they hadn't noticed he had greasy hair.

'That's him. I won it, Charlie,' Nate said, standing tall.

'Did you see anyone else working with him? The tarot reader or Mr Dobrev, Audrey's friend?' she continued grilling them.

'No,' they both answered.

'May I?' she asked, and Nate handed it over, confused.

Charlie ran a hand over the bear and seemed satisfied it was safe, handing it back to Nate. Then she smiled, 'Good job, Nate, well done.'

'Thanks,' he muttered, the moment gone. He shook his head at Adam, telling him not to say anything. He didn't want to give it to Charlie anymore.

Eighteen years later, it still sits in his mother's sewing room; it's one of her favourite gifts from Nate. To think her clever, considerate son went to *Carnival World*, thought of his mother, and won her a pink panda bear.

Chapter 30

Hours and hours of tension. The waiting was the worst. Laura drew a breath as she stood near the window, glancing between the white lace kitchen curtains. It was nearing ten o'clock, and her mother, Susan, had one small light in the kitchen that created enough glow for them to see each other. Tom was on edge, alert, pacing, checking his phone. Keen for action, Laura thought.

The small group shared several cups of tea and a pasta dinner, which Susan threw together. Gavin—the guest neighbour—and Susan had played cards earlier, while Tom and Nate constantly watched and waited, and Laura placed herself in the window.

'How long will you stay?' Susan asked.

'Until midnight,' Nate answered. 'If they haven't acted by then, they probably won't.'

'I'll head home at midnight then if I'm not outstaying my welcome,' Gavin said with a warm smile to Susan.

'That's fine. Maybe Nate or Tom could see you home,' Susan suggested.

'Sure,' Nate said, and his phone rang; he took the call, telling them it was Adam.

'Nope, nothing yet. How about there?' Nate asked, and his eyes widened with interest. Assuring Adam he'd keep him informed, he hung up and said, 'A flare has just gone up nearby. Adam and Audrey saw it from the verandah overlooking the river.'

'That's probably the call to action if there is one,' Tom said, and Nate agreed, ringing Burnsy to check in.

'I wonder what's going on in the carnival grounds,' Laura said by the window. 'There's a strange energy in the neighbourhood. Lights keep going on and off, curtains are being moved and closed.'

'Do you think any existing residents are in on it?' Susan asked.

Nate nodded. 'Yes, the man who just bought the house on the corner nearest to the fairground is in Gerry Dobrev's development group.'

'He got that cheap,' Gavin said with a shake of his head. He was a tall, thin man of similar age to Susan, with salt and pepper hair and strong arms from managing his wheelchair. 'I wouldn't want to sell now even if I was desperate.'

'Me either,' Susan agreed. 'Although,' she added with a look to Laura, 'we'd make our money because we bought here so long ago.'

'Laura, if anyone approaches the house, you and Susan are to go upstairs,' Tom said, ignoring their banter. 'You'll be able to see everything going on in the street and at the entrance to the grounds from there, and you can lie low. Gavin will be fine down here with us. Don't come downstairs until I give you the all-clear.' Remembering she was the client, he added, 'Is that okay?'

'Good idea,' Gavin agreed.

Laura looked to her mother, whom she thought would protest, but her mother agreed. Laura felt a rush of adrenaline. So exciting. So scary.

Adam and Audrey relaxed as they sat by the window, sharing tea and watching the flare fade in the distance. The house was secure, with a large fence and cameras on all the borders.

'I hope you are not missing being part of the action,' Audrey said. 'I am sure being with Laura and Nathanial would be more exciting.'

'No. I am very happy to be here, especially as Tom is there,' Adam said with a smile. Both knew that was the truth. 'Besides, Nate will be telling the ladies about his injuries to get sympathy.'

Audrey laughed at the thought. 'Oh well, if you have a willing audience...'

In the dark street below, car headlights approached the gate and pulled up near the camera. The buzzer, loud in the quiet house, startled them both.

'Who on earth might this be?' Audrey asked.

Adam rose to find out. Moving to the entrance security screen, he saw Gerta Dobrev in the driver's seat. 'It's Gerta!'

'Good grief. What on earth could she want at this hour?' Audrey rose and joined him as Adam pressed the button.

'Mrs Dobrev? It's Adam here.'

'Adam, may I come in and speak with you and Audrey?'

Adam looked to his grandmother, who nodded, and he opened the gate. 'Please, come on in,' he said, leaving his grandmother in the living room as he went to open the door for their guest. She parked close to the garage, which was a nice courtesy, keeping the entrance clear, and exited the car. There was no interior light, which Adam didn't notice or think was odd as he focused on Gerta Dobrev. Nate and Tom, with their training, would have thought otherwise.

Alighting from the car, the small, senior woman who never looked as sinister when away from the carnival environment said, 'I am sorry to come at this hour,' as she approached him.

'That's not a problem; we were both up,' he said, checking that the gate had closed behind her. 'Come in. We were having a cup of tea. Did you not feel safe? Where is Gerry?'

In the doorway, Gerta fussed with her bag for a moment and, with a sleight of hand, unlocked the door Adam had just secured. She followed him into the living area, where Audrey greeted her.

'Gerta, I am glad you came here with all those sirens and flares near your house. Please sit. Tea?'

The fortune teller thanked Audrey and sat, accepting a cup of tea from Audrey's best china set. Adam returned to the window, suspicious of her arrival and scanning the fence line. He mused, *What the hell is going on*, but he didn't want to call Tom or Nate again.

'I am not frightened to be at home alone,' Gerta said, responding to Adam's question, 'but I did want to give you something.' She looked at Adam at the window and added, 'Perhaps it might interest the young lady, Laura.'

Adam moved away from the window just long enough for Gerry Dobrev to alight from the back seat of his mother's car, where he lay, waiting.

Chapter 31

For Nate, what happened next was like being part of an action film on speed. The hours until 10pm had gone slowly – waiting, straining to hear any noise, on edge with anticipation. At 10 o'clock, everything changed – action time. Nate was no stranger to property raids and working with riots from his police days. He and Tom were dressed in black clothing with boots that would allow them to deliver a swift kick or quickly get out of there. He was pleased Tom was present; he knew Adam's fighting experience was limited to the self-defence training James Murphy had paid for or that Charlie had given them – and her first rule of thumb was to run. However, given his injuries, he needed Tom to help protect the women upstairs.

By the window, Laura gasped as the room lit with red. They saw and heard the flares; half a dozen went up in the air and heard sharp commands issued and voices yelling. Everything was locked; Tom had ensured it, but Nate pulled Laura away from the window and turned the light off in the kitchen. They watched in the dark.

'There's so many of them, what are they doing?' Laura whispered as figures ran up and down the street dressed in black, yelling out. Nate could see she was subtly filming as much as she could on her phone and thought it wasn't a bad idea; the police might want the recording. They heard the sound of shattering glass and laughter, then a neighbour's garage door opened, and a car drove out hurriedly, departing before the door closed. Several figures hurled themselves under the garage door as it closed, running into the house.

'Go upstairs now, Laura, Susan, stay back from the windows,' Tom ordered, and with a glance at Gavin, who ushered them up with his hand, the pair left the room, climbing the carpeted stairs quickly and quietly.

Someone rapped loudly on the front door, and Gavin gasped. Tom and Nate braced, waiting, expecting the door to bust open, but the footsteps receded.

'Nate, go check on the ladies and stay with them,' Tom ordered.

Nate grimaced but did what he was told. He fished his mobile phone from his pocket and called Adam on his way up the stairs; it went to the message bank. His eyes locked with Laura's as he entered Susan's main bedroom. 'Tom's not worried; they're just knocking, yelling, and generally pretending to be aggressive, according to him.'

'Good Lord.' Susan's hand went to her heart.

'We should check on Audrey,' Laura said.

'I just rang, and it went to message bank. I'll try again in a minute,' Nate assured her. 'I'm sure Audrey will think it's a grand adventure,' Nate said with a huff of laughter.

And Laura smiled. 'She will.'

The three stood near the windows, watching from the edge of the curtains. Laura, too, was dressed for action in black sports gear. Her hair was back in a single plait, so it was out of the way, and she looked super fit. Her mother, however, was dressed for company. The pair flinched on hearing what sounded like a gunshot.

'Was that a gun?' Susan asked, shocked.

'I don't know, I've never heard one, but it sounded like it,' Laura said, looking at Nate.

'It could have been a car backfiring, but it's most likely firecrackers,' Nate said, his voice calm. 'I doubt Gerry would authorise using illegal weapons; he's got too much to lose.'

Laura pulled the curtains tighter together in the middle but could not resist standing at one end of the window, in the dark, and watching.

'They're coming up the street,' Susan announced from her angle. 'There's a mob of twenty or so.'

Nate moved from Laura's window to Susan's perspective, watching the action, ready to herd the ladies downstairs to the garage and into his car if the action got too rough and they should evacuate. It was frightening for the neighbours, but Tom was right; it was like play-acting. The ex-SAS officer and now security man came noisily up the stairs and joined them, watching the mobs of people running and yelling.

'All okay?' he asked.

'Where's Gavin?' Susan asked, worried.

'He's fine, I'm going straight back down.'

They gasped as a car window was smashed across the road, and nearby, the carnival was on fire.

'It's show and tell,' Tom said. 'The fire is on Gerry's land, and the intruders are like some skit from a bad movie.'

'It's likely Gerry's hired them. I wonder what their brief was,' Nate mused, but then the violence was dialled up a notch.

'Look at that!' Laura yelled as a group ran past on the street in creepy Halloween masks and charged into several houses across the road, breaking windows.

'Now, that's getting aggressive,' Nate agreed. 'I bet that wasn't in their brief.'

'We should have evacuated,' Laura said, and Susan agreed. They were coming towards Susan's house now.

'Nate, you stay here. I'm going downstairs with Gavin to ward off anyone who thinks they might loot the place,' Tom said. 'Yell if you need me. Call Adam and check on them.'

'Let them loot, it doesn't matter, just don't go out there,' Susan told Tom, but Nate shook his head.

'It's better they see someone here, a deterrent,' Nate said. 'If they break their way in, I'll also come down fighting.'

Laura wondered how he would do that in his current condition as Tom raced back downstairs, leaving Nate with the women. Moments later, he reappeared, a finger to his lips to keep quiet. He motioned for Nate to follow.

Nate quietly requested the ladies stay put and silently followed Tom down the stairs. Entering the hallway, they stopped dead in their tracks and turned slowly. Someone was moving around the living area—a dark, shadowy figure.

Tom motioned for Nate to copy him. They flattened themselves against the wall and waited before furtively making their way down the hallway and going full circle back to the lounge room. Tom indicated the empty wheelchair, and Nate's eyes widened.

They silently entered the room; Gavin was standing, the wheelchair abandoned. He was carrying a Halloween mask and wielding a baseball bat as he signalled someone in the window, telling them to move on. Nate shook his head in disbelief.

Why was Gavin here? To save Susan?

To listen in on their conversations?

Lord knows they'd been speaking to security and the police and voicing their opinions about what was happening.

Who was this guy?

Nate's face darkened with anger, and against his better judgement, he stayed put.

Tom moved stealthily behind Gavin, grabbed the wheelchair and hit him in the back of the legs, bringing him down.

Gavin scrambled to his feet, slicing the air with the baseball bat. Tom shoved him against the wall, ordering Nate to, 'Find something to secure him with!'

'Why are you here?' Tom snarled at Gavin. The noise outside was raging now – car horns, yelling, screaming, glass shattering, and sirens in the distance.

'You can go to hell before I tell you anything,' Gavin hissed.

'I'll get you there faster if you don't talk,' Tom threatened.

A huge explosion outside made both men jump, and Gavin made a break, taking advantage of the small distraction. He was at the front door, unlocking it and straight out onto the street, lost in the pack before they could react. Tom ran after him, and Nate followed as far as the door, securely locking it. The sirens were wailing in the streets, and the area was lit by blue and red strobing light; he could smell smoke even if he couldn't see it.

It seems Gavin was leading two lives.

Chapter 32

Gerry Dobrev edged open the front door of the Murphy mansion, relieved to find it unlocked.

Good job, Mum.

He hoped the old girl could keep the Murphys distracted for as long as he needed. He spotted the staircase and knew the Murphy office was upstairs and the first room to the left. Thanks to a tradie mate who had done some electrical repairs for Audrey and was happy to have a bit of cash in hand, Gerry had secured a fairly detailed drawing of the inside of the elaborate home. It made his blood boil to think of Audrey Murphy working with his father to give away his family's wealth to charity while living in this mansion.

Noiselessly, he made his way up the stairs and spotted the office; the door was open – another thing going his way. He could hear his mother's voice downstairs, and now, increasing his pace, he entered the room and half-closed the door. He wanted to be able to make a quick exit, and Gerta had given him half an hour, no more.

The filing cabinet was locked. Damn. No surprise, but oddly, his mother was better at breaking locks than he was. He removed a small screwdriver from his pocket and jimmied the lock; it snapped to his satisfaction. Gerry stopped, listened, heard nothing and opened the drawer. He spotted the file under "D" – the Dobrev name written in capitals.

'Yes,' he hissed and pulled it out, placing it on the desk. Hurriedly, Gerry thumbed through it. Nothing but bloody press clippings, a police report from 18 years ago and some journalist sending a brief to James Murphy.

'Damn it!' he swore and then stopped to listen. It was very quiet downstairs. He hurried back to the cabinet and looked for a file under Alex Armstrong. No such luck. He tried "Carnival" and "Community Groups". Damn, damn, damn! Then he heard footsteps on the stairway.

Adam thought the distant sound of sirens was momentarily louder, as if someone had opened a door or window. He didn't want to alarm his grandmother, so he listened intently, tuning out the conversation the two ladies were having over a cup of tea at the nearby dining room table. Gerta handed over a diary written by her husband, Rayco, during the riots 18 years ago. Why she couldn't have given them that during daylight hours was beyond him, but maybe she did want to get out of the neighbourhood while her son was causing havoc – she was, after all, in her seventies.

Again, a sound. The small squeak of a timber beam on the staircase, one he knew so well from childhood when he didn't want his father or Audrey to hear him sneaking in or out.

He moved away from the window and toward the hallway.

'Adam, what do you think?' Gerta asked, vying for his attention. 'Might it be of use to the young lady?'

Red flag! Something was up. Why would Gerta care what he thought? She was barely civil to them and delighted in telling Laura that she and her son had partnered with Laura's father.

'I'm sure she will be happy with anything that shines a light on the last year of her father's life,' he said distractedly. 'Excuse me.'

As he moved out to the hallway, Gerta jumped up. 'I best be going.'

'Oh, already,' Audrey said. 'Well, thank you, Gerta.'

Adam continued to move upstairs. The office door was half closed, and he knew that was unusual.

'Adam, Gerta is leaving,' his grandmother called.

He didn't answer, not wanting to alert whoever might be in the study that he was nearby. It had to be Gerry, but why? What was he looking for? His phone rang halfway up the stairs, and he grabbed it and saw Nate's number. He paused to answer, not speaking. He heard Nate's voice.

'Adam?'

'Wait,' he said in a hushed tone, putting it on speaker. Adam was no stranger to entering violent situations in prison or mental health facilities, but that didn't make it any easier to walk in unarmed, alone, and not knowing what faced him.

He pushed the office door open the rest of the way and entered.

'Gerry!' he announced, and then everything happened at once. Nate cut the call, Gerry pulled a knife, and footsteps hurried up the stairs behind him; Gerta barged in, Audrey following.

'Mr Dobrev!' Audrey exclaimed.

Gerry stood, knife in one hand, a file in the other, and another file strewn across the desk. 'Where the hell is it?' he hissed, his face flushed with anger. 'Where is it?' He slammed his fist against the filing cabinet, making Audrey jump.

'Go downstairs, Audrey,' Adam said.

'She stays right here,' Gerry said.

'I don't know what you are looking for,' Audrey said quite calmly.

'The will! My father's will, and if you don't give it to me, neither of you will be leaving here,' he snarled, and Adam, who was slow to anger, hit boiling point.

'Why the hell would we have your father's will?' he snapped.

'Because he told me you have a copy with the community village plans. He said he gave it to Mrs Murphy, his wonderful friend,' Gerry sneered.

'The woman whom he thought I should be more like,' Gerta added bitterly.

'I am sorry for that, Gerta. But I promise you both, I have never seen a will from Rayco; I don't know why he would tell you that,' Audrey said.

'Because you were part of it, trying to give away our money, and here you are living in this,' Gerry growled, waving the knife around the room.

'I was not getting a cent of your money; it was going to create a legacy for your name. I, too, give my time and money to help others. But I agree, it is your land and should be yours.'

Adam could see that Gerta and Gerry were surprised by Audrey's support. She added, 'I doubt any court of law would grant it to a community group when you have both worked there as a family business.'

'It's all in his name,' Gerta said, 'that's how things were done then.'

'But the law has changed,' Adam said, watching Gerry and the knife.

'It will be in your favour,' Audrey assured Gerta, 'even if there are community groups who have a verbal agreement with Rayco and might pursue it. My group is not one.'

Knowing that Tom was most likely on the way, thanks to Nate, Adam said, 'Audrey, go downstairs, Mrs Dobrev, stay or go, I don't care. Gerry, tell me what files you want, and I will find them for you,'

Gerry's face was flushed. 'No one goes anywhere. The community village plans, where are they?'

Audrey pointed to a second filing cabinet. 'In there.'

Gerry raced to the cabinet and tugged on it. 'Where's the key? Open it, or I'll break it.'

'I'll get the key,' Audrey said.

'No! He goes,' he said with a nod to Adam.

'That's not going to happen,' Adam said. He had no intention of leaving his grandmother with a volatile Gerry Dobrev. 'Audrey will get it.'

'Fine, Hurry up. Mum, go with her in case she tries to call the cops,' Gerry barked orders to his mother.

The two elderly women exited the office and could be heard heading to Audrey's room on the same level. They reappeared soon after, Audrey holding a bunch of keys, which she placed in Adam's outstretched hand. He didn't want her to come any further into the room. He knew the key in question and unlocked the cabinet.

'It's under "Plans" second drawer,' Audrey said, and Adam found it soon enough. Gerry grabbed it from him.

'What do you think it contains?' Audrey asked.

'Dad's notes to leave the land to the community. If it does, it's the only copy, and it's going to meet with an accident,' Gerry said with a smirk. He placed the folder on the desk and leafed through it, looking up to ensure no one tried anything.

'It's not here,' he said to his mother. 'The will or any instructions.'

'It never has been,' Audrey said.

'Your father was taunting you,' Gerta said, disgusted.

A siren could be heard, and Adam saw Tom's car screaming up the driveway. It was quickly followed by slamming doors, and a loud voice boomed, 'Where are you?'

'Office,' Adam yelled back as Gerry threw the file at him and took off, leaving his mother standing with them.

'Don't worry, Gerta,' Audrey said. 'No one was hurt; there's no need for the police.'

And Adam noticed Gerta's face softened as if the weight of the world had fallen off her shoulders.

'Thank you,' she said in a voice that suggested she was uncomfortable with humility. 'We were desperate.'

The sound of loud footsteps and grunting soon revealed Tom as he wrestled Gerry back up the stairs, pushing him into the room.

'The knife's downstairs, and the cops are right behind me,' he said, struggling to restrain a hostile Gerry Dobrev.

'Thank you, Tom, but please release him,' Audrey said. 'No harm was done.'

'You're kidding me?' Tom gripped the shorter man even tighter.

'Desperation brings out the worst in people,' she said.

Tom shoved Gerry Dobrev away with disgust. 'If I had my way, you'd be locked up.'

'Why didn't you just ask if we had it?' Adam said, and Gerry scoffed.

'Like you'd tell me.'

'Yes, we would have, but would you have believed us?' Audrey asked.

Mumbling the word, 'Crazy,' Tom departed with a shake of his head to tell the police to stand down.

'What now?' Gerry said, looking at Adam and then Audrey.

'Time for bed, I think,' Audrey said. 'Goodnight to you both.' She turned and departed.

'I'll let you out,' Adam said, making sure they left the office first.

Nate glanced up to see Laura racing back downstairs after hearing his urgent call to Tom, who hadn't returned after the scuffle with Gavin; she was obviously not good at following instructions. Susan followed in her daughter's wake.

'Where's Gavin?' she asked, looking around frantically.

'He's miraculously been able to walk and bolted out of here,' Nate said.

'What the...!' she said, shocked.

A group wearing Halloween masks started pounding on the downstairs window of the neighbouring house, making everyone flinch, but the intruders did not come near Susan's house.

'Why haven't they come here yet?' Laura asked suspiciously.

'It makes sense now – you're being protected,' Nate said, including Susan in his observation as she came down the stairs and joined them. 'Gavin was sent here to observe and report back... that's my guess.'

They heard more sirens and saw police and fire trucks approaching. The carnival was well alight.

'Who were you on the phone to just now? Is Audrey all right?' Laura said, an edge of panic lacing her voice. On cue, Nate's phone rang.

'Tom?' he listened and sighed. 'Righto, thanks.' Nate hung up. 'Apparently, Gerry and Gerta paid a visit to Audrey and Adam.' He told them briefly what Tom said. 'It's over... but we're none the wiser for your case.'

'Maybe you should let it go now,' Susan told her daughter.

Laura shook her head in disbelief. 'I had a gut feeling Tom should have stayed with Audrey.'

'I'm glad he was here, with Gavin wielding that baseball bat. Who knows what might have happened?' Susan said, still shaken.

'You're right,' Laura agreed. She peeked through the window curtain. 'Seeing the old carnival go up in flames is so sad.'

'All that history,' Nate agreed.

'How much of this is your doing, Laura?' Susan asked curtly.

'Not as much as you think,' Nate said, stopping Susan's criticism. 'This is about a will and land sales. Laura's timing just happened to give it more oxygen.'

Susan grunted but did not seem convinced.

'There's people everywhere outside,' Laura said.

'The police have closed off the area,' Nate said, but they could still see residents fleeing in their cars; one backed out of his garage so fast that they would have hit anyone who crossed their path. Further up the street, a man hustled his wife and kids into a van. He closed the door, constantly looking around, and moments later, the van sped away.

'It feels like it has been going on for ages, but it's also been quick – so weird,' Laura said quietly.

'Adam calls that a flight or fight adaptation,' Nate said, 'I asked him about it on another case, and that's the sensation, without getting too technical.'

'Really?' she said with interest. 'I must ask him about it.'

Nearing 11.30pm, the streets emptied, sirens quietened, and order was restored. The three walked out of Susan's house and wandered onto the street; the air was heavy with smoke, and the street was littered with rubbish strewn from bins.

Nate approached one of the police officers, and Laura and Susan watched as the fire truck put out the last flames at the carnival. The remaining residents were hesitantly peeking out of windows; the neighbourhood's value had likely plummeted. There would be some real estate bargains in the coming weeks, which is no doubt just what Gerry wanted.

'I hope Rayco Dobrev is safe,' Laura said. Seeing the media vans arriving, they moved back inside.

Laura rang Tom, who assured her Audrey was safe and Mr Dobrev was alive. Tom had told the security team to stand down. For now, it was over.

Nearing midnight, Adam arrived to collect Nate; Tom remained with Audrey. The neighbourhood was deathly quiet. Broken glass glittered like jewels, grass and garden beds were cut up by motorbike tracks, and the acrid smell of smoke lingered. Even in the dark, the skeleton of the carnival rides could be seen, and it was evident that the fire had destroyed several of the buildings.

'I can't believe it,' Susan said as she made coffee for herself and Laura. Nate and Adam declined, keen to depart.

'I didn't see that coming,' Laura said of Gavin.

'He obviously didn't intend to harm you, or he would have. He became aggressive when Tom cornered him,' Nate assured her. 'He had a baseball bat, and I had his wheelchair, so we were evenly matched,' he joked, and the ladies laughed, enjoying the break in tension.

'I think he was sent here to keep the minions from coming to your house, Susan,' Adam said.

Laura shook her head. 'But why? Wouldn't it be more newsworthy to damage the house of the first victim's wife?'

Nate exhaled. 'Maybe they didn't want your father's death dragged up and for that to take centre stage, especially if the letter writer is amongst their ranks.'

Makes sense,' Laura agreed.

'I can't believe it,' Susan said again. 'I've met Gavin half a dozen times, and he has always been in a wheelchair.'

'He was well planted to earn your trust,' Nate said. 'But maybe he does need the chair sometimes. You never know.'

And then Sandra groaned. 'They knew you were coming and that Laura would stay here for the night.'

'How?' Nate asked.

'I saw Gavin on my walk this afternoon and asked after his security. I told him there were rumours of a riot tonight. He asked after me,' she said and scoffed. 'I thought he was lovely to be so concerned with my husband away, and I told him you would all be here. Then I insisted he better come up for dinner until it was safe. I'm an idiot,' she scolded herself.

'No, Mum,' Laura said loyally. 'Who would have guessed that?'

'Exactly, don't blame yourself,' Adam agreed. 'I let Gerta Dobrev in without a thought that Gerry would be loitering somewhere.'

'Neither of you thinks like criminals; it's disappointing,' Nate joked. 'Gavin would have been thrilled with the invitation here. He most likely had his phone on open speaker with Gerry or kept him up to date on what we were doing while Gerry was breaking into Adam and Audrey's home,' Nate said.

'It's a cold-hearted plan,' Adam said.

Laura agreed. 'Yep. Distract from my seeking of justice, run a neighbourhood down, gentrify it, and drive all the residents they class as riff-raff out. Then, make a packet. It will ruin the area's character and culture, all for the sake of profits.'

Susan huffed, her mind still on Gavin. 'It'll be the last time we talk roses.'

Laura stayed up long after her mother had gone to bed. What had she brought upon her family? If Gavin could walk, had he taped the threatening letter to her window and broken into Adam's house, painting the threat on the walls? She tossed and turned, thinking of Tom and Nate downstairs with Gavin armed with a baseball bat. She thought of what might have happened if she hadn't insisted on staying the night with her mother and Susan had been alone with Gavin.

She stepped into the shower, setting the water as hot as she could and scrubbing what felt like smoke, grime, and crime from her body. Laura couldn't shake the vision of Gavin wielding that baseball bat, the ghoulish mask lying nearby.

After the shower and dressed for bed, Laura slid under the quilt, feeling cold and shivering. What if it had just been Nate with them with all his injuries? Would he have handled Gavin? Would she or her mum be lying dead now or injured? She kept imagining that baseball bat's impact, wishing she could talk through her fears with Adam. He'd normalise them; that's what he did for a living.

Laura knew she had to let the thoughts go just like she did at work when she trained herself not to take on her client's pain and not carry the guilt if they didn't win. That was more easily said than done. A glance at the clock told her it was nearing 12.30, and the adrenaline and all the night's tension had left her exhausted and drained.

She tensed. A door just opened, the front door? The screen door of her mother's house made a distinct sound so familiar to her.

Frozen, she listened and waited. There was someone there – low voices. Laura quietly rose and went to the window to look down on the street. She moved the curtain slightly and ducked behind it; a shadow was near the front door. Were there several men out there?

Oh my God, oh my God.

Do I call... who... who do I call?

Mum and I are here alone; I have to warn Mum.

Laura slid between her ajar bedroom door into the hallway and peered down over the stair rail to the front door. She gasped.

Her mother was there. In the arms of Gerry Dobrev.

Chapter 33

'W'e had a fling,' Susan Armstrong told her daughter over a pot of tea after Gerry left. 'And no, it wasn't an affair; your father had passed away, and Gerry was very good to me.'

'Really? A fling with Gerry Dobrev?' Laura asked, her face betraying her astonishment.

Susan smiled with a hint of sadness. 'Gerry wasn't always as bitter as he is now. I've told you your father adored you, but our relationship left much to be desired. Our union was akin to a shotgun wedding – you were due less than nine months after we married, and we tried to make the best of it.'

'But why did you have to marry? It was the eighties, not the fifties.'

Susan shrugged. 'We started dating at 16, and I fell pregnant at 18. We were young and caught up in the silly notion of romance, having a family and a home. Our parents were against it, making it even more desirable. It was only after the reality set in that your dad couldn't spend every night out with his mates and had to earn enough for a mortgage and that I wasn't always as keen for sex because I was exhausted that it went downhill pretty fast. We were burnt out when he died at 24; if he had lived, I don't know how much longer we would have stayed together.'

'And you chose to stay here even if the memories weren't great,' Laura said.

'I loved this house and having my own home, and his life insurance meant we owned it with no mortgage. Your grandfather insisted we have life and house insurance; bless him for that. But Rayco and Gerry looked after us. Rayco contributed to your schooling – he called it a carnival scholarship,' she laughed at the memory, 'and Gerry mowed the lawn fortnightly and did odd jobs for me.'

'Did you have a cold drink waiting for him?' Laura teased, and her mother laughed.

'Yes, actually. He was 20, I was 24 and a fling suited us both. Then his father sent him away to business college for a year—'

'Gerry Dobrev has business qualifications?' Laura exclaimed, surprised, cutting her mother off mid-sentence.

'As I said, he wasn't always a ruffian. By the time he returned, the romance had cooled, but we stayed friends. He's been good to me. You can only judge people by how you find them.'

'Why didn't you tell me?' Laura asked.

'Would it have stopped you investigating?'

Laura pursed her lips before answering, 'No.'

'There you go. Gerry's many things, but he and your dad got on all right, and he wouldn't have killed him or harmed you for that matter.'

The next morning, despite having a late night, Adam was showered, dressed and ready to go to Hopetown Aged Care with Audrey when she returned home from church. He insisted on driving; he liked Audrey's Jag but couldn't bear to be driven either too slow or too fast, depending on Audrey's state of mind, so they took the journey in his Mercedes convertible. Audrey sat with a cake box on her lap.

'I expect a sign to tell me when it is time to go into aged care,' she said. 'Perhaps a fall, or if my mobility fails me.'

'No,' Adam said flat out. 'We'll bring people in if you need help.'

She patted his arm. 'Thank you, darling, but it's not all bad. I'd have plenty of activities and company there, especially if I couldn't drive or get around. And all my meals cooked, washing and ironing done, not to mention medical staff are always on standby.'

'You're right. How old do you think I have to be to get in?' Adam asked, making her laugh.

'You have to have lived a full life, dear, so not for a while,' she said with an affectionate look.

'Are you okay after last evening? You were incredibly brave,' Adam said.

'Goodness, was I? I've known Gerta for years, and I didn't think we were in great danger,' she said stoically. 'I confess Gerry has frightened me on occasion, but he looked weary and not that threatening last night armed with a butter knife.'

Adam laughed. 'He was all bluff and anger. You know, Laura said something interesting to me the other day.'

'I'm sure she did,' Audrey smiled, 'Do tell.'

'She said how alike you and I are. It's weird, but I never considered that. I was always measuring myself against Mum and Dad, even Granddad.'

'I've always thought your father and grandfather, and yes, Winsome, too, were the adventurers… raising the sails and heading into the unknown. You and I, we've kept the boat steady and afloat. They need us as much as we need them.'

'Hmm, nice analogy.'

'I think so. Now, tell me what you hope to achieve today,' she said as they neared the aged care home.

Adam filled his grandmother in, and she listened attentively. He concluded, 'So, I need to ask Rayco to tell me, in his words, what happened that night of Alex Anderson's death.'

'I will try and lead him there with my reminisces,' Audrey offered.

'Yes, please, that would be helpful.' Adam said. 'Laura called this morning with some new information. I don't know what that is yet, but she's coming home today and will fill Nate in.'

'Coming home. Doesn't that sound nice?' Audrey teased, and Adam chuckled.

'How long have you known each other?' He asked.

'About six years. She started work with our community group in year one of her degree. Laura could be a very successful commercial lawyer, but she's determined to help others in the community sector. I have seen her deal with some extraordinary cases, and she always comes through with a quiet confidence that people are inherently good. I find that astonishing.'

'So do I. After a day with my patients, I'm almost convinced that most people are capable of the worst things.'

'That's why you need someone who is glass half-full, maybe even glass three-quarters full,' Audrey joked.

Adam smiled and took it all in but didn't say anything. He liked Laura's lightness of heart; she was very different from Kelsey, who was always reserved and cautious. Even briefly knowing Laura, he felt charged in her company, like she lit the room when she entered. She might be fun to live with – just friends.

Moments later, they arrived at the aged care home, and Adam parked under the shade of a well-manicured tree. They walked through the grounds. At the reception, they were shown to Rayco Dobrev's room; his pleasure at seeing Audrey reminded Adam of the importance of friendship.

'It has been too long, Rayco,' Audrey said while Adam was demoted to tea boy. He organised three cups, a plate and a knife to cut Audrey's cake, which was achieved promptly; they had timed their visit with the morning tea trolley. 'Do you like this place?'

Rayco chuckled. 'I'm going home soon,' he said, and Adam and Audrey made allowances for his confused state of mind.

'That will be nice,' Audrey agreed. 'I was there just the other day, at the carnival.'

'You should have told me,' he declared and thanked Audrey for the large slice of cake before him. 'I would have come out of the office to meet you.'

Adam let them trip down memory lane for a while, and then, when he noticed Rayco getting tired, he received a nod from his grandmother to lead the discussion as he had planned. If Gerry was protecting someone close to him, and if it wasn't Gerta, could it be Rayco, even if there seemed to be no love lost between father and son?

Audrey said, 'Remember that terrible night when that neighbourhood group leader died, Rayco? He was a bit of a bully, though, I have heard.'

'Alex Armstrong,' Rayco said without missing a beat.

'Tell us what you remember, Mr Dobrev. I am sure you are the only person who truly knows what happened that night,' Adam said, empowering the old man, knowing he would not be convicted at his age with dementia.

Rayco sighed and shook his head. 'I didn't mean to kill him, you know. Wrong place, wrong time. He was a nasty piece of work, but he had that lovely wife and child.'

Audrey's face registered her shock, and Adam's breath hitched.

'It was an accident,' Adam said, regaining control. He kept his voice steady and attempted to sound empathic while his mind raced with Rayco's admission.

'It was, it truly was. I would never hurt that young man,' Rayco said as Audrey maintained a calm composure and patted his hand. Then, the truth came out.

Adam found Nate by the pool. After finishing laps, Nate was now drying off on a pool chair. His chest was covered in dark bruises from the beating he had scored Saturday evening, and a red welt ran from his neck down to his ribcage.

Fully dressed, Adam reclined in the pool chair next to him, and Nate filled him in on Laura's discovery – the relationship between her mother and Gerry.

'Didn't see that coming,' Adam scoffed.

'Me either. So, how did you and Audrey go with Rayco?' Nate asked.

'He did it.'

There was silence before Nate said, 'You're serious.'

'Yep. It was an accident.' Adam told him the story, and Nate exhaled with relief at the end of it.

'Wow, it's solved. Do you think he was remembering correctly?' Nate asked, shocked by Rayco's admission.

'I think he remembers it well. I'm no expert on Dementia, but I believe the older, more established memories are more easily recalled than current memories,' Adam said.

Nate nodded. 'You've solved my case for me,' he said with a slow smile.

'Not quite. Rayco's not a reliable witness, not even of his own history. I suggest you get Laura and Burnsy, and the three of you go and talk with

Gerry, tell him what you've learnt and see if he'll come clean; get Rayco's story backed up. Then you've solved the case and can close it.'

Nate swung his legs over the side of the pool chair and stood wincing at the pain. He slapped Adam on the back.

'Thanks. I will. Right now.'

With that, Nate strode off, and Adam looked at the water, tempted. He didn't know where Tom was and didn't care. That left only Audrey home, and she was resting, so he stripped off to his boxers and dived in.

Chapter 34

When Gerry Dobrev saw Laura Armstrong and the private investigator, Nate Murphy, at the entrance to the burnt-out *Carnival World*, he approached them suspiciously. Then he groaned at the sight of a police officer walking over to meet them.

'Come to gloat?' he sneered.

'About what?' Laura asked.

Gerry made a noise that sounded like a low growl. 'What do you want?'

'We need to talk,' Nate said and introduced Sergeant Matt Burns even though the men had informally met when Burnsy followed up the complaints made by neighbours.

'Let's talk about the damage inflicted last night,' Burnsy said.

'And Audrey and Adam have just been to see your dad,' Nate added. 'Let's just say it was Sunday confession hour.'

'The old man,' Gerry said, expelling a long breath.

'I've also got the fingerprint report back from the sign on Laura's window,' Nate added. 'Plus, you were seen last night hugging Susan Armstrong.'

Gerry stepped back, looked skyward and ran his hands through his thin hair. Then he laughed. 'It's all crashing down on me. I'm like a king standing in a defeated battleground with a castle destroyed by war.'

Neither Laura nor Nate could deny him that moment or those feelings.

Gathering himself, Gerry Dobrev unlocked the gate, stood aside, and let them in. He indicated the gazebo, table, and bench within it, which stood erect and undamaged. The four made their way there.

'Do you want to start at the beginning, or do you want me to tell you that I know about the consortium you've set up with your town planner, solicitor, and foreman and the plans to buy back as much of the land and houses surrounding the carnival, to prevent the community getting their hands on it?' Burnsy asked.

'Sounds like you know it all,' Gerry said. 'No crime in wanting to develop real estate, is there?'

Laura held up her hand. 'Please, let's end this, Gerry. Your father confessed, and with his dementia, he is unfit for trial; the game is up. Tell us how it played out then and now.'

Gerry scoffed. 'Why?'

'Because you and I are not our father's mistakes. We have to move on with our lives,' Laura said.

'Feels like we've lived with them for long enough,' Gerry agreed.

'And because I might draw my own conclusions, and I'll have to take you in for questioning,' Burnsy added.

Gerry shook his head and, resigned that the end had come, he began. 'It's this bloody carnival. It's been the curse of my life.' He looked at the burnt ghost train building, the carriages dangling from the Ferris Wheel and the few horses on the merry-go-round that hadn't succumbed to the flames. The carriages were cinder.

'It was created with good intention, to make families happy,' Laura said as a means of consolation.

'Yeah, it was,' Gerry conceded, 'but the old man didn't know when to walk away. I didn't want to continue the business; I made that clear from day one, but he had no time for me after I told him that. I couldn't do anything right. But Mum and I worked every day at that carnival like he did. When the area started to develop, he and Mum were in their sixties. He should have sold up and retired, but he bowed, scraped, and tried to do what the community wanted.'

'You and your mum wanted him to sell?' Burnsy asked.

'You bet. But Dad dug his heels in, and then he started working with Audrey Murphy and her charity do-gooders,' Gerry said. 'He wanted to create this community village and provide social housing or some bullshit. Mum should have been retiring in comfort, and he's offered her the house and a bit of land and wants to donate everything from under her.'

'That's when you went against your father and partnered with the neighbourhood group leader, Laura's dad,' Nate said.

'Yeah. I scared Audrey and her community group away,' Gerry chuckled. 'Then I met with Alex and told him we wanted the same thing. We came up with a few ideas that would put the final nail in *Carnival World's* coffin—neighbourhood riots driving away customers—Dad would have to close and sell up. But then the stupid old bastard...' he stopped talking, wondering what Adam and Audrey knew from their morning discussion with Rayco.

'He ran over Alex Armstrong,' Nate said, and Burnsy inhaled sharply in surprise.

Gerry nodded. 'Silly old bugger. Alex, his men, and my crew were having a fake fight just inside the carnival ground, which ended up spilling out onto the street,' he said, waving his hand in the direction where the fight took place. Not much had changed in the neighbourhood area since then. 'Carnival guests and neighbours were freaking out, and it was a surefire way to get the carnival closed down. But Dad decides he'll get his car, drive through the street riot, and save me, thinking I'm stuck in the middle for the love of God. He's come around the corner, and there's Alex

Armstrong dressed in black, enshrouded in smoke, with lights flashing nearby and the wail of sirens, and with all that distraction, looking around for me, the old man hasn't seen him. I didn't see it all, but I was told that Alex stepped out to hit Dad's car with his bat, but Dad hit him. He's bounced off the bonnet, fell to the kerb and hit his head.'

'And you covered it up for all these years,' Burnsy said.

'What would you have done if it was your dad?' Gerry demanded. 'I started the rioting, and he's never so much as hurt a fly his whole life. He's come to save me for the love of God. We all covered it up, and when the results came that Alex had fallen and hit his head, it was a gift from heaven. Dad never got over it. That's why he paid for your school fees,' he said to Laura.

'Your mum did say to me "be open-minded; not all is as it seems" and she was right,' Laura said. 'Does Gerta know?'

Gerry glanced at the sergeant and back at Laura before answering no. Gerry's comment went unchallenged, but no one present believed that to be true.

'Does my mum know Rayco accidentally killed Dad?'

'No. But she's got a heart. She'd understand it was an accident,' Gerry said. 'Your dad's death increased my dad's determination to give the bloody carnival land to the community. Like he had to buy his way into heaven.'

'And you tried to scare me off with the warning note and trashing Adam's house?' Laura asked.

Gerry glanced at Burnsy and admitted nothing, even though his prints were on the warning letter. 'I'm not saying I did that, but I never wanted you to learn about Dad. The case was closed 18 years ago, and it was an accident; it's still the same verdict even if the coroner didn't know the cause of the accident. Does it make any difference to you now that you know?'

'Hell yeah,' Laura said. 'It does. I can rest knowing that Dad wasn't murdered.'

Gerry gave a small snort but nodded. 'Yeah, okay.'

'What's it all about now then? Why the spook techniques and the scaring away homeowners?' Burnsy asked.

'Despite what you've heard, Dad hasn't got a will, and it was too late to do one once he got dementia. He told me there was a copy with the village plan and that Audrey had it. There wasn't, but the Saturday night riot was a distraction so I could get into the Murphy house. There's some do-gooder working in Audrey's group who still think that they'll get this land and can put up community housing, but it will be over Mum's and my dead body. We're his next of kin, and there'll be no donating our land to anyone.' He spat as he spoke, working himself up.

'They have no legal right to it while you and Gerta are alive,' Laura said.

'Try telling them that,' Gerry huffed. 'They reckon they've got his word, and that's good enough.'

Laura shook her head in the negative. 'That's a hard one to prove, and if there's no will, the Succession Act will distribute the estate, prioritising surviving family members of the deceased.'

'And there's just the two of us,' Gerry said, then smiled. 'Mum's legal guy thinks she might be able to sell it before Dad dies.'

'Ah,' Nate said, 'hence the hurry up to get more properties onto the market at the best price.'

'As soon as I heard that you were opening the cold case and doing some sort of podcast, I thought we could be in trouble,' Gerry said to Laura. 'You'll make the area trendy and interesting, which is our end goal, but not yet, so we had to act.'

'It could be tied up for a while in the courts,' Burnsy said, and Gerry shook his head.

'I've got good people in my pocket. The work has started.'

Silence fell on the small group as they thought about what had passed.

'What is your relationship with Susan Armstrong?' Nate asked, knowing the answer from Laura's discussion with her mum, but Nate wanted Gerry's angle.

'You saw us, didn't you?' Gerry asked Laura. 'I thought I saw your shadow at the top of the stairs last night.'

'I saw you hugging,' she confirmed.

'I love your Mum,' he said unabashedly. 'That surprise you? She's too good for me, always has been. Her second husband's decent; she's done all right there. Alex was never good enough for her.' Gerry shrugged, 'Sorry. I know he's your dad, but it's the truth.'

'What's the story with Gavin and the wheelchair?' Laura asked.

'Protection for your mum. No one was allowed to go near her house, and he's not bad at eavesdropping,' Gerry said with a chuckle. 'I appreciate the updates.'

Nate groaned. He had dropped the ball on that one.

'So, this consortium...' Burnsy started.

'Yeah. I've got some solid investors; we've bought a few properties already, and we've got plans drawn for a new estate on this carnival land. We're going to gentrify the rest of the estate. That's the word that our foreman keeps saying: gentrify, and it will be payday. According to my finance guy, we can use the equity from the carnival land to help with the redevelopment. Mum and I have earned every cent.'

'You might be facing charges for last night's damage yet,' Burnsy said, and Gerry shrugged.

'The damage was mainly on my land, and I doubt you'll find too many neighbours willing to complain. I can't tell you who broke the car and house windows; they were just kids acting up.' He gave a sly smile.

Burnsy added: 'One of the constables bailed up one of the rioters, and he said they were paid to wear the masks and demolish as much as they could on the street. He thought it was a film stunt.'

Gerry laughed. 'Is that so?' He didn't admit to anything. 'Anyone get hurt?'

'Not that we know about,' Nate said.

'There you go then,' he said with a grin to the sergeant near him.

'It's got to stop,' Burnsy said. 'This is a warning, a final warning.'

Gerry agreed with an upward movement of his chin but said nothing that would confirm his actions either way.

'It will be recorded that your father admitted to the accidental killing of Alex Armstrong,' Burnsy said.

'You can't trust the confession of an old man with dementia,' Gerry said, his anger quick to rise.

'We have your testimony as well,' Burnsy said.

'I can't remember saying anything about that,' Gerry said. 'And hell will freeze over before I sign something to that effect. But you have your answer now, Laura. Time to bury your dad for good and not ruin my father's good name.'

Laura studied the wiry man before her, and while she could have bartered, Gerry expected it; she didn't. She said, 'Yes. On that, we agree.'

Nate sighed and looked at the carnival rides. 'Bloody shame the carnival burnt down, though. I'd have loved a final ride on the ghost train.'

Gerry laughed. 'I could give you a good scare if you want to try it.'

Nate laughed and rose gingerly, wincing as he stood to full height. Laura and Burnsy followed, rising to their feet.

'About Dad's diary...' Laura started.

'It's a fake, something to bide time while I rifled the filing cabinet,' Gerry said. 'Sorry.'

'Good luck, Gerry,' Nate said, extending his hand to shake, 'I don't disagree with your right to the land.'

Gerry nodded his thanks and shook Nate's hand. He watched them depart. The carnival was over.

Chapter 35

It had been a strange case. Tom signed off, having had little to do but stay out of Adam's way, which suited them both. But Adam could not resist one more dig as his old security guard entered the kitchen with his duffel bag.

'Well, thanks for the work,' Tom said to Laura. 'I hope you are pleased with the result.' He turned to Adam. 'I guess you could say I came to your rescue again,' he ribbed him.

'I guess you could say you were late to the rescue again, just like last time,' Adam retorted. 'Backed the wrong horse but got there in the end.'

The men stared at each other. Nate quickly rose and said, 'Well, thanks, Tom. Laura and I will see you out. I'm sure you and Adam will have more opportunities down the track to reminisce about those good old days.'

Tom scowled, farewelled Audrey and promptly departed, driving his grey Ford Mustang out of the large black gates again. Maybe for the last time, or so Adam hoped as he watched from the windows in the kitchen of his house wing.

When Nate and Laura returned, Laura grinned at Adam, who looked a little embarrassed and shrugged, 'Sorry, he brings out the worst in me.'

'Perhaps that's the real you!' Laura teased, and Audrey smiled at their antics.

'Analyse that!' Nate said with a chuckle and then sobered. 'I have to apologise; I misread one clue.'

'What's that?' Laura asked, surprised.

'In the audio,' Nate said, crossing his arms as he leaned on the kitchen counter. 'Gerry Dobrev said he had a plan for the woman, but it wasn't you, Laura. It was Audrey. I should have realised when you were referred to moments later as the daughter.'

Laura huffed. 'That was so obscure. Don't beat yourself up. We had the best outcome we could hope for, and I confess, it is a relief to have it over with.'

'As am I, dear,' Audrey agreed. 'Hopefully, I can resume my cemetery visits unhindered.'

'Are you glad Tom's gone too?' Adam joked, and she chuckled.

'No. But I am oddly relieved that Gerry wasn't quite as bad as I always thought him to be. I always held the suspicion that he harmed your father, Laura. I would never have believed it was Rayco.'

'Nor I,' Laura said. 'But, I'm okay with it all, honestly. Knowing it was an accident and that my father started the fight that brought about his demise, well, it's fair to say I have sympathy for Rayco Dobrev. On that note, I best be going.'

'Me too,' Adam said, ready to leave his childhood home again.

'Thank you, Audrey, for your hospitality,' Laura said, hugging the senior Murphy member.

'Anytime, my dear,' Audrey said. 'Nathanial, let us wave Adam and Laura off; hopefully, they will return soon.'

'We'll get our bags,' Adam said, smiling and musing that the concept of being waved off was generational. The pair headed upstairs and met back in their joint living room. Adam grabbed a couple of Laura's bags to help while she juggled her laptop, make-up and sports bag.

'Audrey has always been a waver,' he said.

Laura grinned. 'I, for one, like a good wave.'

'I'll remember that,' Adam joked.

Changing the subject, Laura asked, 'Is Audrey okay with you moving back to your place?'

'Yeah, she's very laid back. I don't think she seriously thought I'd move back here.'

'I'd be here in a shot for the pool, tennis court, and high-security fence,' Laura said, but Adam shook his head.

'It's a big property with plenty of dark corners to scale a fence. I don't feel any safer here than I do at home. Anyway, let's see how it goes. We can always come back.'

Laura had given the landlord notice and was moving into Adam's house as his tenant. A token rent had been agreed upon, and time would tell if both parties could handle each other as flatmates. As they arrived downstairs, Audrey and Nate awaited them.

'I'm waving you off apparently and making sure you leave the premises.'

Adam laughed. 'It's all yours again, go wild.'

As the four left the house and made their way to the garage, Laura said, 'I want to thank you all. It's not the result I expected, but I'm relieved I no longer have to wonder.'

'One of the strangest cases I've had,' Nate admitted. 'A historical crime that wasn't, a client that's happy with the unfortunate outcome, and a community group that misses out, but I'm rooting for the family.'

'Yeah, me too,' Adam said.

'As am I,' Audrey said.

'And me,' Laura agreed. 'But it would be good if they found a way to give something back.'

'That didn't go so well for them last time,' Nate reminded Laura, taking her bags from Adam.

'Are you still going to do the podcast?' Adam asked.

Laura shook her head in the negative as they arrived at her Peugeot and Adam's Mercedes. 'I don't want to "out" Rayco Dobrev when it was an accident. All it will do is ruin his legacy, and it won't bring Dad back. I always envied my school friends whose dads came to everything.'

'Me too,' Adam said, glancing at his best friend. 'Nate's dad was one of those dads. He even came to one of my school sports days once.'

Nate laughed, 'Yeah, he liked to get out of the house.'

They both knew it was more than that. Mr Delaney felt sorry for the poor little rich kid, who had no one there to cheer him on except his grandmother.

'It made me go faster,' Adam joked. 'I didn't want to waste his time.'

Laura laughed at the thought. 'Ah, our parents. Got to love them,' she said with a smile. Unlocking her car, the bags were placed in the back.

Laura and Audrey hugged. She shook Nate's hand and told Adam, 'See you at your place. I've just got a detour to make first. I'm going to see Dad at the cemetery.'

Adam nodded, understanding her need to do so. 'I'll see you at home then.'

'If he's too hard to live with, come back here,' Nate joked as she got into her car, started it, and put down the window to wave as Audrey expected.

'You're only saying that because Laura can cook,' Adam ribbed him as he threw his bag in the Merc.

'Free rent,' Nate continued, trying to entice her. Laura laughed, shook her head at their antics, and slowly drove away, stopping to glance back again at the mansion and wave to Audrey. She went through the large black gates, leaving behind a life she couldn't imagine, and Adam, who knew no different, soon followed.

Then...

Nate pedalled fast through the cemetery, staying on the paths and setting the pace for Adam, who was following. He stopped at the Murphy family vault, and Adam skidded to a stop beside him.

'Are you going to be buried in there too one day?' Nate asked, and Adam shrugged.

'I guess so. My grandfather and great-grandparents are in there. There's probably room. You could come in if you wanted to.'

'Yeah?' Nate brightened. 'Thanks. I'll let you know.'

'Sure. Let's go see the new grave,' Adam suggested, and they cycled around to the dirt mound where Alex Armstrong, the neighbourhood group leader, had been buried the week before.

'Audrey knew him,' Adam said.

'Was he nice?'

'I don't know, she didn't say. But she said the carnival's not leaving now.'

'That's good,' Nate said and grinned. 'I was thinking of asking Dad if we could go there for my birthday.'

'Yeah! That'd be cool,' Adam agreed.

Nate nudged the fresh dirt pile and asked, 'How long do you reckon it takes until he's a skeleton in there?'

Both boys looked at the dirt mound and wondered.

'I reckon it takes ages,' Adam said, sounding like he knew something about the topic.

'Probably. The worms have to eat all through the skin and then lick the bones clean.'

'Gross,' Adam said with a grin.

'Unless you're a worm,' Nate joked. 'Look, there's a funeral car now. Someone else is going to get buried.'

The boys watched a black hearse enter the grounds, with half a dozen cars driving slowly behind it.

'I wonder why they drive so slowly,' Adam said. 'The person's dead; they won't mind some speeding.'

'We'd better get out of here,' Nate said as the line of cars neared. 'Want to go to the creek?'

'Yeah, let's go fishing. So will you ask everyone from your class to the carnival for your birthday?' Adam fished on who might be coming to Nate's party.

'Nuh. Mum said I'm only allowed two parties, and I had one last year. I reckon it's just us. I want to go on the ghost train.'

'Charlie got a scare in there,' Adam laughed.

'Yeah, but she's a girl,' Nate grinned. 'Last one to the creek is a worm-eaten skeleton.'

He took off, and Adam laughed, glancing back at the mound of dirt that hid the bones of a man underneath.

'I'm sorry you're dead, Mister,' he said sincerely.

'C'mon,' Nate called back over his shoulder.

Hurrying along, Adam turned his bike to follow Nate; he usually did.

THE END

From the author

Thanks for taking another trip with Adam, Nate and me. I hope you enjoyed this adventure.

When I was a kid growing up in Toowoomba, we'd sometimes visit the beautiful, historic Drayton Cemetery with Grandma to pay our respects to Granddad, who had a military grave. I have always been fascinated by the headstones, particularly one huge vault. It was the grave of a young boy about Adam and Nate's age – 12. The vault was enormous, with a statue of the boy on the top and an angel behind him. The vault was unlocked for a while, and I'm guessing his family could enter and pray, spending time near their beloved boy. But they secured it after some vandalism. I was amazed by it, with the display of their grief and imagining this kid my age buried in there and his return to dust. Amazing places, cemeteries.

I've always been interested in psychology and have done a little study in the area. However, I am fortunate to have family who are in the business and with bona fide qualifications who put up with all my questions. The field of EMDR (Eye Movement Desensitisation and Reprocessing) is fascinating, as Adam practised with Dane in this novel. The therapy encourages the patient to briefly focus on the trauma memory while simultaneously experiencing bilateral stimulation like watching eye or hand movements, resulting in a reduction in the intensity and emotion that is attached to the trauma. It is amazing what the mind is capable of, and the treatment is proving to be very successful.

I hope no one was too attached to Kelsey; it was time to move her on. But I wish Adam would move back to the mansion.

Also by Jack Adams

The Delaney & Murphy series:

Asylum

Ten-year-old best friends Nathan and Adam really liked Joe. He was their friend, an artist, and the man they spoke to through the wire fence of the lunatic asylum.

But something happened behind those walls, in those rooms, on the grounds, at the river.

The inmate sketched it all – fine lines, truth in the negative space, truth in the pencil strokes.

Then, one day, Joe was gone.

Twenty years later, Nathan and Adamreceived a letter.

Stalker

Adam couldn't wait... his Uncle Allanwas coming to watch his cricket game that afternoon; Adam's father was alwaystoo busy to get there. Uncle Allan believed Adam and his best friend, Nate,would one day be chosen for the Stateside if they kept practising... Adam'sbowling was really improving.

Adam doesn't have an Uncle Allan.

Cult

Eleven-year-old Nate wasn't happy. There was a new kid on the block named Griffin Maxwell, and he wanted Adam to be his best friend. That was Nate's job; they had sworn they would be blood brothers forever. Two days after Adam's birthday party, when Adam received a strange birthday present from Griffin, the Maxwell family was gone.

Twenty years later, Griffin Maxwell is back.

And he wants Adam to come out and play.

Hitched

Twelve-year-old Adam Murphy didn't know anyone who had died, nor did his best friend, Nate Delaney. While testing new speedometers on their Malvern Star bikes, that changed – the pair witnessed beautiful HollyCastle, 16, hitch a ride to Sydney seeking fame and was never seen again. Presumed dead.

Twenty years later, Adam's model mother, the *IT Girl* Winsome Keeley, gets hitched to the nation's favourite singer, Jack Bernham, and the official photographer—Eric Castle—recognises Nate from their school years. The younger brother of the missing girl is still pursuing his sister's cold case.

Adam and Nate are invited to take a ride.

Also by Jack Adams:
Poster Girl (stand-alone title)
Backpacker Soleil 'Sunny' Reyer is gone. Tanned, glowing and star of the *Missing* poster, no one thoughtfruit-picking could be deadly.

Journalist Jessica Steyn was the last person to give Sunny a lift. Assigned the biggest story in her career, Jessica is on the job. Dig, dig, dig … until she buries herself.

The cold case file never leaves his desk like Detective Nick Clarkson is stuck in Strand Harbour fifteen years after Sunny disappeared. Less hair, marriage over, no sign of Sunny.

Author Coen Watson's people are waterpeople; his trust in it is marrow-deep – he's counting on Strand Harbour tocure his writer's block. Unpacking, he forces open a drawer corroded by saltair to find a faded *Missing* poster for Soleil Reyer. The author beginspicking at old wounds.

References

References:

Eye Movement Desensitization and Reprocessing (EMDR) Therapy, American Psychological Association, Retrieved 6 June 2024 from URL: https://www.apa.org/ptsd-guideline/resources/eye-movement-reprocessing-example

Giacomucci Dr Scott, *EMDR Therapy Explained: What is It?*, Phoenix Trauma Centre. YouTube, viewed August 2024 at: https://www.youtube.com/watch?v=AAjkdkHlzYY

Pamich, Dr Abigail, Clinical Psychologist, *EMDR Therapy: Example with a Client in Clinical.* YouTube, viewed August 2024 at: https://www.youtube.com/watch?v=MQeVa6sdRHo